CHERRY
MONEY
BABY

CHERRY
MONEY
BABY

John M. Cusick

CANDLEWICK PRESS

Copyright © 2013 by John M. Cusick

First edition 2013

Library of Congress Catalog Card Number 2013931460
ISBN 978-0-7636-5557-0

13 14 15 16 17 18 BVG 10 9 8 7 6 5 4 3 2 1

Printed in Berryville, VA, U.S.A.

This book was typeset in Bembo.

Candlewick Press
99 Dover Street
Somerville, Massachusetts 02144

visit us at www.candlewick.com

For Sarah

Of course, every girl must respect herself; there's nothing I dislike more than a badly behaved girl.

—Anton Chekov, *The Cherry Orchard*

Cherry

The Loop

Cherry's run was a loop, from her trailer park, down Hope Avenue, up Route 9, past the bottling plant, and back down Webster. The same every day. Same direction, same view.

Except today.

The road ahead was blocked. She slowed a few yards from the sawhorses, stopped, bent, stretched, and spit onto the pavement. The kid in the traffic vest made a face.

"What's going on?"

"The road's blocked," said the kid.

There were police cruisers and wooden barriers and detour signs.

"No kidding," said Cherry. "I mean, why?"

"They're filming a movie," said the kid. He was maybe in college. He had those super-geek glasses that actual geeks bought when they decided to embrace geekdom. He was probably wearing old-fashioned sneakers. Cherry stretched her calves and checked.

Yup.

"What movie?"

"It's a remake of *Alive and Unmarried,* the one about Stewart Cane, the guy who, like, invented soda."

"And they're filming it here?"

Aubrey didn't have much to recommend it besides a nightclub, Shabooms, and they had one of those over in Worcester, too.

"Yeah. So the road's blocked. You gotta go around."

Cherry put her palms out. "Okay, okay, I'm going. Easy."

She spit one more time for good measure and started back home. She jogged past the nice houses, then the slightly scrubbier houses farther down, then the just-plain-scrubby houses, and at last came to the entrance of her trailer park, two streets of mobile homes called Sugar Village. Next to the village was Sweet Pond, which was clear and dead, thanks to runoff from the cola bottling plant. The lake sort of smelled sweet. She always liked that.

A weed-clogged crack separated the darker concrete of Hope Ave. from the paler cement of Sugar Village, and some part of Cherry, left over from avoiding cracks and broken backs, hopped over the threshold.

That hadn't been too bad. She didn't flip out or swear at the glasses kid. See? She could be chill. She decided today was Day One of her new life of not flipping her shit at people. Today was Day One of not being a crazy bitch.

Their trailer was small, even by trailer standards. Cherry's bedroom was half a bedroom, split down the middle with a flimsy wall of Sheetrock. Her younger brother, Stew, had the other half. No wall was more than two inches thick, which meant a stray elbow or angry fist could easily knock through to the next room. Every snore, conversation, or cough was audible through the walls. Privacy was a dream—except in the glass phone booth of the shower, which was a great place to get some thinking done.

The faucet sputtered and gagged, releasing a jet of scalding water and steam. She stood under the flow, letting her thoughts wash away with the sweat and road grit. Hot showers were the best, with the water so hot it turned your skin pink, as if you could shed it gecko-style. And just when she couldn't stand it any longer—*twist, crank, rattle*—she'd torque the cold water to full. The shock *nuked* conscious thought.

A quick change and Cherry flounced into the kitchen in her work uniform. Burrito Barn staff were required to wear vomit-yellow polo shirts with matching visors. She'd spent the previous evening scrubbing a chipotle stain off the lapel with a toothbrush.

The percolator bubbled, filling the trailer with an oaky, burned smell. Cherry's father sat at the kitchenette table, palms enveloping his favorite mug. She kissed his forehead.

"Morning, Pops."

Grunt.

"I'll make you breakfast."

Pop flipped a page in the *Aubrey Times*. "Donuts in the fridge."

"No donuts." She retrieved the frying pan from its drawer. "You gotta eat healthier, Pops, or your heart's gonna 'splode."

The sink was filled with last night's pasta dishes. No one asked her to wash them, but the men were just *fucking incapable*. Pop and Stew might be content to eat off a plate with congealed gravy stuck to the underside, but *someone* had to have standards.

"How was your run?"

"Aborted," said Cherry. "They're filming a movie at the bottling plant, I guess."

"You couldn't just go around?"

"Nah. If I can't do *my* route, I'm not running."

"You're a crazy girl."

"I know."

She set the eggs sizzling and retrieved a Yow-Gurt

from the fridge. According to the package, it was both nutritious *and* delicious. Pop eyed the pink sludge as though he doubted both counts.

"How come I gotta eat eggs and you get to eat that shit?"

"I'm not fat, Pops."

Pop huffed, turned a page. "I'm big boned."

"And your big bones are covered in clogged arteries," said Cherry. "You're like a bacon-wrapped dino skeleton."

Pop chuckled and handed her the comics page. Charlie Brown missed the football. Cherry missed *Calvin and Hobbes*.

"Your quarterly report card came in."

Her eyes jerked up a little too quickly. She lowered them. "Oh?"

"Yeah. Apparently it came a week ago, but somehow it fell out of the mailbox."

"Weird."

"And into the trash."

"Huh."

"And got ripped into a million pieces."

Cherry ate her yogurt. "Must have been mice. I told you we need an exterminator."

He pushed the document across the table. It had been reassembled with Scotch tape, roughly, but the writing was still legible. Next time she'd burn it.

"Look, what does it matter?" She tossed the empty Yow-Gurt cup over her shoulder. It landed squarely in the trash. Pop raised his eyebrows, duly impressed. "I'm graduating, aren't I?"

"Yeah, *high school*," said Pop. "What about college? How do you expect to get in with report cards like this?"

Cherry allowed herself a peek at the Aubrey Public stationery. The details had not magically transformed:

Lacks drive.
Vulgar language.
Impulse-control problems.

"That last one is bullshit," said Cherry. "I do *not* have fu—" She took a breath, smiled, turned her palms out. "I am rage-free. And my language isn't *vulgar*—it's . . . colorful."

Pop chuckled. She started to stand, but he stopped her with a gentle hand on her wrist. "You're not getting off easy because you make me laugh, Alice Kerrigan."

Cherry swallowed. "I hate that name."

"Cherry."

"Pop."

He released her. "What do you wanna do?"

"I want to save your eggs before they vulcanize."

When your pop's an auto mechanic, you pick up some choice vocab.

Pop sighed like a deflating bouncy castle and turned out his palms—a family gesture.

She wasn't sure how it had happened, this Grand Canyon of a misunderstanding between her and Pop. She was on one side, missing early decision for college, pretending to forget early enrollment, dropping hints about taking a year off. Then way the hell and gone on the other side was Pop, who usually respected her decisions, but now he was wringing his hands, waiting for those applications to go out, still expecting Cherry to be the first Kerrigan to go to college, the family vanguard, the one with *potential*.

She wasn't going to college, and she just couldn't bring herself to tell him.

She added some chopped peppers to the eggs. (In addition to washing the dishes, the boys were incapable of shopping for anything other than microwave pizza and beer.) She served it up on Pop's favorite Patriots plate.

"What's all this green shit?"

"Vegetables," said Cherry.

"No cheese?"

"Are you serious?"

She flicked away the report card and tossed it in the bin with the coffee grounds, browned paper towels, and other garbage.

Something smacked her on the back of the head.

"Goddamn it, Stew!"

7

"Language," said Pop.

"Morning, family!" Cherry's brother opened the cabinet and took down the Cap'n Crunch. "How is everyone this fine Sunday?"

Cherry socked his shoulder, then leaned in close, sniffing. Stew looked at her like she'd just farted. "What?"

"You stink like weed," she said in a whisper.

"You can't smell shit," he hissed.

"You better have left some hot water for me," Pop said, examining a green-and-yellow wad at the end of his fork.

"I got hot water for about two seconds. Blame Cherry," said Stew. He arranged himself in Cherry's seat with the cereal and a carton of milk. Cherry checked the clock on the stove and sat between the boys.

"Eat quickly, all right? We gotta go soon."

"Go where?" Stew asked.

"I got work, genius," Cherry said. "You're driving me, like always."

"Can't today," said Stew, mouth full of cereal. "Pop's got me driving out to Marlborough to pick up a new muffler."

Cherry's jaw dropped. She looked to Pop. "Why didn't you tell me?"

He shrugged. "You can walk it. It's not that far."

"Work starts in five minutes, and it's a fifteen-minute walk!"

"Then I guess you better start running," Stew said.

"Fuck!" Cherry jumped up, knocking over her chair. "*This* is why I need a fucking car, Pop! You said you were gonna fix up one of the old junkers at the shop for me!"

Pop leaned away as if her anger were a hailstorm. "I will, soon as I can."

"You been saying that for two years! *Goddamn it!*"

She grabbed her keys and slammed open the screen door, making for Hope Ave. at a dead sprint.

For the record: Cherry knew she was a crazy girl. She had been since forever. The oldest example, the earliest moment of craziness Cherry could recall, transpired on a humid Tuesday afternoon, after a morning spent doodling with chalk on the sticky-hot driveway. Cherry was bent over her flower, scribbling with a diminishing pink nib, when she heard shouting inside the trailer. She was seven, knees tacky with driveway grit, pink tint on her neck and shoulders from two hours in the hazy sun. The screen door slammed open.

Here the memory skips a frame. It was later, the humidity had hatched thunder and rain, and Pop sat at the kitchen table, just . . . paralyzed. Cherry's mother dragged a flower-print suitcase to a big red sports car of a make and model that all of Cherry's subsequent automotive education could not discern through memory's downpour. There was a man at the wheel. Her mother did not look back or say good-bye. The suitcase's casters jittered over the driveway where Cherry's chalk flowers were rapidly dissolving.

She was too young to get it, what was happening, but knew she now hated her mother. In her childish understanding of the situation, the chalk, which her mother had purchased, was somehow to blame. To hurt Momma, Cherry threw the yellow Crayola chalk box at the big red sports car and screamed, "I don't even *want* it!"

Momma didn't notice. Trunk slam. Door slam. Lightning flash. The brake lights flared, and the red mystery car was gone, taking her mother with it.

This is what Cherry discovered about herself: while her brother hid in his room and her father stared glumly into his coffee, it was Cherry alone, seven-year-old Cherry, who, in so many words, told their selfish, disloyal, inconstant mom to go fuck herself.

Chapter Two

The International Sign for
Help Me, I'm Dying

She'd worked at Burrito Barn since freshman year, when it was Jeb's Chicken Jamboree. In addition to her perfect attendance, Cherry Kerrigan was a master burrito roller. A monkey could fold a taco, but it took an artist to make the perfect burrito. Roll too tight and it exploded in your mouth, too loose and the filling landed in your lap. Burrito rolling wasn't a career plan or anything, but she liked having something she was good at, unlike school. Working hard, getting paid—these were things to be proud of.

Cherry arrived at ten thirty, soaked through and breathing hard. Her manager glanced up from the break-room whiteboard.

"What are you doing here?"

Cherry took a drink from the bubbler. "I work here. Remember?"

"Not today you don't." He pointed at the whiteboard, a grid of indecipherable squiggles. "You're working tomorrow, the twenty-fifth."

"I can't work on Monday. I go to school."

The manager squinted at her, looked back at the board. "You do? How old are you?"

"Also, you didn't tell me I had the day off."

The manager tapped his chin with the marker, leaving an ink soul patch. "Oh, yeah."

"So?"

"So, you're still not working today. It's not on the board." He gestured to the squiggle grid as if this explained everything. "See?"

Cherry plucked the marker from his hand and wrote her name in the 10:30–4:30 slot. "Voilà. It is written." She handed him the marker. "Okay?"

He swallowed and nodded. He was a little afraid of her. That was fine by Cherry.

The burrito station was a long table with a sneeze guard and a sink at one end. The blotter was stenciled with burrito-rolling instructions, which Cherry largely ignored. Above the sink was a three-paneled safety poster. The poster featured two characters: Red Guy and Green Guy. Red Guy was choking, and Green Guy was performing the Heimlich maneuver. Some joker had drawn a fourth panel in which Red and Green were smoking cigarettes, like they'd just had sex. The poster *did* look dirty. Once you saw it, you couldn't unsee it. Though in Cherry's version, Red Guy was a skinny burrito roller with her hair dyed blond, and Green Guy wasn't green at all, but coffee colored, with a leaf-rustle voice and warm, soft hands.

Working the register was Ned, a boy Cherry knew from school. Kids called him Ned the Sped because he took special ed classes. Cherry and Ned were Speds together until eighth grade, when Cherry had graduated to Below Average while Ned stayed Way Below Average. Cherry just called him Ned. When you took special ed, you called *yourself* a Sped. You didn't need reminding.

The morning passed. The lunch rush came and went. Cherry reheated her twentieth package of Zesty Amp-inadas. Ned was picking his nose when two girls approached the register. They weren't local. Their fancy clothes were from catalogs with deck chairs and sailboats: visors and white polo shirts and bug-eye sunglasses that hid their features. They were probably wearing high-heeled sandals. Cherry pretended to need something under the counter and checked.

Yup.

Nobody dressed like that in Aubrey, not even in the nicer parts.

The girls read the menu, the dark-haired one tapping her chin. Her blond friend's lips kinked at the end in a perma-grimace. The bitchy blonde mumbled something, and the pretty brunette giggled.

"Hush, Span. Not everything can be Nobu."

She had a British accent. Because, of course.

Ned cleared his throat. "Howdy and welcome to Burrito Barn. Would you like to try our Border Burrito with Chimmi-Salsa Tater Stackers?"

The dark-haired girl gave Ned a megawatt smile that made her look somehow familiar, though maybe it was only that all rich people looked like they came from the same crystalline gene pool.

"Two . . . Win-Chiladas," she read from the menu, her accent making the ridiculous words sound sophisticated. "And Perrier."

"Who?" said Ned.

"We don't have Perrier. Just soda," Cherry said with her best customer-service smile. "I recommend cherry. It's my favorite."

The brunette smiled back. "Two cherry colas, then."

The blonde made a face like she was choking something back.

Cherry rolled the Win-Chiladas, and the girls took a corner table. Ned stared at them.

"How's the view?".

"I'm pretty sure she's famous," said Ned.

"How can you tell?"

"Famous people wear sunglasses inside."

"Oh, yeah. Good point."

It was the typical midafternoon lull. Standing still drove her ape-shit bonkers, so she wiped down her station and worked to unclog the finicky soda fountain. Her mind wandered as she worked, drifting back to her poster fantasy. The coffee-colored hands had unfastened her bra (and here was where *real* imagination took over; Cherry was seven-tenths a virgin) and were working their way south when a noise yanked her out of the daydream.

Someone was screaming. The bitchy blonde jumped to her feet. Necks swiveled. The other girl, the brunette, was doubled over like she was laughing, but no sound escaped her throat. She clawed at her collar, clutching her neck in the international sign for *Help me, I'm dying.*

Burrito Barn was frozen. The patrons, the manager with his mop, Ned the Sped mouth-breathing at the register—everyone stood stock-still, staring at the choking woman like she was doing performance art.

They can't move, Cherry thought.

They can't move.

I can move.

She dropped her rag, ran one-two-three steps to

the counter; she swung her legs up and over, and then another four strides across the dining-room linoleum, slipping once on the spilled cola. The choking girl's face had turned lavender, not red like the poster. Cherry slipped her arms under the girl's and heaved. She folded her hands into a big fist and punched *in and up, in and up,* just like the poster said. The girl's visor had fallen off, and Cherry could see the dark swirl of hair and the pale scalp underneath.

With a wet, thick hack, something popped out. The girl held her hands to her mouth and caught the gummy brown obstruction. Cherry helped her to a chair and knelt in front of her. Color was returning to her face. Damp hair clung to her cheeks and forehead. All the beauty had been squeezed out of her.

"You okay?" Cherry said.

The girl nodded, clutching the obstruction to her chest like something precious. Her eyes, tearful and bloodshot, fell to Cherry's name tag.

"Cherry?" she wheezed, her voice the texture of powdered soap.

"That's me."

The paralysis in the room was broken. The girl's friend rushed to her side, weeping, kissing her forehead. They hugged each other. A sound like rain filled Cherry's ears.

Applause.

Cherry wandered, dazed, back to her burrito station. People clapped her on the back. Her manager appeared—he'd lost his visor, too—and took her by the shoulders. Cherry felt herself ushered into the back room, a fog filling her brain like steam from the morning's shower. She couldn't think. She wasn't sure she could breathe.

"Holy shit, holy shit." The manager literally jumped up and down. He locked the break-room door. "Oh, my God. I need to call the cops. No! The paper! No, fuck the paper. I'm calling *People* magazine."

"I need some water," Cherry said. The room was spinning much more than usual.

"Cherry, snap out of it. Don't you realize what you've done?"

"Huh?"

"That was Ardelia Deen!" the manager said. "You just saved a movie star!"

You searched for Ardelia Deen.

Related searches: Arden Deen, Lucifer Deen, Maxwell Silver, Cyrus Dar, Cynthia Sundae.

Ardelia Deen

Born: <u>January 1, 1989, London, England, UK more</u> >>

Mini-biography:

Ardelia Deen, daughter of acclaimed film director Arden Deen (1954–), made her cinematic debut at the young age of . . . more >>

Trivia:

An amateur architecture historian, Deen has published several academic papers on Edwardian mansions . . . more >>

Up 71% in popularity this week.

Awards:

Nominated for 2 Golden Globes. Another 15 wins & 24 nominations . . . more >>

Ardelia Deen and Maxwell Silver slated for remake of 1961's *Alive and Unmarried,* to film in Massachusetts

(From Retrovid.com, February 1, 2013, 2:02 PM, PDT)

Cyrus Dar discusses his torrid affair with costar Ardelia Deen

(From Filmgasm, January 21, 2013, 2:58 PM, PDT)

Filmography:

1. *Alive and Unmarried: The Stewart Cane Story* (2014) (*in production*) . . . Olive Aubrey

2. *Lady of the House* (2012) . . . Jane Austen

3. *Cinema Royalty: Arden Deen's Family of Stars* (2007) . . . Herself

4. *Low in the Morning* (2006) . . . Hazel Low, age 14; age 16

5. *Red Shift* (2003) . . . Ruby Blue

6. *The Rented Girl* (1997) . . . Rachel Spatz; Rebecca Spatz

---

You searched for Cherry Kerrigan.

Your search yielded no matches.

Did you mean cherry cola?

Chapter Three

You're Blowing Up

Burrito Barn was like a crime scene with no victim. News vans clogged the parking lot, stacked bumper to bumper along Hope Ave., a forest of satellite dishes rising over the treetops. On the ground, crews reported within earshot of each other:

"No news yet whether Ms. Deen survived the attack . . ."

". . . largely due to unsanitary eating conditions . . ."

". . . was saved by local high-schooler Alice Kerrigan . . ."

Yokels strained against police tape, while the cops crooked their fingers in their belts and everyone craned to catch a glimpse of Keira Knightley or Nicole Richie or whoever it was (reports varied). Other onlookers were gossip fiends who'd seen the news on Twitter and rushed over.

#BurritoBarn was trending.

Squawker Squawker Magazine   2 min ago

@therealArdeliaDeen suffered from an obstructed wind-
pipe, sources confirming she is okay guys! #ArdeliaDeen

CelebsTalker Stan McDonald   4 min ago

@therealArdeliaDeen saves local girl from choking at
some barn! http://brd.ly/6B04R

---

ardentforardelia Nicole   12 min ago

@therealArdeliaDeen is dead??? Someone please
confirm! #panicked #sayitaintso!

---

shutthefunkup Olivia Fenchetti   17 min ago

Pic of #BurritoBarn parking lot. Craziness! Anyone
else hear @therealArdeliaDeen was saved by
@CherrySmack? #IKnowHer! twittpic.com/6mD4s

Ardelia and her blond friend had vanished, escaping in a
little Italian sports car just before the press arrived. The
manager was more than eager to give his statement, but

no one cared what he had to say. Cherry, on the other hand, was cornered in the break room by half a dozen news crews. The reporters were packed shoulder to shoulder pad in the tiny room. The cameramen stood just behind, like a second layer of shark's teeth, squinting into viewfinders. The sound guys were at the back, balancing fuzzy boom mikes that bumped against the ceiling, making headphones squeal. The wall of plastic, paisley, and heavily made-up faces formed an advancing semicircle around Cherry. Now she understood why they were called the *press*.

"What went through your mind when you saw that Ms. Deen couldn't breathe?" a woman in a neckerchief asked.

Cherry took a breath and tried to gather her thoughts. There weren't many to gather. Her brain felt emptied. Was this really happening? No, obviously not.

"I think it was, *That woman can't breathe,*" she replied.

A cameraman chuckled. She hadn't meant to be funny.

"Are you a big fan of Ms. Deen's?"

Cherry shrugged. "Not really."

She judged from their expressions this wasn't the answer they expected or wanted. "My brother's obsessed with her, though. He's got a poster of her above his bed."

More laughter from the camera guys. This time even some of the reporters smiled.

"Which poster?" a girl in a Freaktallica T-shirt asked, holding out her mini-recorder.

"What's the one where she plays Jane Austen and hunts vampires?" Cherry asked.

"Lady of the House," everyone seemed to say in unison.

A few of the reporters chuckled this time. The bored newspaper guys glanced up, pens poised.

"Yeah, that's the one," said Cherry. "She's in that white nightgown and holding the bloody stake. The movie was okay. I heard the book sucked, though."

"Were you excited to meet a celebrity?" the local news lady asked, inching forward.

"No," said Cherry. "I mean, I dunno. I didn't really know who she was. I just thought she was some hot chick in a polo shirt who didn't know how to chew her food."

This time, they *all* laughed.

"So, you didn't recognize Ms. Deen when she entered?"

"No, but I knew she was rich."

"How's that?"

"Her clothes are from Star and Liberty," Cherry said. "We don't really have swanky shit like that in Aubrey." She winced. "Shit. Can I say 'shit'?"

"Sure!" said the girl from TMZ.

"We can edit it out," said the Worcester Cable News guy.

"You seem pretty unimpressed with celebrity," the *Boston Globe* man said.

"I don't know," said Cherry. "I never met a celebrity before."

"So, how does it feel?"

She thought about it, searching for something profound. "She's so . . . small. She looks big on-screen, you know? Not *fat* just . . . like a *giant*. And in reality she's this tiny person. I mean, I could wrap my arms around her twice."

"Are you worried that Ms. Deen has an eating disorder?"

"Could this incident be related to bulimia?"

"Why do you think Hollywood is so obsessed with body-image issues?"

"Whoa!" Cherry put out her palms. "I just said the bitch was fit. I don't know if she's anorexic or whatever. In fact, she ordered some pretty fatty food, so . . ."

"I love it!" someone said.

"I have a question," a woman in no-nonsense glasses asked. "The restaurant was full of people, and by all accounts you were the farthest from Ms. Deen."

"Yeah," said Cherry. "That's right."

"Why do you think *you* ran to her aid, and no one else did?"

The room got very quiet, and for the first time Cherry was aware, *really* aware, that she was talking to an audience of millions, to more people than she had ever or would ever meet in a lifetime.

"I guess it's because most people, when something goes wrong, they think about what to do," said Cherry.

"And you knew what to do?" someone offered.

"No," said Cherry. "I just don't think."

"Amazing," someone said. "This is way better than Christina's leaked photos."

More questions. More photos. She felt faint. She was going to go down like a prizefighter if they didn't give her some air. They loved her, they couldn't get enough of her, but Cherry'd had more than enough of them. Finally she said she had to pee and locked herself in the bathroom. There was a skinny window near the ceiling. It took a few attempts, but soon she was able to squirm through the small gap and out into the alley behind Burrito Barn. She dropped to the pavement, her top streaked with grease and grit from the windowsill.

Ned was there, smoking a cigarette.

"What's wrong with the door?" he asked.

"Those fuckers don't know when to quit." Ned offered her the smoke. She shook her head. "See ya, Ned."

She started down the alley, but Ned stopped her.

"You wanna go the back way." He nodded over his shoulder. "There're still a bunch of news guys in the parking lot."

Cherry smiled. "Thanks, Ned."

• • •

She jogged up Hope Ave., a crazy girl with wild hair in a filthy Burrito Barn uniform. She was halfway home when her brother's tricked-out Dubber came over the ridge. She flagged him down.

"I was just coming to get you."

She slid into the passenger seat. "Work let out early. On account of extreme craziness."

"Holy shit, so it's true?" Stew showed her his cell phone, a text from his latest girlfriend:

> Stewie ur sis saved Ardelia Deen from poisoning!

"Choking, actually."

"Damn."

He pulled into traffic, reaching across her lap for the glove compartment. Stew extracted a joint and lit up.

"You're kidding, right?"

Stew shrugged. "This is a *situation*. You want?"

"No." She waved the smoke away from her face.

"Okay, so, you gotta tell me."

"Tell you what?"

His voice was like a frog, smoke tumbling out with his words. "Are they real? Her tits?"

"Jesus, Stew!" She punched his arm, and the Dubber swerved a little.

"I'm just saying, when you did CPR or whatever,

you probably got a good feel. I mean, you're in the position to answer a question many a young man has pondered...."

"You are *such* a guy."

"That's what they tell me." Stew smiled around the joint in his lips.

"All right," said Cherry. "Yeah, they're real."

"Oh!" Stew let go of the wheel, throwing his hands up like he was on a roller coaster. "She noticed! I *knew* you were a lesbian!"

"You *fucker*." She socked him again, plucked the joint from his fingertips, and flicked it out the window.

They were both laughing so hard, Stew had to pull over a block from their driveway, just so they could contain themselves.

Pop was MIA. Cherry and Stew booted up the family's HP. The dial-up buzzed and sang its weird music.

"Cherry, you are blowing up," said Stew.

It was true. Not only did she have 217 new friend requests, but her followers on Twitter had tripled. The YouTube video of her interview already had 127,000 views. Cherry read the comment stream:

LOL fucking hick
Mrjazz 1 min ago
don't be a hater dickhead shes sweet
starcrusher45 1 min ago

WE LOVE YOU, CHERRY!
    Believerbelieves 1 min ago

That girl is tooo skinny someone tell her to eat something
    stacKED27 1 min ago

Is anyone else fantasizing about her giving Ardelia the Heimlich maneuver?
    FallGuy 1 min ago
        I am!
        anonymous 1 min ago

the squawker.com clip is higher rez check it out on myfeed
    ArdeliaTube 2 min ago

Squawker, TMZ, all the major celeb blogs were talking about her. The front page of Trip'd featured a publicity shot of Ardelia next to a photo of . . . *shit.*

"I look terrible!"

The photo they'd used was from the Burrito Barn break room. Cherry was sweat stained, pale, and haggard. It had been taken while Cherry was midsentence, midblink, possibly mid-sneeze.

"*'I just thought she was some hot chick in a polo shirt who didn't know how to chew her food,'*" Stew read. "Did you really say that?"

"*Jesus.*" Cherry gripped the sides of the monitor. "I sound like an idiot! It didn't sound that stupid when I said it."

"Check it out," said Stew. "You're even on Auto-Tune the News."

"You're kidding me."

Someone had set a clip from Cherry's interview to music, editing her words together so it sounded like she was singing.

"No, but I knew / I knew / I knew she was riiiiiich," the web Cherry sang. *"Shit! / Can I say 'shit'? / Well. / I knew she was riiiiich!"*

"My sister the meme," Stew said. "Also, thanks for mentioning the poster thing, asshole. You made me sound like a skeeve."

Cherry leaned her forehead against the desk. "Damn it. Why can't I just keep my mouth shut?"

"Maybe this is the reason." Stew brought up SweetWear.com, the design-your-own T-shirt site. Top rated was something called the Cherry Tee, a red-and-black tee with a message in white lettering over the outline of a cherry. It said:

I DON'T THINK.

"Fabulous," Cherry said. "Fucking. Fabulous."

"Where are you going?"

"Out," she said, unlocking the back door. "If Pop asks, I'm at Lucas's."

Chapter Four

Constant Velocity

The Kerrigans' backyard was a small patch of scrub surrounded by a chain-link fence. An elm stood in the corner, its branches extending over the yard and their neighbors', the DuBoises. Cherry used the tree to hoist herself over the fence. Somewhere above her, near the wooden plank Pop had nailed there years ago as a tree house for her and Stew, a heart had been carved into the trunk. Etched inside were these words: CHERRY + LUCAS.

The tree had continued to grow, smoothing the rough edges of the lettering, rounding the curves of the heart; the exposed bark had darkened over the years, but it was still legible. It was still true.

Cherry dropped onto the DuBoises' back lawn. The rear window of their trailer, the counterpart of Cherry's bedroom, glowed. Lucas leaned over his desk, carving a new design into the hacked-to-shit blotter. Cherry rapped on the screen. He grinned now, his teeth looking immaculately white against his dark skin.

"Hello, you gorgeous thing." She leaned her arms against the sill.

He raised the screen and leaned out for a kiss. He tasted like coffee. He always tasted like coffee. It was enough to make a girl a Starbucks freak.

It was widely acknowledged that Lucas DuBois was the only dude chill enough to date Cherry Kerrigan. He was the mellow ying to her manic yang, the silent partner to Cherry's chatter, responding in monosyllables with the occasional New Orleans drawl he'd inherited from his Creole father. (Cherry referred to these honeysuckle-dipped phrases as "panty remover.") Kids who liked Cherry referred to their relationship as adorable; kids who didn't joked that no matter what Lucas had in his shorts, Cherry Kerrigan had the bigger balls in *that* relationship.

But really she was wrapped around his finger.

"*Mmm. . . .*" She laid her head on her arms and batted her eyelashes at him. "I've been waiting for that sugar *all* day."

"You and me both." He handed her a piece of paper. "Latest design. What do you think?"

She considered the sketch. Like all of Lucas's artwork, it was hysterical and vibrant. He spoke softly, but the boy painted *loud*.

"I love it." She traced the contours with her finger-tip. "Where you going to paint it?"

"I got the spot picked out."

"Let's go!"

Lucas checked his watch. "Now?"

"I got to get out of here," Cherry said. "I had a crazy day I'd rather not think about."

"What happened?"

"I take it you haven't been online lately."

Lucas didn't do Facebook or Twitter, and he'd only gotten e-mail at Cherry's insistence. The TV was usually turned to sports in the DuBois household.

"Not recently."

"I'll tell you on the way," she said. "You'll laugh your ass off."

They trekked down the darkened path along Sweet Creek. Lucas's duffel of paint cans went *poing!* and *clang!* as it bounced against his leg, echoing across the ravine. The wet weather had turned the gentle slope to slick mud, and they clung to each other, sneakers pressing into the slime as they clutched each other's sleeves.

Lucas shook his head. "So you're a web celebrity now. A *webrity.*"

"It's awful."

"Why?"

She blew a wisp of hair. "All these comments on how

I look or talk or act . . . Like I *asked* for it. Like I deserve getting hated on because I wanted attention in the first place. Which I didn't."

"It'll blow over," said Lucas. "What's that line about fifteen minutes of fame?"

"I fucking hope so. Jesus, I hadn't even thought about school."

"Nobody will care."

Cherry let out a humorless laugh. "Oh, yeah, they will. This is, like, the biggest thing to happen in our town since that girl found a potato that looked like Mother Teresa."

"It was an apple. And who cares? You don't care what people think."

She smirked, threading her fingers through his.

"Is Badass Cherry Kerrigan actually feeling a little *vulnerable*?"

"How's this for vulnerable?" She twisted his arm until he cried out in pain.

"All right, all right! Jesus."

"Come on, you like it."

Lucas rubbed his sore knuckles. "So what did your father say?"

"He hasn't seen it yet, I don't think." She sighed.

"Oh?"

She explained the latest chapter in the college saga. The message was clear: *Go somewhere, because here isn't good enough*. But what was so bad about Aubrey? She looked up through the branches. Bats were wheeling in the sky, disappearing in front of the water tower, and reappearing again like black sparks. She loved her hometown. It was part of her. Aubrey was a silent family member. She couldn't just abandon it.

"He's just worried about you," said Lucas. He knew there was no changing Cherry Kerrigan's mind once she'd set it.

"What about you? You worry about me?"

"Never."

They came to a quiet stretch of Route 9 that ran over the creek. The water disappeared into a drainage pipe. Together they climbed up the embankment and crossed the pavement. A dirt road led into the woods, and there was a sign that read:

UTILITY ACCESS ONLY
NO ADMITTANCE

They sidled over the chain and made their way down the potholed path, Cherry using her toe to dig out rocks embedded in the soft earth, kicking them down the lane. At last they came to a train bridge, towering over the riverbed like a dinosaur in the moonlight. It was just bright enough for working. A cement canvas twenty feet wide and sixty feet high.

While Lucas set up his gear, Cherry stretched out on a flat rock overlooking the creek bed. She could see the stars through the railroad struts above. She listened to the rattle and hiss as her boyfriend began the first outlines of his piece, which would be sixteen feet across and incorporate seven different colors. Lucas hated the word *graffiti*. His artwork wasn't bubble lettering or crazy script (he'd call that *too nineties, too Fresh Prince*). Instead it resembled his favorite subversive street artist, Bonzo. He liked to paint people, often children, clinging to the real cracks in the pavement, hiding behind a real drainage pipe, interacting with the surface he painted on. Cherry felt that Lucas's people seemed to want to jump off the wall.

"Why'd you choose this spot?" Cherry asked, sitting up. "I mean, it's real romantic and all, but no one's gonna see it."

"Less likely someone will paint over it, then," Lucas said, shaking the chromium yellow. "Besides, we'll know it's here. We'll be old and ugly, and this will still be here and still look fine."

Like Cherry, Lucas had no plans for college. He'd work as a janitor at the high school like his dad. Her man was an *artist,* and he didn't need a college degree or a generous grant from the White People Foundation to make art. This was one reason Cherry loved him. He didn't need to *go somewhere* to be amazing.

He stepped back and admired his work. He'd

embellished a crack in the cement, widened it, length-ened its offshoots into tree branches, and added leaves and blossoms. Below he'd painted a small girl in a dress, her hand pressed to the tree, as if feeling its bark.

Cherry snuck up behind him and wrapped her arms around his waist. He twirled her around and pressed her against the strut. Cherry giggled. She wasn't a giggler, a blusher, a *girl*—Lucas brought it out of her.

"So . . . what *do* you want to do?" he asked.

"Right now?"

"After school."

Cherry shrugged, fiddling with the buttons on his shirt. "I dunno. Get a job? Maybe an apartment downtown?"

"All by yourself?"

"Why, you got a better plan?"

Lucas licked his lips.

"What? What is it?"

She could hear the roar of the creek where it got deeper up ahead. She could hear the roar of the highway. There was a roar in her ears, too.

"Let's get married."

"I beg your *what*?"

The moonlight glinted off Lucas's teeth. Pressed against him, she could feel his heart racing under his spat-tered painting shirt. "Why not. You love me, right?"

"Yeah . . ."

"And I'm pretty into you—"

She shoved his shoulder. "Jerk."

"So, let's get married. I don't want anyone else."

Cherry opened her mouth, hoping the right words would just fall out. She felt dizzy. She'd only had one other boyfriend (Big Mistake). She'd known Lucas since preschool, when his family moved into the trailer behind hers. One morning she found him carving his name into *her* tree and said if he didn't stop, she'd beat him senseless. He offered to carve her name, too, which she'd accepted as a compromise. They were bound together thereafter, first as friends and for the last two years as a couple.

The bridge began to hum.

"Jesus, Cherry. Say something!"

Cherry's breath quickened. Tiny freight trains coursed in her veins, rushed through the hub of her heart. Her bones vibrated with the approach, the engine, the wheels, the noise, the track humming all the way from now into the endless future, and she had to hop on or let it blast by because life would not slow down for her. And really there was no question because there was only one place she wanted to go, an inner place, a place with Lucas.

She breathed *yes* into his mouth just as the 8:21 to Boston blasted, *exploded* overhead, quaking the bridge and rattling the paint cans in their duffel bag, vibrating the happy couple pressed against the strut. Once it had passed and Cherry and Lucas pulled back from their kiss, the train was gone, but she was still rocketing on, moving forward, breathless with velocity.

Chapter Five

A Thing of Beauty

Once, on a dare, Cherry had chugged an entire twenty-ounce Red Bull. The effect of all that caffeine, aside from making her jaw clench, was a kind of relaxed hysteria, like a tiny, insane Cherry was doing jumping jacks inside her skull. She felt something similar now, saying good night to Lucas at his door. Like life was set, certain, and simultaneously so fucking exciting, she might piss her pants (another side effect of the Red Bull).

But the dreamy-giddy thing lasted only as far as the chain-link fence, and then something began to grate at the edges. She'd have to tell the fam. She didn't want to tell them. The news was perfect so long as it was just hers. Stew would laugh it off, make a joke like he always did. Pop . . . Pop would be trouble. He'd see it as the nail in Cherry's college coffin, an idea that was already sealed and buried.

She crossed the backyard, auditioning her tone out loud.

"Lucas asked me to marry him. . . . Pop, I'm marrying Lucas." No, that was taking the offensive, which made her feel like a sneaker-stomping little girl. Climbing the rear steps, she tried again, imagining her father in his armchair, staring up at her in glum disbelief. "Poppa, there's something I need to tell you. . . ." Too dramatic. Keep it light. "Okay, you wanna hear something *nuts* . . . ?"

No.

Fuck it. If Pop didn't like it, tough. She wasn't going to make a production.

She opened the door.

"Hi. I'm engaged."

The trailer was empty. She checked the bedrooms; the garage was dark and vacant. No note. It was 9:30. At this hour Pop was usually watching TV, halfway through a six-pack of Silver Bullets. She checked her phone, also lifeless. She was on her way to charge it when she heard a car pull in, an engine die, a door slam. Now she pictured Pop lumbering up the walk, fist stuffed in his jean pocket, searching for his keys.

Cherry opened the front door.

"Hi. I'm *ennnn* . . ." The last word teetered over the edge like Wile E. Coyote. Cherry steadied herself against the door frame to keep from tumbling off the stoop. The mental image of her father snapped back like a rubber band, leaving Cherry brain-numb, completely stalled.

There was a movie star on her doorstep.

Ardelia Deen looked much recovered. She was dressed in a swimming green cocktail dress, her flawless features touched with makeup.

"Cherry, right?" She offered a manicured hand. Cherry shook it.

"Yeah."

"Sorry, you must think I'm absolutely *bonkers* just dropping in like this. My manager got the address from *your* manager, ha-ha." She swallowed.

Cherry's brain was still stumbling. Pop, the engagement, Lucas . . .

"I'm sorry, what's happening?"

"I wanted to say thank you. I'm sorry I didn't this afternoon. I was so distracted, and Spanner—that's my manager, the friend I was with—she insisted we rush off before the press showed up. And then there was a checkup at hospital, and with one thing and another . . ." She took a breath. "Anyway, I am sorry it's so late, but I had to see you in person. *Thank you,* Cherry."

"Oh! Yeah, sure." Cherry tried to clear her head, shaking it. "You're welcome. I just did . . . It was nothing."

"Not to me!"

The intensity of her tone startled them both; Ardelia's voice was for amiable after-party interviews and gracious *your welcome*s while signing photographs, not life-and-death talk. She smiled and flipped her hand to lighten the tension. Cherry squinted. She didn't seem like that afternoon's Burrito Barn customer or the towering goddess Cherry knew from the big screen. Ardelia Deen in person was something new, something huge and vague, reduced in size. And sharpened.

She had no clue what to say.

"So . . ."

"I love your"—Ardelia waved absently—"caravan."

"What? Oh, the trailer. Yeah it's . . . I like your dress. It's really"—she groped for something intelligent—"green."

"Chartreuse, actually."

She nodded vigorously. "Oh, yeah. Chartreuse. I love their stuff."

"Actually chartreuse is the *color*," Ardelia said, blushing. "The designer is . . . It's Faviana, but . . . Wow." The starlet took a breath. "I just sound incredibly pretentious, don't I?"

"No! No, no. It's me. I'm retarded."

"Don't use that word." Ardelia cleared her throat. "I mean. Well."

"Well." Cherry made a gee-golly gesture. "I guess this wins for most awkward conversation ever."

Ardelia Deen chuckled. Cherry had actually made a movie star laugh. "Yes, I guess it does," Ardelia said.

Cherry looked around for something, anything to talk about—and that was when she saw Ardelia's wheels.

"Oh. My. *Lord.*" She rushed to the gleaming silver sports car. "You drive an *Alfa Romeo?*"

"Is that what it is? I had my manager pick it out for me. I just told her I wanted a car like the one from *La Dolce Vita.* Sort of a present to myself, but to be honest, I barely ever drive it."

Cherry peered inside. "This is a Series 2 Spider. This shit is *vintage.* You can tell it's from the seventies, after they chopped off the tail and put in the padded dash." She stepped back to take it in all at once. "I need a cold shower after seeing this."

Ardelia seemed impressed. "You certainly know your cars."

"Pop owns a garage. I was conceived and born in the back of a Fiat."

Ardelia laughed again. "Honestly, I'm a useless driver. I learned on British models, and this whole other-side-of-the-road thing? Impossible."

"This is really . . ." Cherry pressed her palms to the hood. It was hot and cool at the same time. "This is a thing of beauty."

She hadn't noticed Ardelia watching her, admiring her admiration, or maybe just thinking she was nuts. The movie star smiled.

"Do you want to go for a spin?"

"Really? I mean, could we?"

"Would you like that? I don't particularly like driving, but if you want to . . ."

Cherry was already behind the wheel. Ardelia climbed into the passenger seat. Cherry sank low, running her hands over the console.

"I'm going to have to make love to your car now."

"Well, buy it dinner first."

The girls laughed. The keys were in the ignition.

"Listen to that! She *purrs.*"

"Now," said Ardelia, "I've noticed it's a little touchy, so go easy at—"

Chapter Six

Whooo!!!

Ardelia's sentence was cut short as both girls were thrown back into their seats. Sugar Village blurred, reeled, and was gone before Ardelia could fumble with her seat belt.

"*Whooo!!!*" Cherry howled.

"Well, I didn't know it could do *that*."

"Not *it*. *She*. A car like this is definitely a *she*." She pulled onto Hope Ave. and reduced speed. "That was *fun*."

"It was, wasn't it?" Ardelia bit her lip. "How fast do you think it—*she*—can go?"

Cherry shrugged. "Specs claim 158 miles per hour."

"What's that in kilometers?"

"I have *no* idea."

"Hmm." Ardelia thought, eyeing her driving companion. "What do you say we find a highway and see what she can *really* do?"

"I dunno. You think? If we get pulled over . . ."

"Speeding tickets are on me!"

Cherry squeezed the leather steering wheel, rubbing her fingers into the grooves. "All right, Ms. Movie Star. You're on."

Route 290 zigged and zagged, winding itself under the wheels like measuring tape zipping back into its casing. In a few minutes, they'd reached the edge of Aubrey. Cherry took the last exit before Worcester and plotted a return course on Route 9, a smaller street-level highway that traced the outskirts of town. In no time they'd reached the Webster border, having circumnavigated Aubrey entirely. It gave her a chilly shock. The world felt so small at this speed.

"Tell me about yourself!" Ardelia said too suddenly. She sounded nervous, but that made no sense. Movie stars didn't get nervous around normal people. Not that Cherry knew many movie stars. Or normal people, for that matter.

"Not much to tell. One time I gave Ardelia Deen the Heimlich maneuver."

"Oh, I'm sure there's more than that."

"Well . . ." A smile crept onto Cherry's lips. Was it weird to tell a stranger before her family? The news was so big, so crazy in itself, it made a strange kind of sense that the first person she told was Ardelia Deen. In an Alfa Romeo.

"I got engaged. Today. Just now."

"*What?* That's wonderful news!"

Ardelia's glee was disarming. Cherry took her eyes from the road to glance at her. "You actually seem excited."

"I am!" She flashed her perfect teeth, bouncing in her seat. "What's his name? Who is he? How did he ask? Tell me *everything.*"

"His name is Lucas. We've been dating for a few years, but I've known him since we were little kids. He lives in the trailer behind mine."

"He's *literally* the boy next door." The starlet sank low in her seat. "That is *so* romantic. I wish I had someone like that."

"He's perfect," said Cherry. "He's . . . he's a street artist."

"Like Bonzo."

Cherry nearly took her eyes off the road again. "You know about *Bonzo?*"

"Darling, he's a cultural icon, not to mention a Brit. I mean now, he's a little . . ."

"Played out," finished Cherry.

"Exactly."

"*No one* around here knows who Bonzo is. They think he's a TV clown from the sixties."

Ardelia laughed. "We *must* celebrate. Why don't I

take you to dinner? Do you know Ascot in Boston? They do the most fabulous *amuse-bouches. . . .*"

Cherry's good cheer evaporated. She imagined strolling into a fancy restaurant looking like an idiot in her sponge-gray track shirt. International Internet humiliation was bad enough for one day, thank you. Plus, who could afford a restaurant that served French-sounding food? And *Boston*? That was light-years away.

"I've got a better idea," said Cherry.

The Spider huzzed into a 7-Eleven parking lot, stopping just short of the concrete benches and cigarette canisters guarding the entrance.

"What's this?"

"You want food? This is food!" said Cherry. "This is what me and my friends do for late-night eats."

"Oh! Fabulous. Never been in one." Ardelia hopped out of the car, striding toward the chaotic glow of the convenience store, dress swirling like an anemone. She managed to make 7-Eleven look like a red-carpet event.

The store was empty save for Jim the Clerk, who in the movie version, Cherry thought, would have been reading a magazine with Ardelia's picture on the cover. Jim barely noticed them.

"What's on?" Ardelia said, rubbing her hands. "I'm *famished.*"

Cherry steered her toward the candy rack. "*This* is

my favorite." She handed Ardelia a length of rubbery something in a foil sheath.

"What is it?"

She expected Ardelia to recoil in horror. Instead, the starlet unwrapped the candy right there and took a bite.

"Oh, my God," she said, mouth full. "This is *divine*!"

That was unexpected.

"Really?"

Ardelia considered the rack. "Are they all this good? What's this?" She took a box of brightly colored straws.

"You've never seen Pixy Stix?" Cherry said, now genuinely shocked. "Pixy Stix are, like, an *institution*. Didn't you have a childhood?"

"Clearly I've been deprived."

Cherry laughed. "You need to be educated." She slapped the Pixy Stix and the remains of Ardelia's Laffy Taffy on the counter, fishing in her shorts for spare change.

"What about this?" Ardelia said, holding a small plastic package.

"Bubble Tape? It's bubble gum. It's awesome." Cherry counted the meager handful of quarters. "I think we can only get two things, though."

Ardelia waved. "Nonsense, it's on me."

Cherry ruffled. She leveled a Pixy Stix at Ardelia. "I don't let people buy me things, *comprende*?"

Ardelia snatched the Pixy Stix away.

"Oh, get *over* it, Cherry Kerrigan. I'm paying and that's final."

The clerk clicked the register. "Is that all?"

"Wait . . ." Cherry blinked. What just happened?

"No," said Ardelia. She stepped back, examining the rack of candy. "I can't decide."

"They're all good," the clerk offered.

"Are they? Fine, then," said Ardelia. "How much for the whole rack?"

Wrappers littered the Spider's floor, the cramped space behind the seats stuffed to the wheel well with boxes and boxes of Nerds, Bottle Caps, Mike & Ikes, and every other bad-for-you whatsit the 7-Eleven had to offer.

"What is it?" Ardelia asked.

A length of licorice rope dangled from Cherry's lips. She chewed, quiet since 7-Eleven, working her thoughts into a soft, gummy paste.

"I don't know," she said. "You're not like most rich people."

Ardelia tipped back a box of Sno-Caps. "What are most rich people like?"

"I couldn't imagine them eating Sno-Caps, for one thing. You're kinda . . ." She swallowed the licorice rope. "I like you."

"Well, thank you. I like you, too." Ardelia tossed a

crumpled carton into the backseat. "Most of the poor people I know make unfair generalizations about entire swaths of the population."

Cherry rallied a comeback, then caught herself. "Ahh, I see what you did there."

"Clever, right?"

Cherry smirked. "Very clever, movie star."

Ardelia offered her a bag of candy. Cherry took a piece.

"What are these called?" Ardelia asked.

"Marshmallow Circus Peanuts," said Cherry.

"That's what they *are,* but what are they *called*?"

"That's their *name.* Marshmallow Circus Peanuts." Cherry was laughing. She was actually having a good time.

Ardelia held one up. "Absolutely brilliant."

There was a *crack,* and the wheel spun free of Cherry's hands. The Spider swerved, sending a landslide of sugary orange puffs into the foot well. They wobbled into the right lane, Ardelia shrieking. Cherry steadied the car.

"Bloody Christ, twice in one day," Ardelia gasped, clinging to her seat belt. "What happened?"

"Wait," said Cherry. "Listen."

Something made a warbling sound underneath the car.

"Did we hit something?"

Cherry signaled into the breakdown lane, and the girls stepped onto the shoulder of Route 9. This stretch of road was dark, with thick forest beyond the reflectors and guardrails. A green exit sign gleamed up ahead. A semi blasted by. They came around to the rear of the car. The bottom of the right tire lay flattened against the asphalt, air hissing from an invisible puncture.

Ardelia pressed a hand to her forehead. *"Shit."*

"Fuck. It's my fault," said Cherry.

Ardelia sighed. "It was an accident. What do we do now, though?"

"You have Triple A?"

"Triple what?"

"Okay." Cherry considered their options. "We'll change it ourselves. I'm sure there's a spare in the —"

She popped the trunk. It was tiny and packed with luggage, a field of *L*'s and *V*'s.

Ardelia winced. "I took the tire out."

"So you could fit . . ." Cherry started.

"So I could fit my new luggage," Ardelia finished.

"Right."

"Right."

"So?" Ardelia brandished her smart phone. "Tow truck?"

"There's only one mechanic in town, and right about now he's watching *My Name Is Earl*." Cherry nodded toward the exit sign. "Pop's auto shop isn't far. We can get a spare tire there."

"How do we get there?"

Cherry patted the rear bumper. "We push."

"As in . . . the car?"

"Yeah. I'll put her in neutral. It'll be easy with the both of us."

Ardelia gazed at her phone with a pained expression. "Why don't I just call someone to get us?"

"Movie Star, we can't leave this car here. It'll get towed or, worse, stripped. And besides . . ." She pushed the other girl's shoulder, a gentler version of her usual punch. "Why pay someone else when you can do it yourself?"

"I was about to say precisely the opposite."

Another truck rumbled past, honked twice, didn't slow.

"Well?" said Cherry.

Ardelia tucked her phone away. "Fine. Let's just get it over with."

Cherry climbed behind the wheel, shifted into neutral, and popped the emergency brake. Too late, she realized Ardelia was already braced against the rear. The Spider lurched forward and the other girl disappeared in the rearview mirror. Cherry rushed to the back of the car, where Ardelia was on her ass, spread-eagled in the grime, hair hanging over her face.

"Oh, fuck! Are you okay?"

Ardelia was convulsing. Cherry pictured twisted ankles, sprained wrists. The starlet turned her face to the sky. Her cocktail dress was covered in mud, dirt speckled her ivory complexion, and she was laughing.

"What's so funny?"

Ardelia sniffed, trying to catch her breath. She looked down at her ruined dress.

"Chartreuse!"

Cherry was speechless, dumbfounded by this weird-ass, bat-shit, mind-blowing, star-studded, heartbeat-y, pulse-racing, head-spinning, face-melting *brain-fuck* of a day. She laughed too, so hard she couldn't stand anymore and dropped into the mud. The girls leaned against the crippled car and filled the vacant road with their cackles.

Chartreuse. It *was* a ridiculous word.

Chapter Seven

Kerrigan Auto

The Spider jerked, heaved, and rolled into the lot of Kerrigan Auto on Main Street, pushed by two sticky, filthy, bruised young women. They lurched the last few feet into the waiting garage.

"If only my friends could see me now," Cherry said.

Ardelia picked at a leaf sticking to her rear. "I was thinking the same thing."

Cherry turned on the shop lights, casting a glare across the chrome and metal tools. The light was on in Pop's office, a half-finished beer on the desk, still cold, as if they'd just missed him. Ardelia, refreshing herself with a bottle of water from the mini-fridge, inspected the guts of a turbo engine, then peered into the undercarriage of an elevated pickup truck.

"This is where your father works?"

"It's his business," Cherry said. "This is my inheritance."

Ardelia hefted a menacing-looking power drill. "Very impressive. Will we get to use this?"

"Not to change a tire," Cherry said. "But if you want to put holes in shit, there's an old Gremlin out back."

"Delicious."

The girls positioned themselves on the dusty floor. Cherry showed Ardelia a length of beveled piping with a crosspiece. "This," she said, "is a tire iron."

"I bet I know why it's called that."

Cherry started on the busted tire. "Now, you wanna pop the bolts before you jack up the car. That way the weight on the wheel gives you extra leverage."

"I'm learning so much today," Ardelia said. "No more shall I be a damsel in distress."

"I hate damsels, especially distressed ones." Cherry grunted, popping off the last bolt. "Okay, now we jack." She rummaged under Pop's table and came back with a jack. "You should always keep one of these in your trunk."

Ardelia saluted. "Roger."

Cherry showed her how to position the jack under the car and started to crank. After a few revolutions, she felt Ardelia's gaze.

"Do I have something on my face?" asked Cherry.

"Yes. Grease. And possibly caramel?" Ardelia wiped

Cherry's cheek with her thumb. "But I was wondering why you dye your hair."

Cherry cranked with a little more force. "You can tell?"

"Darling, I may not be able to change a tire, but I know a home dye job when I see one. Your eyebrows don't match."

Cherry let out a breath. "I dunno. I like blond better." *Crank, crank.* The Spider wobbled higher. "Also, Pop always says I look like my mother, and I'm not too wild about that." She wiped her brow. "I never told anyone that."

"Mum's in Cabo with a yoga instructor named Juan," Ardelia said.

"You're kidding."

"I'm not."

"Mothers, right?"

"Who needs them?"

Cherry sat back, sweating from the effort. "Well, Ms. Oscar Nominee. Ready to change your first tire?"

Ardelia wrapped an arm around Cherry's shoulder. "My *God,* yes."

As they pulled into the trailer park, Ardelia texted something on her phone.

"You're seventeen Sugar Village, right?"

"That's me. And we're here."

Cherry brought the Spider to the curb and killed the engine. Ardelia turned in her seat.

"This was . . . magical."

Cherry shrugged. "What can I say? I'm a good time."

"You certainly are. Thank you. For everything."

They hugged.

"I guess I'll see you on the big screen."

"I suppose so."

The girls climbed out, and Cherry headed for the door. She turned. "Take care of that car, will ya? She's a beauty."

"Cherry."

"Yeah?"

Ardelia tossed her something shining, tinkling. Car keys.

"She's yours."

"What?"

Ardelia patted the hood. "You'll take better care of her than I can. It's the least I can do."

"Holy shit." Cherry stared at the keys like they might suddenly turn into Marshmallow Circus Peanuts. "Holy. Shit. You're giving me your *car*?"

"Well, one of them."

"I . . . I can't take this!" She gaped at the gleaming automobile. "Jesus, what am I saying? Of course I can!" She ran to Ardelia and hugged her, squeezing until her back cracked. "Thank you!"

"Don't break me!"

"You want me to drop you at your hotel?"

"No need," Ardelia said.

An engine growled, and a black SUV rounded the corner. It parked across the street, and a kid in a Paramount polo shirt climbed down from the driver's seat and opened the rear door.

"Car service by text," Ardelia said, waggling her phone. "A nice perk."

"You're officially my new favorite movie star."

Ardelia waved. "See you around, Cherry Kerrigan."

The SUV pulled away, disappearing onto Hope Ave. Sugar Village was quiet again.

Cherry tested the weight of the keys in her hand and rubbed her thumb across the Alfa Romeo bobble that hung from the ring like a lucky rabbit's foot. They were *hers*. She jumped, pumping her fists, and whooped at the moon so loud, every dog in the neighborhood started barking.

She could hear voices as she approached the trailer door. She came in to see Stew waving his hands like he was putting out a fire.

"She's coming, she's coming!" he hissed.

"I can hear you, jackass," Cherry said, laughing. "You guys are *not* going to believe this—"

Pop stood at attention by the side door like the world's fattest palace guard. He cleared his throat.

"My lady, if you'd step this way."

Stew patted her back, grinning. "Oh, man, are you gonna love this."

"Have you two gone completely mental? What is this?"

She was ushered into the garage.

"I was going to wait for your birthday, but after all the craziness this afternoon, I figured we could do this a little early," Pop said.

"Do what?"

He flicked on the overhead.

Bathed in the halogen light was a rust-spotted Gremlin, freshly refurbished with new (though mismatched) doors and side-view mirrors, a bumper from a Volvo 950, and a beautiful chrome muffler, brought out special from Marlborough.

"Ta-da!" Pop spread his arms wide. "And she's all yours."

"I mean, she's no Dubber," said Stew, opening the driver's door and getting behind the wheel. "But she's fucking tricked *out,* Cherr. Specialty dials to track your fuel efficiency . . . And I found this *killer* radio in a Prius that some kid rolled in Springfield." He turned the dial and Lynyrd Skynyrd began to play.

"So," said Pop, touching her shoulder. "What do you think?"

"She's speechless!" Stew said. "Wait for it—here comes the screaming."

Cherry managed two words, drowned out by the radio. Stew switched it off.

"What was that?"

Cherry swallowed.

"Fuck. Me."

The three stood on the lawn, admiring the gleaming Spider. It looked entirely out of place, a time machine dropped in the middle of the shit-pot Stone Age. Pop let out a long whistle.

"Well," said Stew, "this is ironic." He glanced at Cherry. "Am I using that word right?"

"I'll give it back," said Cherry. "I should give it back."

Stew leaned on the hood, pressing his cheek to the curves. *"Mmm."*

"Please don't molest the car," Cherry said. She glanced at her father. "I'm sorry, Pop."

Pop puffed out his mustache. "What are you sorry for?"

"She just *gave* it to you?" Stew said.

"These are the keys." Cherry dangled the key ring. "It's a thank-you present, I guess."

"Some thank-you," Pop mumbled.

"Well, I did save her life," Cherry said. Pop cocked an eyebrow. "What? I *did*."

"Can I drive it?" Stew asked.

"You *have* a car."

"I don't have an Alfa Romeo. Wait, if *I* save her life, can I get one, too?"

Neighbors peered through their curtains. Mrs. Budzenia was walking her German shepherd, Grover. She stared. Grover peed.

Pop cleared his throat. "Let's go inside."

"Come on, Pop!" said Stew. "Can Cherry take me for a spin—?"

"Now!"

Stew walked backward into the house, clutching at his heart, pining for the car.

Pop and Cherry stayed a moment.

"Are you mad at me?"

"Why would I be mad at you?" Her father rubbed his chin, his stubble going *shhhh-shhhh*.

"You seem kinda . . ." Cherry made a grouchy face.

Pop shook his head, then said, almost accusing, "It's just . . . I can't give you a *Spider*."

"I know, Poppa! I know." She hugged his arm. "I love the Gremlin. It was made with love."

Pop grunted.

She nodded toward the sports car. "Besides, think of all the speeding tickets I'd get in that thing."

Pop grunted again at a higher pitch.

They stood arm in arm. The Spider seemed to grin back stupidly, like a new puppy.

"It really is beautiful," said Cherry.

"Yes, it is."

"I can't give it back, can I?"

"I would disown you."

She leaned her head on his shoulder. "Thank you, Poppa."

He put his arm around her. "You deserve it."

At 1:04 a.m., Cherry plugged her dead phone into its charger. The little Nokia played its cloying jingle and began to *ping-ping!* with texts from her best friend, Vi.

> 12:01:
>
> > Hi. Sundays suck. I'm bored. Call me.
>
> 2:30:
>
> > What's going on down there!!!!! It's all over fbook.
>
> 2:43:
>
> > Gaaaaaa!!!! Holy shit call me call me!!!!
>
> 2:52:
>
> > I'm coming down there.
>
> 3:31:
>
> > Where are u? This place is a madhouse.

4:25:

Ok ned says you went home. Call me k?

She turned off the light and crawled into bed. Curled into a ball, sheet tucked to her chin, she dialed Lucas's number.

"Just calling to say good night and that I fucking love you."

"I called your house line, but your bro said you were out."

"Yeah, I had an insane evening," Cherry whispered. "I'll tell you about it in the morning."

"Did you tell your dad about us?"

Cherry stared into the gloom. The glow from Lucas's window bled through her drapes. She pictured him at his desk, sketching. "Not yet. You?"

"Yeah. Dad said good for me 'cause I'd never do better."

Cherry smothered a laugh. "Hey," she said.

"Yeah?"

"You're the most amazing thing that happened to me today."

"You, too."

The exhaustion settled on her like a blanket, and they whispered their *good-nights*. She dreamed of piloting a rocket car across the sky, an endless ocean sweeping beneath her wheels.

Chapter Eight

Don't Freak Out

Cherry's alarm chirped at 5:05. Her pre-dawn run was comatose. Her eyes passed over the pavement without seeing it, her ears filled with the rush of her breath. She showered, dressed for school, and was pulling on her sneakers when the previous day began to climb her like ivy. The sun was bleeding through her blinds. It was a new world out there. Or maybe she was new. Or both.

"Can I drive the Spider to school today?" Stew asked. He stood in the hallway wearing nothing but a towel. With the toothbrush in his mouth, it sounded like, "Cahwah dah da shaydah wa oolooway?"

"No chance."

He removed the toothbrush.

"I hate you."

She patted his cheek.

Pop was at the kitchen table. Red Sox mug. Sports section. His mustache was dusted with white powder.

"You've been eating donuts."

"Good morning to you, too."

She checked the fridge. The Entenmann's box was half empty. "Jesus, do I have to start putting a padlock on these?" She turned with a grin. "It's fine. Everyone deserves a treat once in a while."

Pop fluffed the paper. "Uh-oh."

"What oh?"

"I never get off that easy. What did you do?"

Cherry took a seat, folded her hands, and assembled her most winning grin. She worked in some daddy's-little-girl eye gleam for good measure.

"Don't freak out."

Pop lowered the paper. "You're pregnant."

"No!"

"Thank Christ. All right, out with it."

"Lucas asked me to marry him. I'm getting married!" She opened her arms for a hug. Pop didn't budge. Cherry waited.

Pop continued not budging.

"Nope."

"What do you mean, *nope*?"

"That's not happening."

Her smile tightened. "Yes, it *is*."

"Oh, yeah? And where's the reception? Mel's Diner?"

"This is *good news.* I'm *in love,*" she said, hating how childish that sounded.

Pop puffed his mustache. "I'm waiting for the 'good-news' part."

Cherry pushed back from the table. "You're an asshole."

"You're a moron."

"Why are you being this way?"

Pop folded his hands over the table just as she had done, except minus the hopeful grin.

"So what, you'll just be a housewife?"

Something inside her turned to poison. "Yeah. Cook, clean, shop. You know, all the shit I do now. Really, not much'll change."

"Like hell it won't." He stuck a fat finger in her face. "You are going to *college.* You are going to *do* something with your life."

"Having a family *is* doing something."

"No, it *ain't.*"

"Is that what you told Mom? Maybe she would have stuck around if you didn't think her life was bullshit."

The Red Sox mug exploded against the wall, chunks pinging and skittering over the counter and tile. A sliver of glazed ceramic executed a pirouette on the sink's edge and tumbled in with a deafening *clink.*

Cherry was frozen, her bluster vaporized. The mug hadn't been aimed at her, but she felt its shatter in her spine, the shards under her skin.

His voice was still. "That was clever, the way you turned that around on me." She met his eyes, and they were exhausted. He seemed so *old*. "*You're* clever. And you're wasting it. You think I *want* you to work until you die? If I could give you a *mansion,* I would. I can't. But I'll tell ya something else." He pointed to the backyard, to Lucas's trailer. "Neither can that guy."

He took his paper and made for the back door. The screen door slammed, bounced once, and slammed again.

Stew rushed in, pulling on his shorts. He took in the coffee running down the wall. He gaped at her.

"Holy shit, are you *pregnant*?"

She took the Spider to school.

Chapter Nine

Self-Appointed and Seriously Superior

At 7:55, Cherry pulled into the Aubrey Public parking lot with "Superb Ass," the new single from Cynthia Sundae, buzzing through the Spider's modified speaker system. Nothing vented aggression like hip-hop played at eardrum-splitting volume. Swarms of kids slowed, stopped, and turned to watch her pass. She found an empty spot in the section reserved for seniors. Mr. Butkey, the assistant principal, was in conference with a sophomore on the front steps. He whistled as she got out of the car.

"Win the lottery, Ms. Kerrigan?"

"Something like that, Mr. Butkey."

She pulled her bag from the rear and locked the Spider. The vintage locks clicked with a satisfying *ker-CHUNK*.

"Cherry!" Vi Ravir waved from their usual meeting place by the spruce tree and ran over, as much as she could run in heels and a skirt. "Oh, my God, where have you been? Whose car is that? What happened yesterday?" She squeezed her knees together. "I'm so excited I have to pee!"

Cherry leaned against the Spider, hooking a thumb in her cargo pants like a trucker. "Yep, yep," she drawled. "She's *all* mine."

"Where did you get it?"

"Ardelia Deen gave it to me." Shrug. "Came by my place last night to say thank you for saving her life. This was her way of showing her gratitude, I guess."

"You *hung out* with her?"

"She's actually pretty cool," Cherry said. "Not like you'd think. I taught her how to change a tire."

"Cherry, *I'm dying.*" Vi put a hand over her heart. "I'm dying! I'm dead. I'm dead now. You killed me."

Cherry straightened, getting into the swing of it. This was *really* going to blow Vi's mind.

"Listen, though. I've got even *bigger* news!"

Vi folded her hands, literally quivering in anticipation. Times like these she reminded Cherry of a Chihuahua.

"Oh God, oh God, oh God, *tell me.*"

"Lucas asked me to marry him!" She inflected these words with Vi levels of hysteria. Their effect was to freeze Vi in her place, jaw petrified into the same demented grin of a girl in a McDonald's poster.

"He . . . did?" Different parts of Vi's face seemed to be registering different emotions.

"Yeah! Last night! Before the whole Ardelia thing."

Vi's brow furrowed as she desperately tried to square this with the other, unrelated, news. "Cherry, that's . . . amazing!"

The girls embraced, Cherry testing the hug for weaknesses, signs of hesitancy. When they separated, Vi had composed herself.

"Honey, I'm so happy for you."

"Thanks," Cherry gushed. "I mean, we didn't set a date or anything. It won't change much. Just, like, we'll be together like we're together now. But forever."

"That's . . . wow." Blink, blink.

"Yeah."

"Yay . . . marriage!"

Vi squealed and squeezed Cherry's hands. They hugged again, but the hug deflated too quickly. They started toward the doors. They strolled arm in arm, quiet a moment, before Vi spoke up.

"So."

"So?"

"You were telling me . . . about changing a tire with Ardelia Deen?"

"Oh."

Oh.

Vi was more interested in the three hours Cherry

had spent with Ardelia than the lifetime she would spend with Lucas.

"Yeah. The car got a flat. So we pushed it to Pop's and changed the tire."

"You *pushed it*? That must have been hilarious!"

"I guess."

"Then what happened?"

"Then we went home."

"I mean, was she mad? Did she meet your father? Had she already given you the car? Or what?"

The bell rang, clattering in the tiled foyer. Cherry disentangled herself and re-shouldered her backpack. "I gotta get to homeroom."

"See you at lunch!" Vi shouted. Cherry waved without turning, a gesture that looked like *Sure!* or *Go away!*, depending on what angle you saw it from.

The morning passed without incident. Cherry wasn't sure she felt relieved or disappointed that no one remarked on her brief Internet celebrity. Something distracted her from the usual, homey boredom of class. The reading seemed pointless, the teachers shabby and hopeless. Her future with Lucas secured, school was irrelevant, and she couldn't wait for it to be over. And there was something else, too. An excitement hangover. She was disappointed to discover that after her outrageous day, life was dragging on just as she'd left it, one bell after another.

Nothing had changed. *She* hadn't changed.

At last a long, stuttered ring announced lunch period, and Cherry headed for the cafeteria, walking a little slower than the hustling students around her.

As she neared the cafeteria's double doors, Olivia Dunrey (who spelled her name *Olyvya,* which gave Cherry a migraine) rounded the corner with her entourage. Olyvya dressed and acted like the Queen Bee of Aubrey Public, a self-appointed and largely ceremonial title, since apparently no one but Olyvya and her friends realized she was the most important girl in school.

During freshman-year orientation, Olyvya had attempted to distinguish herself as Seriously Superior by joking that Cherry dressed like Gwen Stefani circa 1994 (a good burn, Cherry had to admit). The three chicklets who would become her entourage giggled. Cherry turned in her assembly chair and punched Olyvya in the jaw, knocking her flat on her back and liberating her right front incisor. In a sense this moment divided their class. From that point on, some regarded Cherry Kerrigan as a freak show, a maniac, a dangerous lunatic. A near majority thought it was the most awesome thing they'd ever seen. Either way, from then on, Cherry Kerrigan was legend. But nobody saw the aftermath, when Pop explained with uncharacteristic calm that *he'd* be the one to pay for Olyvya Dunrey's expensive oral surgery. On that score, Cherry still felt horrible about the whole thing.

Now, to Cherry's utter shock, Olyvya was waving at her.

"Hey," she said, flashing a two-toned smile. "I saw you on the news. That was pretty amazing. You saved her life."

Of course, Olyvya was the *one* person to mention it. "I was just . . ."

Before Cherry could finish, the other girl swooped in for a hug. Her eyes moistened. She let out a shuddering breath. "I just don't know what I'd do if I *lost* her."

Cherry recalled Olyvya had come as Jane Austen, Vampire Huntress, to last year's Halloween dance.

"You don't even know her," Cherry said, dumbfounded.

"She's so brave, you know?" Olyvya sniffled. "I heard she went right back to work today. Isn't that courageous?"

"I went to school the day after my appendix burst," said one of Olyvya's friends.

"If you see her again, will you give her this?"

Cherry watched in horror as Olyvya took an envelope from her purse. Ardelia's name curled across the front in pink pen, sprouting flowers and butterflies.

"Jesus," Cherry said, recoiling. "Listen, I'm not gonna see her again—"

Olyvya pressed the letter into Cherry's hand. "Thank you."

"I'm not giving her this." She looked to the toadies for help, but they all wore Olyvya's expression of eager concern.

"*Thank you,*" Olyvya repeated with a little more force, and departed, head high, a saint with her disciples.

Cherry tossed the letter in the trash.

"Were you just talking to Snaggletooth?" Vi asked, coming out of the girls' restroom. They started for the cafeteria.

"She wanted me to give Ardelia a love note. Can you believe that? We're not like *buds* or anything."

"You're not?"

"No!" Cherry shifted her bag. "I mean, is that what people think?"

"I did hear someone say you were 'summering' at her mansion in England."

"Oh, *man.*"

"And some dude was spreading this rumor that you guys are secretly lesbian lovers. But I'm pretty sure he was just fantasizing."

"(A) Gross. And (B) We're not friends. We're certainly not *lovers.* She came by to say thank you. That's *it.*"

"Okay! Don't shoot the messenger. *Jeez.*"

"Sorry," said Cherry. "It's been a weird twenty-four hours."

They took their usual seats near the vending machines. "Well, cheer up," Vi said. "Soon we'll be out of here, you and Lucas will get hitched, and then me and Neil, and we'll live across the street from each other, and our daughters will be besties."

Vi offered Cherry an orange slice.

"Danke," said Cherry, demonstrating half her German vocabulary.

"Bitte," said Vi, using the other half. "On that note, I've got to study for the quiz. Herr Bergmann will kill me if I fail another one."

Chapter Ten

You Gotta Go Around

Final period was study hall, and as a senior, Cherry was practically obligated to skip. She wanted to see Lucas and so descended the scary west staircase to the boiler room, where Mr. DuBois had his office. She found Lucas's dad tipping back in his ancient wooden chair like a private eye, reading the *Aubrey Times* and drinking a ginger ale.

Cherry knocked, raising her eyebrows.

Leroy smirked. He was a founding member of the Cherry Kerrigan Fan Club.

"Someone puked in the faculty bathroom," he said, explaining Lucas's absence. Cherry gave a thumbs-up and was turning to go when Mr. DuBois called her name. "Hear we're gonna have a celebration soon."

"Assuming Pop doesn't throw me in the trash compactor first."

"Hermann'll come around," said Leroy. Mr. DuBois and Cherry's father were old poker buddies. "After all, as father of the bride, he's the schmo who's gotta pay for everything."

Leroy meant it as a joke, but Cherry felt a ripple of panic. The actual *wedding* hadn't occurred to her. She'd pictured herself with Lucas, an endless stream of days in his company. She now struggled to imagine a dress, a band . . .

Oh, God. The Funky Chicken.

"Maybe we'll elope."

Leroy laughed, crushed his soda can, and tossed it into the basket. "Certainly cheaper that way."

She found Lucas in the main hall, dragging the wet mop behind him. They both held their arms out as if to say, *Where the hell were you?* She kissed him and grabbed his ass.

"Hey! PDA much?"

She grinned. "This is mine now. I get to grab it as much as I want. Hey," she added, "where were you at lunch? I thought I'd see you."

"Dad needed help. I have to stay after, too."

Cherry withdrew, her excitement spoiled. "I wanted to take you for a spin in my new whip."

"Yeah, I heard you made quite an entrance this morning. Hermann got you a sports car?"

"Not exactly," said Cherry. "And P.S., your dad

shouldn't make you clean puke during the school day. You're still a student."

Lucas shrugged. "He's getting old, and I don't mind helping. He wants me to start working for him right after graduation."

"Oh."

"Uh-oh," said Lucas. "What is it?"

"No. It's just . . . I thought we'd have a summer together before you had to work a full-time job." Plans Cherry hadn't known she'd made evaporated like ammonia off a boys' restroom floor. Ninety days of uninterrupted sunshiny bliss, the last summer before work and adulthood. *Nope. Sorry!*

"Dad works through June," Lucas said, his tone an apology. "Closing everything down. So that means I work, too."

"That really sucks. I'll never see you."

"You can come visit. Dad won't care."

"I guess. . . ." A thought tickled her. "We could hook up in the classrooms."

"On the teachers' desks?"

"Exactly."

He kissed her forehead, totally insufficient; Cherry pressed her lips to his. Someone cleared his throat. It was Principal Girder, heading for the door with briefcase and trench coat. They hadn't heard him coming. The guy moved like a ninja.

"Surely, there are better places to do this," he grumbled. It wasn't a question.

"Sorry," Lucas said, backing away from Cherry.

She snaked an arm around his shoulder, pulling him back. "It's cool, Mr. Girder. We're getting married."

Girder looked at them over his spectacles. *"Mazel tov."* He shuffled away, mumbling to himself. "We'll hold the reception in the auditorium."

Vi was buckling her seat belt, one of Nurse McKinley's free lollipops jutting from her mouth. It rolled and clacked against her teeth in a way that made Cherry wince and run her tongue against her own.

"I can't believe Girder said that."

"He's a cranky old fuck." Cherry let the car's growl soothe her. The Spider loved her. The Spider understood her pain.

"This car is epic," said Vi, stretching across the leather seats. "I feel like a Bond girl." She fiddled with the stereo, which had been modified with an iPod adapter. She plugged hers in and cranked Cynthia Sundae, a shared obsession.

"'He's got that superb ass . . .'" Vi sang through the open window. *"'Sup-sup-superb ass-ass-ass.'"*

Other kids in other cars lined up to exit the parking lot, their booming stereos jostling for dominance. Loud music playing on a sunny afternoon and kids' voices—all a reminder that summer was gearing up and soon school would be over for good. The idea that Cherry alone would be hanging out in the humid, dark halls of Aubrey Public through the swimming-pool months was a serious bummer.

They pulled onto Sturbridge Street, the Spider bucking against the stop-and-go traffic, which was heavier than usual. At their turnoff, a kid in an orange vest waved them past, the street blocked by sawhorses, a white truck, and something that looked like a black umbrella on complicated rigging.

"Oh, shit. Not again."

Cherry slowed and rolled down the window.

"You gotta go around," the kid said. The script on his T-shirt was partly visible through the opening in his vest: IVE AND UNMA.

"What's going on?" Vi asked.

"We're filming."

"Who's *we*?"

"The film crew," the kid deadpanned.

"Is this Ardelia Deen's movie?" Vi turned to Cherry. "It must be, right?"

"I can't talk about the talent," the kid said, turning demurely and opening his vest. The movie's title was written in cheap iron-on lettering: ALIVE AND UNMARRIED. "But yes."

Vi clacked her Blow Pop. "Cherry, you wanna go say hi to Ardelia?"

"You know Ms. Deen?" The kid cocked an eyebrow.

"Oh, yeah, Cherry's like her bestie. She saved Ardelia's life."

His eyes went wide. "You're *that* girl? Holy shit!" He stepped back. "Isn't this her car?"

"It was a gift!" Vi said.

"All right," Cherry said with finality. "Where's the detour?"

"Up Carlton Street," said the kid. "Hey, can I give you my résu—?"

Cherry pulled away. "Carlton Street, seriously?" She was fuming. "It'll take us forever to get home."

"Why would anyone want to make a movie *here*?" Vi asked. "Though Squawker said it's a remake. The one about the guy who founded Cane Cola. Are they filming at the bottling plant? I bet that's it." *Click-click-clack-clack* went her lollipop.

"You keep clacking that thing against your teeth, and I'm going to throw it out the fucking window," Cherry snapped.

Click.

Clack.

"Sorry," said Vi.

Chapter Eleven

Bizarro World

As the week wore on, a few more kids said something to Cherry about her web celebrity. Commenting online was one thing; saying something in real life apparently required a grace period of seventy-two hours. Cherry ignored the new Facebook friend requests, many of which turned out to be reporters and bloggers looking for inside info. On Wednesday an envelope bearing Paramount's blue insignia arrived for Cherry. Inside was the title and paperwork to Cherry's new car, along with a note written on soft, feathery stationery in Ardelia's immaculate hand:

> *For C—*
> *Hope you're treating her well. I know you will.*
> *—A*

By Thursday the fervor over Cherry's celebrity had died down, and then Tina Needle, a rock star everyone expected to die of an overdose, was hit by a bus on the way home from the organic market, and people stopped mentioning the Cherrdelia story entirely.

Things weren't mentioned at home, either. Pop didn't bring up the marriage, and neither did Cherry. She and Stew held a few late-night conferences in Stew's room, Cherry calling Pop controlling and *vicarious*—a word she'd picked up from TV—and Stew getting stoned and somehow always guiding the conversation back to a favorite song lyric or the universe or the unconscious.

In the evenings she saw Lucas. Watching movies, going for long drives, and hanging out at the park hadn't changed, a fact Cherry needed to verify constantly. She was nervous that "engagement" would somehow alter their relationship. She didn't want Lucas to start acting "husbandly" any more than she wanted to be his "little woman." She wanted them to go on being best friends exactly as before. An engagement was a promise that nothing would change and no one would ever leave. She'd hoped it would ensure her present happiness would last forever. Instead, it was all about planning for the future and the least happy topic of all: money.

"I have some savings," Lucas said Wednesday evening. They were lying on their backs in the gazebo in

Aubrey Park. It was sunset, but some little kids were still making the miniature merry-go-round go 'round. "Maybe enough for first month's rent on an apartment."

"I mean, we can't live at home," Cherry said. "Right?"

"I don't think it works that way."

She closed her eyes, imagining that the conical roof of the gazebo was focusing her thoughts and shooting them into space. *This will all be all right. This will all be all right. This will all be all right.*

As an alternative to thinking and planning and worrying, she and Lucas made out. Like, a lot. More than usual. A car meant mobile privacy. The Spider's hard leather seats were inferior to the Gremlin's spacious, cushiony rear, which was the only thing the old girl had over her prettier little sister. Cherry hadn't planned to save herself for marriage, but since they'd be tying the knot so soon, wasn't it better to wait and make it Super Special? In the meantime they were trying some new stuff, exploring new territory, at her pace and her insistence. Lucas was affectionate, but Cherry discovered she preferred to be the one in the driver's seat. She was less comfortable when the focus was on *her* body. She didn't like being the center of attention. She was much better as *caretaker,* making sure a good time was had.

He offered to go down on her more than once.

"Verboten," she said Thursday after her German quiz. They were parked in a secluded corner of the Aubrey High lot, behind the outbuildings.

"But I want to," he said. "Believe me, it's hot. I'm into it."

"No. It's weird and it's gross."

"Would it be gross to go down on me?"

From anyone else, that would have sounded like a request. But her boy was more concerned with her comfort than his own pleasure.

Cherry couldn't keep the smirk off her face.

"No," she said, letting the word linger in the corner of her mouth. "And maybe *that's* something I can give you for your birthday."

"What about *your* birthday?"

"Ice-cream cake," she said, kissing his neck. "And *you, you, you.*"

Fridays and Saturdays Lucas was a late-shift busboy at Willie's family restaurant, so weekend nights were Vi territory. The girls had barely seen each other since news of the engagement. Vi answered her phone with, "Who is this? The name Cherry sounds familiar, like someone I used to know. But it's been *soooo* long—"

"Har-har," said Cherry. "You want to do something?"

"Yes, I do."

. . .

They caught an early movie, another romance-zombie mash-up called *A Walk to Dismember,* and cruised the main "strip" in the Spider, enjoying attention from Worcester college boys and guys in lowriders who whistled and wanted to drag race. They buzzed Shabooms, and Vi pointed out that some of the kids in line were dressed too fancy to be local. Cherry wondered whether the movie people might actually deign to visit Aubrey's only night-club. They didn't see anyone they recognized.

Around ten they stopped for eats at Mel's Diner. Vi swirled her fries in some mayonnaise (a gross tic she'd picked up visiting her cousin in Montreal). "So, where are you and Lucas going to live?"

Cherry stared at her plate: a mountain of hash browns with a pool of ketchup on top like a crater of lava. Usually Hash Browntain was her favorite late-night snack, but she'd lost her appetite. It was all this future talk.

"I don't know. We'll get an apartment, maybe."

"Yeah, but . . ." Vi repeated the swirling motion, this time heavenward. "How are you going to support yourselves? Will you work?"

"Jesus, Vi. Do you have to be such a bring-down?"

"What? I'm just asking a totally reasonable question. You guys aren't gonna live at *home.*"

"Yeah, I know that," said Cherry. "I'll figure it out. I don't have to think about it right now."

The SweetWear T-shirt page flashed in her mind.

I DON'T THINK.

Dudes stumbling out of Shabooms swaggered past their window. A chach in white chinos licked his lips.

"You wish!" Cherry shouted. They probably couldn't hear her through the glass.

"Okay, change of subject," Vi said. "How was it?"

"What?"

"The sex!" said Vi. "Hello?"

"We haven't done it," said Cherry. "You know that."

Vi blinked with exaggerated slowness. *"Quoi?"*

"We didn't do it."

"You got *engaged* and you didn't *fuck*?"

A woman in the next booth scowled in their direction.

"No," said Cherry. "But there was stuff. I mean, new stuff."

"Did you . . . ?" Vi made a fist, bulged out a cheek.

Cherry laughed. "Not yet. I've actually never done . . . that. Not even with Deke."

"Well, you should," said Vi. "Dude puts a ring on it—he should get *something.*"

"Well, technically there was no ring, so . . ." said Cherry.

There was a tap on the window, which they ignored. The tap came louder, and Cherry put her middle finger to the glass, not wanting to bother with more douches in chinos. Vi's eyes turned to dinner plates.

"Cherry, look!"

Cherry looked. Ardelia was standing on the curb. She waved and made a *Why?* gesture. The blond girl from Burrito Barn was with her, texting.

Sorry! Cherry mouthed, and leaped up. She tripped past the *ding-ding* of the diner door and ran into Ardelia's hug.

"Fancy meeting you here!" she said. "Cherry, this is my best friend and manager, Spanner Grace."

The blonde glanced up from her phone long enough to twitch her eyebrows.

"Hi," Cherry said lamely. "Looks like you been out clubbing."

Ardelia wore a form-hugging red dress. Her bitchy friend was in a ramrod-straight black skirt. Even made-up, she wasn't as pretty as Ardelia. Cherry rolled that thought around in her head, savoring it.

"We were at the club up the street, but I was mobbed, so we left." She glanced at the diner. "What are you doing?"

Mel's Diner suddenly seemed toxically lame. Old biddies, the high-school boys. Cherry shrugged. "Nothing much."

"Ohh." Ardelia rubbed her hands together. "I would kill for a milk shake. Span, what do you think?"

"We're expected," said Spanner. She was also British, but while Ardelia's accent fluttered and weaved, the other girl's stuck to its perch, wings clipped. She bet this girl would never try Laffy Taffy — or Hash Browntain, for that matter.

"Oh, right, the thing," Ardelia said. She took Cherry's hands. "Do you want to come?"

Spanner and Cherry exchanged matching glances. "Come where?"

"Maxwell's having a party. Just a small thing at his suite in Boston. Friends and cast members."

Maxwell Silver. Movie star. Heartthrob. Ardelia was inviting her to an after-hours party at his *hotel room*. She glanced down at her cutoffs and tatty halter. "I'm not really dressed. . . ."

"Oh, come *on*. Nobody cares. It'll be fun! Besides, you can save me from the boring studio people." She leaned in close. "Not *one* of them knows how to change a tire."

Spanner slipped her phone into a tiny black clutch and closed it with a *snap*.

Had Vi been right there, Cherry's response would have been an instant and firm *no*. Vi would beg, Cherry would put her foot down, Ardelia would go, and they'd probably never see each other again.

But.

No one Cherry knew was standing there to make sure she acted like her usual self. Right now she was *Ardelia Deen's* Cherry, who maybe could do things Regular

Cherry couldn't. Maybe Ardelia's Cherry could say *fuck it* and go to parties . . . in Boston . . . with celebrities . . . in her Daisy Dukes. Shit, anything was possible.

"Okay," she heard herself say. "Can my friend come? She's inside."

"The more, the merrier!"

"Not really," Spanner mumbled. Cherry pretended not to hear it.

"I'll be back in a second," Cherry said. "Don't go anywhere."

Vi did not raise her eyes as Cherry relayed the invitation. She contemplated her tuna melt instead.

"I can't."

"What?" said Cherry, unbelieving. Vi turn down a party? They were now officially in Bizarro World. "I mean, *what*? I thought you'd freak. Why not?"

Vi glanced out the window. Ardelia was taking a picture with a passing gaggle of girls.

"Cherry, I just . . . with them? It's too much. I'd be too nervous."

"Don't be like that. She's nice."

Vi shook her head.

Ardelia was waving to her again. A black SUV pulled to the curb. It was all sparkles and chrome out there.

"I'm going," said Cherry. "You're invited. You should come."

"I'll just go home," said Vi, her voice small.

"You don't have a car."

"I guess I'll walk, then."

Cherry wanted to smack her, to snap her out of it, to punish her for this guilt trip. Instead, they hugged good-bye stiffly, and it was Cherry who held on a little too long. She wandered back outside, realizing too late she'd stuck Vi with the bill, but she was too embarrassed to go back. Suddenly Mel's Diner was the warmest, friendliest place ever, and she was stepping into a cold night with strangers.

"All good?" Ardelia said.

Cherry nodded. She climbed into the plush SUV, glancing back. Vi was texting, sipping Cherry's milk shake. She looked content enough.

The car, the party, the jealous gaggle on the sidewalk . . . and Cherry was *something,* but *all good* wasn't it.

Chapter Twelve

To Play or Not to Play

Stars of *Alive and Unmarried* stayed at the Parcae, a scalloped and terraced hotel in the shadow of the John Hancock building. At midnight the facade was lit white as a wedding cake, and men in gold frogging held open the doors.

Cherry felt her pockets.

"Did you lose something?" Ardelia asked.

"Should I tip the door guy?"

Ardelia laughed and took her arm. It was just the three of them in the elevator, and Cherry was possessed by a childhood impulse to push all the buttons. But this elevator had no buttons at all.

"It'll take us straight to the master suites," Ardelia explained.

"First time in a lift?" Spanner asked.

"No. Obviously," said Cherry. "And in America we call them *elevators.*" This was out before Cherry realized she might also be insulting Ardelia. Spanner pounced.

"Did you hear that?" Spanner asked her friend. "*Elevator.* What a novel word! Why, I must remember it next time I'm taking the *lorry* to the *loo* to find my *bumbershoot.*"

"Oh, stop it," Ardelia said, smirking.

"Is this the new thing in America?" Spanner asked Cherry's reflection. She pointed lazily to Cherry's cutoffs.

"Sort of."

"Very rustic."

"Well, I didn't know I was going out tonight."

"No, Spanner's right." Ardelia tapped her chin.

"She is?"

There was an Emergency Stop button. She could always hit that. Why wasn't there a Teleport Home button?

Ardelia snapped her fingers. "I know! Let's switch shoes."

Cherry obeyed, exchanging her frayed Converse for Ardelia's pumps. Unused to high heels, Cherry tottered over the other girls. She considered the effect, Ardelia in her gown and sneakers, Cherry in cutoffs and blazing red stilettos.

"Voilà," said Ardelia. "Now it's *fashion.*"

As if this were the secret password, the elevator *ding*ed and the doors slid open. There were five master suites on this floor, including Ardelia's. Maxwell's was in the northeast corner, down a length of vanilla carpet, past two pearly double doors. Music, voices, and the chatter of glasses and ice cubes sounded on the other side. Ardelia pulled the silvery handle, grinning at Cherry, and then they were in.

She couldn't make out anything about the room beyond its size, so thick was the press of human bodies, satin, and skin. A fog of perfume, beer, and pot smoke hung over the crowd. A yellow feather bobbled toward the bar, an outcropping of someone's ridiculous hat. There was a woman's shoe in the chandelier.

"Ardelia!"

Something shiny entered the clearing by the door where Ardelia, Cherry, and Spanner stood. The shiny thing pressed a martini glass into Cherry's hand and swallowed Ardelia in a hug.

"Maxwell!"

Maxwell Silver was dressed in a glossy black shirt with the top three buttons unfastened. In her new heels, Cherry had three inches on the man she and Vi had swooned over in *Heavy Metal Pirates.* Maxwell's hand cupped Ardelia's lower back. She seemed to lift a little with the pressure. The costars exchanged words from the sides of their equally perfect mouths, Maxwell letting slip some inside joke that reduced Ardelia to giggles. Cherry felt a flash of jealousy and took a sip from Maxwell's martini. Gasoline and vinegar.

"Max, this is Cherry," Ardelia said, gesturing Vanna White–style. Maxwell's eyes followed Ardelia's gesture down to Cherry's toes and up again.

"Charmed." He offered his hand, which Cherry moved to shake, but he dived for the martini glass instead. "In the business?"

"She isn't!" Ardelia said with glee.

"Thank Christ. This way."

Maxwell took her hand now, and Cherry was dragged bodily through the masses while her mind still wobbled by the door: *Maxwell Silver had checked her out.*

Maxwell held one hand; Ardelia trailed behind holding the other. Bodies parted for their host. Then they were at the bar, something out of Ariel's undersea bower in *The Little Mermaid*.

"What's your poison?" It took Cherry a beat to realize Maxwell was addressing *her*.

"A . . . beer?"

She wasn't a drinker. You had to stay soberish to keep an eye on Vi, whose hair usually needed holding. But she was no one's designated tonight. The bartender handed her a brown bottle with a German label.

"So what *do* you do, if you don't do what we do?" Maxwell said in his ticklish accent.

"Bup!" said Ardelia, removing Maxwell's hand from where it brushed Cherry's—she hadn't even noticed it there. "Not this one, Max."

"I'm making *conversation*."

"On the make, more like it."

Maxwell groaned. "She's such a Mama Hen, isn't she?"

Again, Cherry didn't realize she was being spoken to. She kept forgetting this wasn't happening on a screen but live, and she was an active participant.

Ardelia's hand was on her right arm now, Maxwell's on her left. "Don't let those blue eyes fool you. He's a scoundrel."

She was supposed to say something now, and not wanting to look like an idiot mute, Cherry said, "Don't worry. That play don't play."

It was an old line, but Maxwell cackled. " *'That play don't play.'* I love it! Can I use that?"

Cherry was mid-sip, and by the time she'd lowered her bock lager or whatever it was, a pale hand had snaked around Maxwell's waist and he turned away.

Cherry hid behind her beer bottle. "What am I doing here?"

Ardelia puffed a stray strand of inky hair. "I know,

it is a bit much, isn't it? But I mean it about Maxwell." The humor left her voice. She was like a news anchor transitioning from the weather report to "Buyer Beware." She squeezed Cherry's elbow. "Steer clear of him. He's the devil incarnate."

Chapter Thirteen

Where Did You Find Her?

Ardelia guided Cherry through the room, introducing her to beautiful people of both sexes and the occasional distinguished old fart with white hair and a black turtleneck. But soon Ardelia was called away, and Cherry had to fend for herself. She was good at parties, typically, but these people talked about things entirely foreign to her, about places she'd never heard of, like Croatia, and the best place to buy organic cheese. But more than anything else, movie people talked about *themselves.* They talked about other times they had been at parties and talked about themselves.

And then, as sometimes happened, something clicked in Cherry's head, and she suddenly *got* these people, from their understated shoes to their overstated hair. They were just popular kids. Perhaps *slightly more popular* popular kids, but popular kids, nonetheless. Popular kids liked to shine, but not at the center of anything. A crowd of popular kids wanted to be a *halo,* which was why they always stood in circles (dorks and losers lined up against the wall like a mass execution). Once she understood this, she instantly relaxed. By midnight a crowd of models, actors, and older film people encircled her. The beer was making her loose, and the added height of the heels gave her authority. She was a tipsy Titan. A wobbly Amazon.

"So it was me, Vi, and Sharon Hanniford," she explained, revving up another story.

"The one with the lazy eye?" a girl in a teal cocktail dress asked.

"You're thinking of Sharon Gregory," said her date. "Sharon Hanniford's the one from the beer-bottle story. Right?"

"Exactly," said Cherry. "So, Sharon's all heartbroken because of the whole Danny cheating thing. I mean, the girl is *tore up.* So, I got this box of M-80s—"

"Pardon," said a French fashion model. "M-80s?"

"Fireworks," said the model's husband, also a model.

"Yeah, but *serious* fireworks," Cherry corrected. "Vi's cousin brought them down from Canada. *Anyway,* we got this box of M-80s, and we pull through the parking garage where Danny is in the backseat with this skank from Aubrey Private."

"That asshole," said the girl in the cocktail dress.

"I hate Danny," said her date.

"Totally," said Cherry. "So we pull up real slow and

quiet like we're just another car looking for a spot . . ." She paused for dramatic effect. This story had slayed the Aubrey football team at last year's homecoming. "And then I just let loose from the passenger seat. I'm throwing them under his car, on the roof. M-80s are going off—*bang! Bang!*" Cherry made explosion shapes with her hand. "It sounded like a drive-by. They were *shitting* themselves."

The crowd applauded. A woman in a frosted bob held her hand against her chest. "Oh, that is too much."

"Serves him right," said the director of photography.

"It was *sick,*" said Cherry, flush with attention and booze. Everything she said was fucking *fascinating*. And once you got past the goofy accents and conversations about cheese, these people weren't so bad. Cherry said so and got a big laugh.

Ardelia appeared at Cherry's side, putting an arm around her waist.

"Ardy, *where* did you find her?" asked the frosted bob.

"In a burrito place," Ardelia said. "And she's *all* mine, so none of you go and steal her. Anise, don't give me that look. I know you're searching for a new PA."

The teal cocktail dress fluttered her eyelashes. She leaned toward Cherry with a confidential air. "Well, I *am*."

"Tough!" Ardelia said, snapping her fingers. She did

that a lot, Cherry noticed. She imagined Ardelia snapped things away, or snapped them into existence, all day long. *Quickly, more wine!* Snap-snap. *Bring the serving boy to my boudoir!* Snap-snap. *Take this girl away—she is vulgar and boring.* Snap.

Just then the music cut out. Maxwell was standing by a grand piano in the corner, waving.

"Ardelia! Come do the thing."

"Oh, yes!" someone shouted. "Come on, do it!"

Ardelia waved them away, but the crowd wouldn't let her go, urging her toward the piano. She resisted for all of ten seconds.

"Fine! Fine."

The room applauded.

"Ladies and gentlemen," Maxwell announced, "as some of you may know, our little Olive"—Cherry guessed this was the name of Ardelia's character—"recently had a scare."

The crowd went, *"Awww."*

"We're just so happy she's all right," Maxwell said. By now Ardelia had reached the piano. "So let us celebrate the fragility and sanctity of life," Maxwell added with mock reverence, "with a private performance."

"Stop! Stop!" Ardelia waved at the cheering crowd, laughing. "What do you want to hear?"

"Do 'Night and Day'!" someone shouted.

"Do 'Love for Sale'!"

General laughter. Ardelia's eyes found Cherry.

"Cherry! Any requests?"

The room's eyes were on her. What were they asking her, exactly?

"Uh . . ." She cleared her throat. "How about 'Superb Ass?'"

She'd meant this as a joke, but the room went nuts. Ardelia shrugged.

"Well, if it's all right with Cynthia . . ." She gestured to somewhere in the room. The yellow feather, its owner obscured by the crowd, bobbled.

Maxwell sat at the piano and began pounding out the bass line. Ardelia climbed onto the grand's glossy top, Cherry's sneakers squealing. When the vocals came in, Ardelia began to sing, and Cherry was surprised by the sweetness and emotion she was able to wring from a song about a nice ass. Ardelia hammed it up, turning the hip-hop anthem into a torch song, about love and loss, and when she sang, *"'I'll die if I don't get it, I'll cry if I don't get it, I need you . . . !'"* Cherry believed her.

She was the brightest spot in the room. Even among the rich and famous, Ardelia Deen was important.

She finished to wall-shaking applause. Ardelia curtsied and let Maxwell help her down. Cherry clapped — difficult while holding a beer bottle — and let out a wolf whistle.

"So, what is it you're doing here, exactly?" said a pert

voice in her ear. Spanner was at her side, smoking a slender brown cigar. It smelled awful.

"Sorry, what?"

She exhaled a jet of blue smoke. "I mean, it can't be fun for you. Being a party favor."

Cherry waved the smoke from her eyes, her stomach turning queasy, her fingertips going tingly with the realization that she was being insulted. At school, digs were hurled down the hall, unmistakable. Spanner's words *seeped,* like poison. The toxins detected, Cherry shifted into Fightin' Mode. She didn't take shit from jokers like Olyvya Dunrey, and she sure as hell wouldn't from a copper-bottom bitch in a too-tight dress.

"All right. You got a problem with me?"

"Problem? I *have* no problems. I fix other people's."

"Ooh, good one," said Cherry. "How long you been sitting on that little gem?"

"Right now I see *one* problem," Spanner continued. Her coolness flustered Cherry a little. "And I plan to solve it, *pro bono.* Do you know what *pro bono* means?"

Cherry didn't, though she'd heard it on *CSI: Miami.* "N-no . . ."

"Not surprising. *Pro bono,* from *pro bono publico* or 'for the public good.' Colloquially, 'for free.' I'd explain what *colloquial* means, but we'd be here all night." Spanner sighed. "I'm guessing they don't teach Latin at your school."

Cherry's face was on fire. Was it uncool at Hollywood parties to savagely beat another guest, or would it be considered part of the general mayhem?

"Ardelia *asked* me to come, okay?"

"Oh, you're not *her* problem," said Spanner. "You are *utterly* inconsequential. *She* is *your* problem."

"How is she my problem?"

Spanner tapped her cigarillo. The ashes drifted toward the floor and seemed to disappear.

"You see, this is what Ardelia *does*. A new production, a new city, a new friend. She likes *new* things. Year after year, I have seen new friends, like you, come and go. But none of them *lasted*." She pronounced the word like something sharp and unbreakable. "So, when this production is over, Ardelia will go home, and you will stay in your awful town, in this awful country. You will go back to the trailer where she found you, and your life will snap back into shape like a rubber band. And it will *hurt*." Spanner's eyes met Cherry's, and they were smoky and blue. "So, this is my professional advice. Cut out now, and save yourself the heartbreak. There's a good girl." She glanced at Cherry's beer. "Are you old enough to have that?"

Spanner removed the bottle from Cherry's fingers and dropped it in a wastebasket, then disappeared in a puff of smoke.

Chapter Fourteen

New York Movie

After her performance, Ardelia was absorbed by the crowd. Cherry searched for her, feeling like Invisigirl. Bodies didn't part for her the way they did for Maxwell and Ardelia. Nobody seemed to hear her say "Excuse me" or "Coming through." Women threw back their hair in fits of laughter and struck her in the face. Men swept their arms like batteries in a gauntlet. She wished Vi were here. No, she wished *she* were wherever Vi was.

Something large and yellow bumped her elbow.

"Excuse you!" snapped a woman with a feather jutting from the top of her hairdo. She was covered in feathers. A sexy Big Bird. Disturbing on many levels.

"Have you seen Ardelia?" Cherry asked.

"Ardy? In there."

Big Bird nodded toward a far door, her feather dipping into Cherry's face before returning to the full upright position.

Cherry wedged herself through the crowd and at last reached the bedroom door. It stood ajar, the room beyond dark. Cherry knocked once, praying her friend was alone.

Ardelia stood in a rectangle of yellow window light, holding a cigarette. She'd removed Cherry's sneakers, which lolled half under the bed. It was quieter here. The view from both windows was stunning, but it was the painting on the wall that Ardelia was looking at. She jumped when Cherry cleared her throat.

"I'm gonna bounce."

"Oh, no! Are you bored?" Ardelia's pout fell. "Sweetie, have you been crying?"

Cherry wiped her eyes. *Fuck, fuck, fuck.* "Smoke makes my eyes watery."

"Oh, sorry." She held her cigarette away. "I was just thinking about what Maxwell said. About life being fragile. Max was just being Max, but . . . he's right. Life *is* fragile. You know what I thought that day, when I was choking? I had a full thought, apart from, you know, *I can't breathe.*"

Ardelia's eyes searched the middle distance. She licked her lips. "I was sitting there, choking, convinced, you know, *this is it.* And I thought, *I'm all alone.* Isn't that silly? What a thing to think when you're dying." She looked at Cherry. "Do you ever feel that way?"

She thought about Lucas, about Pop and Stew, about

Vi. Her life was full of people. But why did it sometimes feel like she was constantly gathering sand into her arms? Sand that was always rushing away from her, through her fingers, between her arms, no matter how much she scooped, no matter how hard she squeezed?

"I worry a lot. About people." She'd never realized this before. But she did. She worried. All the time.

"Intelligent people always do," said Ardelia. Before Cherry could ask what this meant, she'd turned back to the painting. It was just a boring watercolor, like the kind hanging in the Aubrey Public Library.

"I love this painting. It's an Edward Hopper. His paintings always make me cry. So many lonely women."

The painting *was* lonely. A woman in blue leaned against an orange wall at the back of a theater. The back of an audience member's head was visible, the stage obscured.

"Who is she?"

Ardelia shrugged. "I always thought an actress. Waiting for her cue."

Cherry looked closer. "She's an usher."

"Hmm?"

Cherry pointed to the girl's trouser leg. "She's got an orange stripe down the side of her pants. That's a uniform." Cherry thought about this. "She can't see the show from where she's standing."

Ardelia looked again. She traced the band of tangerine

down the girl's side. She turned to Cherry and seemed to consider her with the same surprise, the same interest, as if there were a colored band on Cherry she hadn't noticed before.

"Listen, stay, won't you? You and I will have fun. Fuck everybody else."

Cherry laughed. "It's weird hearing you swear."

"I don't usually. You bring it out of me."

Cherry considered the blonde in the painting. She looked bored. She looked sad.

"All right," said Cherry. "Back in a sec. I gotta do something."

She found Spanner amid a circle of girls, speaking in a low voice through cigarillo smoke. The girls hung on her every blue word.

"Hi," said Cherry with a grin. The others smiled politely.

Spanner turned with exaggerated slowness. "Yes?"

Cherry leaned in so only she could hear. "Fuck with me again, and I'll break your face. Got it?"

The other girl swallowed. She looked even paler, if that were possible. Cherry was all grin. She nodded to the others. "Ladies."

She crossed to the bar and drummed on the counter. "Another one of those German beers, please, and keep 'em coming! It's a party!"

Chapter Fifteen
Play Grown-up

Cherry woke hours later in the bedroom with the Hopper painting on the wall. Light from the partially drawn curtain crisscrossed the bed like rays from a heat lamp; she felt like she'd been sleeping in a boiled, damp, loosely rolled burrito.

She kicked off the soggy sheets, revealing Ardelia, still in her party gown and curled in a fetal position, clutching one of Cherry's sneakers like a teddy bear.

"What time is it?" Cherry asked in an unrecognizable voice. An investigation of her phone revealed six missed calls from home. She didn't bother to check the voice mails. Pop was going to flay her for being out all night.

Ardelia opened her eyes with visible effort. She glanced up at Cherry, raised herself on one elbow, and looked around. "Well," she mumbled, "I'm all sunshine and rainbows."

They found Maxwell in the wreckage of the living room, asleep on a foldout with a blonde who turned out, much to Cherry's surprise, to be Spanner. Ardelia stood over them. Cherry couldn't detect any hurt in Ardelia's swollen eyes. She stooped to pick at a wad of gum tangled in Spanner's hair. Spanner batted her away sleepily.

They rode the elevator in silence. She didn't want to see her reflection in the mirrored doors. While Ardelia took care of some business with the concierge, Cherry waited on the curb. She'd helped herself to a pair of sunglasses a guest had abandoned on Maxwell's carpet. Even with the shades, the early afternoon light was punishing. No, not just the light, the wind too. Being *alive* was painful. So, this was it. Her first-ever hangover. She was used to the pain of overexertion, from running too far or overdoing it in a push-up contest. This was different. This was damage. She felt like she'd swallowed a cheese grater. She resolved to never make fun of Vi's hangovers again; no one should have to suffer through *this*.

Two younger girls teetered past in matching Hello Kitty T-shirts. They were giggling and screaming about something, and Cherry imagined a million tortures for them. They glanced her way, and she wondered what she must look like to a pair of middle-school girls. She'd never been *that* girl before, the one heading home in last night's clothes, mascara turned to ash, all disheveled and hungover and looking roughed up in a way that was maybe slightly sexy. She'd always thought those walk-of-shame zombies were pathetic. But now, despite the throbbing in her head, Cherry felt like kind of a badass. She felt older and, yes, a little damaged, like she'd left a part of herself behind in Maxwell Silver's hotel room. Like she'd spent a little of her life's currency, diminished a precious supply, just a tiny bit.

It wasn't a bad feeling at all.

The hotel door opened, all flashes and squeals, and Ardelia emerged, wearing her own face-masking shades. She took a look at the world and sneered.

"Isn't it hateful?"

"Yes," said Cherry, wondering if her voice would ever sound normal again.

"Breakfast?"

"I gotta get home. My father's going to kill me."

"I'll drop you." Ardelia touched the doorman's elbow. "Greg, could you have them send my car around?"

Buses thundered past. Cherry stuffed her hands in her pockets and shivered, thinking of bed and maybe pancakes. She heard the snap of a lighter. Ardelia lit a cigarette. Cherry plucked it from her lips and crushed it on the pavement.

"Wha . . . ?"

They were being watched. She nodded toward the middle-schoolers waiting for the light. The girls giggled, pretending not to stare.

"You're a role model."

Ardelia gave her a once-over. She looked formidable in her shiny shades and rumpled party dress. *Snap-snap.* "You know, usually the only people who tell me what to do are my agent and my manager."

"If they're not telling you to quit, they're idiots."

The SUV pulled up, and the girls climbed in back. Cherry worried she'd crossed a line. Ardelia was quiet, looking out the window until her cell hummed "God Save the Queen." She checked the ID and silenced it.

"Who was that?" Cherry asked.

She leaned her head on Cherry's shoulder and removed her shades. "Oh, you know," she said with a sigh. "Just some idiot."

Ardelia dropped Cherry by Mel's, where she'd left the Spider last night. Cherry drove with the window down, worried she might puke. The pavement near Sweet Creek Bridge was a swirl of skid marks; someone had nearly gone into the guardrail, it looked like. The black squiggles and stink of recently burned rubber made everything worse, and Cherry experienced a kind of nauseated déjà vu.

She made it back to Sugar Village, killing the engine and sitting in the driveway, mustering the energy to face Pop. The stomachache, she realized, wasn't only physical. Guilt circled her insides like a spiny blowfish. Somehow being with Ardelia, her fellow debaucheress, had shielded her from it, but alone now, Cherry felt disloyal. Disloyal to her father for breaking curfew, disloyal to Vi for abandoning her at Mel's, and weirdly, she felt disloyal to Lucas, though she hadn't done anything wrong at the party. Having a great time, feeling so awesome, having something that was just *her own*—this felt like a betrayal. As if in the communal world of Sugar Village, memories were supposed to be made together and shared, and here was Cherry with her own little gleaming evening tucked in her pocket like a found coin. It was all hers. It made her feel selfish and sleazy.

When she came in, Pop was at the kitchen table. It was littered with paper, shredded envelopes, a yellow-ruled notebook on which he'd scribbled columns of diminishing numbers. Here was Pop, quietly working away on a Saturday. Here was Cherry, coming home at one o'clock in the afternoon, looking like hell warmed over. See Cherry squirm. Squirm, Cherry, squirm.

He glanced over his reading glasses.

"Morning."

"Morning."

He gathered her appearance, mentally turning it over like the problem part in a malfunctioning engine. "There's coffee."

"Thanks."

Cherry didn't drink coffee, but the smell of Chock

Full o'Nuts (or as Stew called it, Chock Full o'Shit) was intoxicating. She poured a mug of the acidic brown stuff and added a heap of powdered creamer to soften the blow to her stomach.

"Let me know when you're ready," Pop said.

"One sec."

Cherry arranged herself across from her executioner. The papers were bills. *Shit.* She recognized the cheery red Verizon checkmark, the blue Con Edison seal, those monthly harbingers of stress and cutbacks. The first of the month, Pop would go on a rampage: If it was winter, he'd torque down the heat; summer, he'd unplug the air conditioner; and Cherry and Stew would get a lecture about leaving the lights on when they left a room. The next week it would blow over, and they'd all return to normal habits. It was best to just keep your head down and above all stay out of the house when Pop did the finances. Stew was nowhere to be seen. That was smart.

I Don't Think, thought Cherry.

Pop sealed an envelope, removed his glasses, and folded his hands.

"You okay?" he asked.

Cherry nodded.

"Good. First things first. You're grounded. Two weeks. No television, phone, Internet. No going out on the weekends. After school you come home, or you go to work, then you come home. Got it?"

Cherry got it. She'd gotten it the moment she climbed into the Escalade outside Mel's. Pop meted out punishments, or rather collected them, with the same neutral efficiency of the printed bills on the table. Misbehavior had a price, and you better not fuck up if you couldn't pay. Sneak out while grounded? Your choice, but the penalty fees would stack up, your days of incarceration would grow, until you had no choice but to grit your teeth and take it. Action and consequence, it was all up to you. And really, two weeks for one all-nighter wasn't a bad deal. Cherry had built up a few months of good credit.

Except for one thing.

"What about Lucas? Can he come over?"

"No."

"But, Pop—"

"You'll see him at school."

"You're not letting me see my *fiancé*?"

Pop rubbed his eyes. "Don't call him that."

"Why not? That's what he is!"

Pop broke his composure. "Where's the ring, then, huh? Where's the *plan*? Where's the job and the place to live? You're too old to play house, Cherry."

"I'm too old *not* to," she snapped. "I gotta do *something*."

"I'm not arguing with you about this. You're grounded. That's final."

"Whatever." Cherry pushed back from the table.

"We're not done here."

She made an exasperated noise. "Fine. What?"

Pop clicked his pen. She wanted to snap it in two. She hated his officiousness now. He was showing her how *reasonable* he was. How *adult*. There was still a dent in the wall from the coffee mug.

"I'm going to ask you for something," Pop said. "I thought long and hard about this. It's your life, so I'm *requesting* that you *consider* something. For me. Because I'm your father."

He waited. Cherry held up her hands. "Well?"

"I'm asking you to wait. Wait to get married. Just a year or so. You can live here as long as you want, rent-free. You could maybe apply to a few schools. . . ." She began to protest, but he stopped her with an outstretched palm. "I'm not saying you *gotta* to do this. I'm not asking you to not be engaged. I'm asking you to give yourself time to see what other options are out there."

"Options," said Cherry, "in men?"

"In life," said Pop.

"Don't you think I already considered the options?"

His expression told her no, he didn't think she had, but he was going to let her figure that out herself. He took her hand. Her skin was pink and soft, so unused next to the tanned, time-roughened, craggy terra firma of her father's. "I love you, Snack Pack."

The old nickname buckled Cherry's armor. She tried not to smile.

"I'll think about it," she said softly.

"Good." He squeezed her fingers and stood. "Now, finish paying the bills."

"What?"

"You wanna play house? This is part of it, and you gotta learn sometime."

"That's not fair!"

"That's part of your punishment." He kissed her forehead. "Have fun."

He retrieved a beer from the fridge. A moment later, Cherry heard the TV pop and hum to life.

The coffee did shit. She still had a headache.

Chapter Sixteen
Solitary

And so began a weekend in isolation. No TV, no car, no freedom. Her confiscated phone disappeared into Pop's junk drawer. Cherry didn't mind. She wasn't up to talking to Vi, who was probably mad at Cherry for ditching her. As for Lucas, Pop granted her one supervised phone call, like she was in prison or something, to say simply: "I'm grounded. I'll tell you about it on Monday."

"Oh, shit. You okay?"

The sound of his voice made her chest constrict. She wanted to melt into the receiver, twist down the curly cord, and zip across the yard to his room.

"It's fine. I'm—"

Pop pressed the switch on the cradle, killing the connection.

"That's enough," he said. "Homework. Now."

They were not phone talkers, Cherry and Lucas. Growing up next door to each other had removed the need for constant chatter. She didn't need to fall asleep the way Vi did, cell to her ear, boyfriend's breath crackling in the receiver. If she wanted to feel Lucas there, she could just open her eyes. His pillow was visible from her pillow, with only two screens and a hash of wire fencing between.

But not telling him about the party was agony. She had no reason to feel guilty, but, okay, it had been a *serious* party, and she did get *seriously* drunk, and there were *seriously* cut dudes there, including at least one *seriously* famous one. And though she didn't feel like she'd done anything wrong, the need to clear it with Lucas was overpowering. The news lodged somewhere in her sinuses, an entrenched rock snot she was desperate to expel but couldn't.

As usual, Lucas was away all Saturday night busing tables at Willie's. Cherry normally liked her Saturday nights Lucas-free. They kept her feeling independent, like she had a life outside their relationship. But now she just wanted to see him, hit the Refresh button, convince herself that one night in Boston hadn't changed her into someone else.

At eight Pop let her watch *Archer* with Stew, but she just couldn't get into it. The boozy antics on-screen made her feel dirty. *God,* she was such a fuck-up.

Stew noticed something wasn't right. When Pop wasn't looking, he nudged her shoulder.

"You wanna . . . ?" He nodded toward his room and mimed smoking a joint. This was the last thing she wanted to do.

"*No,*" Cherry said. "Why do you think I would *ever* want to do that?"

Stew shushed her. "Jeez! Okay!"

"Stoner dumb-fuck," she growled. "Has to make everyone as much of a loser as he is. Jesus shit, Stew."

Her brother shrank into the couch, at once shocked and petrified Pop would hear her. "Cherry!" he hissed. "Wow, holy shit, I'm *sorry.* I just thought you looked stressed—"

She stood up, blocking the television. "Get your shit together! It's not all about having a good time, you know?" She slapped the edge of the plastic bowl in Stew's lap, showering him with Doritos. Pop looked up from the kitchen table.

She went to her room and slammed the door, shaking the trailer.

"What did you do?" she heard Pop say.

"I . . . I don't know."

Cherry noticed a catch in his throat, like he was going to cry.

Pussy.

Chapter Seventeen

April Fools' Day

She barely slept. She had coffee again for the second time in a year. How fast could you develop an addiction? By 7:35 she was so wired, the other cars on Hope Ave. seemed to pass in slow motion. She felt like an angry god at the wheel of her Spider, the front grille prowling over the streets of Aubrey. Faster. Stronger. That's right, *look at it*. God, caffeine was good. She tapped her fingers on the wheel, humming with the radio, and made it to school eighteen minutes earlier than usual.

Sitting still was not an option, so she locked up her bag and paced the empty halls. Cherry cruised around the school like a tube in a centrifuge, her feelings separating out, the euphoria of the caffeine, the need to see Lucas, her anger at herself, and at the very bottom, the heaviest feeling of all, her fear she'd done something wrong.

All at once she had to pee like crazy. She altered course and was in sight of the girls' room when Lucas, a ring of keys jangling from his belt, exited the boys' room, whistling tunelessly.

When he saw her, he smiled. The sight of his teeth filled her with a different kind of urgency.

"Hey, girl! What's—?"

She yanked him into the girls' room.

"Cherry! I can't be in here."

"That mouth's too pretty for talking." She pressed her lips to his. They stumbled backward into a stall. "How long has it been?"

He let her kiss his neck. "Seventy-two hours? About?"

"Too long."

"Mmm-hmm."

They bumped against the stall walls, reorienting. Cherry nibbled his ear.

"So, what happened?"

"I went to an all-night party." She fumbled with his fly. "With Ardelia."

"Ha-ha," said Lucas. "April Fools."

"No, for realsies. Crazy, right? Vi and I just ran into her."

"Did you—whoa—have fun?"

"I got really drunk," she said. "Hey, since when do you go commando?"

"Since it's laundry day. You could have called me."

She grinned, working for a better angle. "Maybe I didn't want you falling for Ardelia."

"Well, I *do* have a thing for accents."

"Oh, *Lucas.*" Cherry did her best Ardelia impression. "Why must we fornicate in such undesirable surroundings. Wow!" she said, noticing his reaction. "You really *do* like accents."

Lucas blushed. "Told you."

Relief coursed through her. She'd told him everything, and everything was fine. *He was here, he was here, he was here!* His hands were on her, and wasn't she just the most rock-star girlfriend in the universe? "Oh, *dahling,*" she whispered. "I'm all sunshine and rainbows."

Grimy-kneed, breath freshened with a Life Saver, Cherry headed to the library, feeling like she had helium in her joints. There were still a few minutes before homeroom, and she was aching to find Vi, who would be so impressed that Cherry'd done what she just did on school grounds. Was there a more awesome girlfriend in the world? And it wasn't as weird as she'd expected it to be. She'd made his knees buckle. That was a good thing, right? Maybe she was really good at blow jobs. Maybe that was her hidden talent.

"Saw you on TMZ again," said Kaya Melton as they passed in the hall. Cherry swiveled, blushing, as if what she'd been thinking about were visible on her face. After a beat, Kaya's words actually connected.

"April Fools?" Cherry tried.

"Naw, really," said Kaya. "It was you going into a hotel with Ardelia Deen."

Cherry stalled. Had there been cameras? She hadn't noticed any.

"Come on," she heard herself say. "You think *I* go to hotels with Ardelia Deen?"

Kaya crinkled her nose. "I *thought* it was kind of weird. But you met her, so I just figured it was you. It *looks* like you."

"Can't believe everything you see on TMZ," Cherry said, and went inside.

Maybe it was residual thrill from what had just happened in the bathroom, but Cherry wasn't at all upset about the alleged photo. In fact, it was kind of exciting, and she could always deny it was her. She found an empty computer terminal and tried to log on to TMZ, but the school's site blockers said no. With her home Internet privileges revoked, she'd have to wait two weeks to see the photo, and by then it'd probably be buried or taken down. She'd have to ask Vi.

Cherry checked her e-mail. There were a few

messages from university mailing lists she'd signed up for months ago, just to appease Pop. Otherwise it was all spam. One subject line jumped out:

From: Edith Hughes <u>EdithMWBHughes@gmail.com</u>
To: Cherry Kerrigan <u>cherrybomb95@gmail.com</u>
Subject: It's Ardelia

Hey, hon,
Sorry about the e-mail address. It's a nom de plume.
Are you free around 5? Do you want to swing by the set? I'd love to show you around. Today we're filming <u>here</u>. I'd also like to talk to you about something. Don't fret if you can't make it.

Xoxo
A

P.S. Bring Lucas.

Running into Ardelia at Mel's had been a coincidence, but this was an actual premeditated invite. Cherry tried to read it as friendly, but the "talk to you about something" freaked her out a little, like maybe she was in trouble. Like she was about to get dumped. But that was ridiculous. Ardelia wanted to show her the set. She

wanted Lucas there. These were good signs. After reread-
ing the e-mail five times and analyzing every word,
Cherry wrote a reply:

I'm there like shareware.

XO,

C

Remembering she never signed her e-mails and definitely never wrote *XO*, she deleted the sign-off and
hit Send.

Chapter Eighteen

Full Crisis Mode

Vi was waiting for Cherry in the hall after homeroom. She was in full crisis mode, clutching her book bag to her chest like a life preserver. Her concealer barely masked the purple bags under her eyes, and when she spoke, Cherry detected a lipstick smudge on her front tooth.

"Where were you? I've been calling all weekend!"

"Pop took away my cell," Cherry said. "What's up?"

She glanced up and down the hallway, then pulled Cherry into the same girls' room where an hour before Cherry had pounced on Lucas.

"Vi, what's going on?"

Vi checked under the stall doors, making sure they were alone. The bell rang. They were officially late for first period.

"Okay, so. Last weekend, you know? I was with Neil, and we were fooling around and stuff, and I guess we sorta . . . did it."

Cherry waited for the bomb. "That's . . . nothing new, though, right?"

"Without a condom," said Vi. "And I didn't get my period on Sunday."

Cherry's smile fell. She'd expected the typical crisis *du jour*. Another fight with her mother or some new too-pricey lip gloss she *had* to have. Not . . . *this*. This news was panic-worthy. Cherry's periods were maddeningly unpredictable, but Vi's were like clockwork.

"Why didn't you use a condom?"

"I don't know!" Vi chewed at her hair, a nervous tic Cherry hadn't seen since grade school. "Neil likes it better without, and I don't know . . . It just happened!"

Cherry had thought Neil was a dog ever since he and Vi slept together on their first date. She wasn't a prude, but Vi had been sloshed (she'd downed three nervous shots of her dad's sambuca before Neil even arrived). Neil treated her okay, but Cherry never forgave him for taking advantage of an obviously plastered girl.

And now? This.

"I'll kill him," said Cherry.

"Cherry, what am I gonna do?" Vi wailed. "My parents will *kill* me! I can't be pregnant! I don't even know if I *want* kids! I can't go to Rutgers with a baby!"

Wait.

"Rutgers?"

"I got in." Vi looked away. "I found out a month ago."

Cherry's knees buckled. All thoughts of killing Neil vanishing in cold shock as the damp sink pressed against the back of her thighs. "Why didn't you tell me?"

"I don't know. I thought maybe . . ." Vi met her look. "I know you don't want to go to college and everything, Cherry, but *I do.* They have this amazing study-abroad program where you can go to Japan for a year."

"Japan."

"Yeah." Vi shrugged. "I'd like to go to Japan."

"Japan." The word was a cork in her brain. As long as it was stuck there, other words, other thoughts, couldn't come gushing out.

"Stop saying *Japan,*" Vi said. She cinched her eyes tight and shook her head. "Now none of that's going to happen."

When Vi's eyes opened again, her gaze was distant. Cherry could see Vi imagining her future. Puke-stained shirts and warm formula and baby books. Books and books about babies. How could Vi raise a baby, or go to college, for that matter? They both involved so much reading, and Vi *hated* reading.

Rutgers. Japan. Baby. Holy shit, holy shit, how did this day suddenly get so *real?* Vi was the possibly pregnant one, but Cherry felt like *she* was going to puke. She wanted to shove Vi away — and hug her so closely and so tightly, her bones would snap.

It was all so impossibly hard. So impossibly hard to keep simple. Safe. *Here.*

It started to prickle and boil and bubble in Cherry's brain. Heat surged up her solar plexus and turned her face the color of her Coca-Cola T-shirt. Vi recognized the crazy look in her friend's eyes.

"Cherry, what are you going to do?"

She shoved the restroom door so hard, it smacked against the outer wall. Her rage was deafening, her vision tunneled, so all she saw was the tapering tiles of the second-floor hallway.

Mrs. Jordan's room was on the first floor. Genghis Khan scowled at Cherry from the poster on the door, his bloody scimitar barring the way forward. She pushed right past him.

The students' heads were bent, taking a quiz. Mrs. Jordan sat at her desk, doing Sudoku. She didn't notice Cherry come in. Neil was in the front row, brow furrowed like early man trying to master this new pointed tool. Cherry slapped her palm over his quiz. The sound was like a gun going off. A girl nearby gasped.

"You selfish piece of shit."

"Ms. Kerrigan!" Mrs. Jordan may or may not have said. Cherry only heard the blood roaring in her ears.

Neil blinked at her, trying to compute.

"You low-life buzz-cut douche bag. Do you know what you've done? You've ruined her *life*."

Kids looked back and forth from Cherry to Neil to Mrs. Jordan.

"Wha . . . ?" Neil said intelligently.

She slammed her fist on his desk, knocking it into his fat knees. "I swear to God, if she's pregnant, *nothing* will save you from the *Kill Bill*–style rampage I will unleash on your ass."

"W-wha . . . ?" Neil tried again.

Mrs. Jordan was standing now, toddling over in her tiny shoes. "Cherry Kerrigan, you will report directly to —!"

Cherry balled up Neil's half-finished quiz and threw it at him. It bounced off his stupid face and fell to the floor. Before Mrs. Jordan could reach her, Cherry turned, making sure to give Genghis an extra-hard slam on her way out.

Halfway down the hall, the reality of what she'd just done began to wheedle its way into her brain, but she'd think about that later.

I Don't Think.

"Come on," she said when she found Vi.

"Where are we going?" Vi asked. Cherry tugged her toward the exit.

"7-Eleven. We're getting you a pregnancy test."

• • •

Vi, according to the little blue dash in the window of her Sure! test, was not pregnant. As they sipped iced lattes at Starbucks (Vi's treat), she kept pulling the little stick out of her pocket and rechecking it.

"It's not going to change," Cherry said.

"I know." Vi'd been wearing a perma-grin for the last hour. "So what class are you missing right now?"

Cherry winced. "A pre-calc retake."

"Cherry! You'll get a zero!"

She shrugged, curling herself around the tall, frosty cup. "So? This is more important."

It was important she be with Vi. Vi needed her. (And who would be there for her at Rutgers? In Japan?)

During the "90 Seconds or Less!" promised by the test's blue-and-yellow box, Cherry had paced outside the 7-Eleven bathroom like an expectant father. She'd felt conflicted. Would it be so bad if Vi had a baby? Heck, they could raise it together. Cherry wanted kids. Maybe not right after high school, but life didn't always go like you expected. She imagined herself and Vi taking little Cynthia to the playground on Center Street, buying baby clothes, attending PTA meetings at Elm Elementary. These images filled Cherry with a guilty pleasure. *Because now she'll have to stay,* a voice whispered. Cherry told the voice to shut up.

It should have been Cherry getting her ass reamed in front of Mrs. Jordan's history class. She wanted exactly what Neil had done: to tie Vi forever to Aubrey, to home, to Cherry.

Then the bathroom door had opened, and Vi waved the pee stick over her head. *"Not pregnant!"*

"I'm so relieved." Cherry was never very good at lying. "So . . . relieved."

Now Vi used her straw to swirl the soggy sugar residue at the bottom of her cup. "So was Neil mad?"

"He just made that gorilla face."

"Gorilla face?"

Cherry did an impression. Vi laughed.

"I can't believe you stormed in there. You could get expelled!"

Cherry did a mental checklist of recent infractions, adding up her column of detentions. She'd definitely earned a suspension. She pictured Principal Girder's girlie handwriting: *Demonstrates severe impulse-control problems.*

"What are they going to do, expel me two months before graduation?"

"Listen," said Vi. "I'm sorry I didn't tell you about Rutgers."

Cherry shrugged. "That's okay. So, you're really going?"

Vi's eyes went dreamy again, except this time instead of diapers it was quads and frat parties and lecture halls, maybe. "I guess so, yeah. That's why we should really have an awesome summer together."

The meaning of this landed, bounced once, landed again. "Oh. Like, one last good time before you go away."

"No!" Vi said, and then, "Maybe a little."

"Forget it," Cherry said casually. "It's not like I thought you were going to stay here forever."

"Maybe you could apply next year? We could be roomies!"

Cherry imagined sharing a dorm room in New Brushnow or New Bradford or wherever Rutgers was, one side a version of Vi's current bedroom, all scented candles and military-straight sheets, the other littered with Cherry's track shorts and empty yogurt cups. How had they stayed friends all this time? They were so different, really.

"Yeah, maybe," said Cherry, slurping up her latte until it was all gone.

Chapter Nineteen

Star Hauler

The link in Ardelia's e-mail indicated a warehouse on the edge of town, up a long gravel road lined with vans, flat-beds, and double-wides. A kid in a production T-shirt stopped them at a makeshift checkpoint. He tapped the window, and Cherry rolled it down. Dorky glasses. Vest. Did they get these guys from the same family or what?

"Hi, can I help you?" the kid said. His tone sounded like, *Please die immediately.*

"We're here to see Ardelia Deen."

"This is a closed set."

"We're invited." She pointed to his clipboard.

The PA checked his list, nodded, and tapped the roof of the car. "Go ahead. We're all good."

"Yeah, I *know.*" Cherry pushed the accelerator.

Lucas chuckled from the passenger seat. She'd worried he'd be uncomfortable around the movie people. But this wasn't the hotel party crowd. The set was workaday. Guys in jeans hopped in and out of trucks. PAs spoke into headsets and checked clipboards, and everyone moved with the serious focus of people with a job to do and not enough time to do it in.

"Little bigger than the spring semester play, right?" she said. Lucas had done tech on a few school productions. He'd been recruited as the only kid who knew how to work the lighting board, the only one who could fix a thing if it broke.

"Sure is."

"Maybe you could get a job as a set designer."

"And work in Hollywood? I'd rather be eaten by wolves."

"Whoa. Little extreme?"

"You read about how fake everyone is in Hollywood, shaking your hand while they stab you in the back. And besides, so many movies suck these days." He glanced at her. "Right?"

"Totally," she said, not sure if she believed it. She'd liked *Heavy Metal Pirates* okay.

They came to a chain of trailers with STAR HAULERS written on the side in spangle paint. Cherry parked, and the pair stepped into the evening breeze. They waited for a pickup to rumble by before crossing the road.

Lucas read the names stenciled on the doors. "Stewart. Olive. Lucy. Desi."

"She's Olive," said Cherry, and knocked on the door.

Ardelia answered in a thigh-exposing bathrobe and slippers. From the neck up, she was in character, hair parted in the center and gathered in waves over her ears in an old-fashioned, unflattering style. She squealed.

"Hooray! I'm so glad you came. And this must be Lucas! Hello!"

She hugged him. Lucas managed a "Hey."

"Come in! Come in!"

The interior of Ardelia's trailer was Maxwell's hotel suite in miniature. Minibar, mini-kitchenette, even a mini-chandelier. It was smaller than Cherry's home, but every surface gleamed or bristled with luxury. It smelled like vanilla.

"That's all, Jan," Ardelia said to the woman in white standing by the massage table. "Just leave the table — you can get it later."

Jan smiled politely and excused herself.

"I know, it's decadent," Ardelia said in a guilty tone. "But, honestly, most of the day is just waiting around, so you might as well pamper yourself, right? What do you think of my hair?" She fluffed her waves. "It only took them *three hours* to do it. I've been here since four in the morning!" She rolled her eyes.

Ardelia was cheerful, beleaguered, self-effacing, scattered, and attentive all at once. She offered them drinks from the mini-fridge, apologized for the lack of variety (there were seven kinds of soda, water, bubbly water, and a tiny bottle of champagne), and finally sat with an *"Oof!"* on the velvet couch. She gestured for them to sit on the raspberry love seat.

"Sooo," she said, half speaking, half taking a breath. She turned to Lucas. "Cherry's told me a lot about you."

Lucas looked Cherry's way, as if to verify this. "Oh . . . yeah?"

"You're a graffiti artist. And also the love of her life." Ardelia flashed her teeth.

"Ardelia's into Bonzo," Cherry offered. Lucas nodded. This was where he was supposed to say something. He nodded some more.

"Oh!" Ardelia patted Cherry's knee. "I meant to tell you. Maxwell says it was a joy having you there on Friday. He said you were the life of the party."

Lucas perked up. "Maxwell?"

"The guy who hosted the party," Cherry said quickly.

"Like, Maxwell Silver? As in Captain Keith?"

"Oh, you've seen *Pirates*?" Ardelia said.

Lucas studied Cherry. "That's . . . cool."

"Oh, you don't have to worry about Maxwell," Ardelia said. "He's a cad. Only a floozy would fall for his charms."

Cherry recalled Spanner on the futon. Heh.

"Okay," said Lucas.

"So," said Cherry, ready to change the subject, "was there something you wanted to talk to me about?"

"I think . . ." Ardelia started, her eyes moving to the clock. Just then "God Save the Queen" tittered from the side table. "Well, speak of the devil!" She answered her phone. "Hello? Oh, hi, B!"

Lucas made a withering expression, and Cherry shoved his knee.

"Why, yes, he's here right now. Do you want to talk to him? Just a moment." She put her hand over the receiver. "Lucas, do you have a minute? Someone would like to speak with you."

He glanced at Cherry, bewildered. Cherry shrugged.

Confused, Lucas put the phone to his ear. "Hello?" His face went slack. *"Seriously?"*

Cherry mouthed to Ardelia, *Who?*

Bonzo, she mouthed back.

"Wow, I mean. It's . . . an honor." *Holy shit!* Lucas mouthed to Cherry. "Yeah, I'm a *huge* fan." He stood, paced. "Yeah, I tag. I mean, not like you. Just . . . right. It's amazing to talk to you. I always wanted to ask, on the Obama piece, did you lay down an aerosol base or . . . yeah, exactly! I knew it!"

"Come on," Ardelia said, taking Cherry's arm. "Let's leave the artists alone."

They stepped outside. It was cooler now; the sun

had sunk behind the tree line. Ardelia gathered her robe around her neck. Cherry's shorts and tee exposed more skin, but she wondered if Ardelia didn't feel a little weird walking around in her tiny robe. No one seemed to notice, though. Stagehands carried a plaster buggy to a flatbed truck; PAs shouted at one another.

"You know Bonzo?" Cherry said.

"Not really, but I made a few phone calls. Amazing what a pair of premiere tickets can buy you."

"You just made his whole year."

"Listen." Ardelia touched Cherry's arm. "I wanted to talk to you about something. I've got a . . . personal problem." She made a so-so gesture with her hand. "Well, not a problem. More like a personal *project*."

"Oh, shit."

"What?"

Cherry sighed. "You're leaving, right? The movie's wrapping, and you're gonna go do your indie film somewhere." She pictured one of those groaner indie films that movie stars did to up their street cred. All handheld cameras. Someone gets cancer and comes home for a shitty wedding. Lots of crying and screaming and whiny music. She hated those.

Ardelia laughed. "No! We've still got a few more weeks of shooting."

"Oh," said Cherry. "So, why'd you get all serious?"

"I'm screwing this up royally, aren't I?" Ardelia

said. "I'm getting serious, Cherry, because I want to offer you a job."

Cherry stopped in her tracks. "A job? Like, working for the studio?"

"Not the studio," said Ardelia. "I want to put you on my payroll. I want you to work for *me.*"

"Doing what?"

Ardelia placed her hands on her tummy, jutting out her hips so her flat stomach looked round. "I want a baby," she said. "And I want you to help me find a womb."

"Um," said Cherry. "April Fools?"

Money

Chapter Twenty

An Honest Day's Work

On April 3, Cherry worked her last day at Burrito Barn. The manager who'd witnessed the Ardelia incident had returned to grad school. His replacement, the *new* New Manager, was only a year older than Cherry and a freshman at Holy Cross.

"I'm just doing this until my summer internship starts," she said, accepting Cherry's folded uniform and visor. "Two months is about all I can take of this place."

Cherry raised her hand. "Three and a half years."

New New looked horrified. "You should get a gold watch."

"It's just a break," said Cherry. "I'm doing this other thing for a little while, but I'll be back."

New New snapped her gum. *"Why?"*

For old time's sake, Cherry purchased a burrito (New New didn't roll it right—way too loose) and ate it in the parking lot, no longer an employee, just a paying customer. Tossing away the soggy wrapper, she felt like she was leaving behind the only thing she'd ever done well.

Her paychecks from Burrito Barn had paid for her cell and incidentals, like nights out with Vi or Lucas. She'd also contributed to family expenses, sometimes stopping at Hadwin Market, throwing eggs, bread, and milk in with her personal items. Pop never asked her to do this — it was just something you did, like making your bed or plucking hairs off the Irish Spring after a shower. Now Cherry had a new, better-paying job, and that meant she could help out more. She kept reminding herself of this, since she wasn't sure she deserved her new paycheck.

As Ardelia's "consultant," she would be paid for her opinions, but how could her opinions be worth money since they just *happened*—she just *had* them—without any effort on her part? She wasn't sure the job constituted work. Work was supposed to be hard, unpleasant, or at least *produce* something—like a burrito. How could she justify charging for something that cost her nothing? It didn't seem fair.

"It's supply and demand," Ardelia pointed out. Cherry had come to pick up her first week's pay in advance. A night shoot was scheduled, and though it was four in the afternoon, Ardelia's workday hadn't started yet. She poured herself a protein shake and took a thunking swallow. "Your candor and perceptiveness are of value *to me.*"

"One man's trash is another man's treasure," said Spanner, cutting a check. "You start Saturday. The first candidate arrives at eleven, so get here at ten thirty. Don't be late."

Ardelia powered through the rest of her breakfast and daintily dabbed her lips. "So, how's school?"

Cherry shrugged, marveling at all the zeros. "I don't know. I haven't been in two days."

Cherry was suspended for a week after reaming Neil. Pop had gone ballistic. This, coupled with breaking curfew, would have normally earned her a life sentence. But he calmed down later when Cherry told him about working for Ardelia. And he forgot her grounding entirely when she mentioned the rate.

"Don't be an idiot," Pop said, holding Cherry's check up to the kitchen halogen. "You don't turn down a soft gig."

"I feel like I'm scamming her." Cherry was scrubbing the breakfast pans, sleeves rolled to the elbow, hair tied back in a bandanna—her standard ensemble for housework. Being home during the school day, she helped out more; the trailer had never been so spotless. She'd even de-mildewed the bathroom, and the heady taint of bleach floated through the trailer and out the open windows. Her home with Lucas, whatever it would look like, *would not* smell like a boys' locker room, damn it.

"This Deen seems pretty smart. You should have asked for more."

He handed her the check and returned to his Eggos and sausage links, dribbling syrup on the table she'd just wiped down.

"It's not a career, Pop. Just a few interviews."

"Better than rolling burritos."

Cherry's eyes stung (stupid bleach). She'd always assumed Pop was proud of her Burrito Barn job. He was always going on about *honest work* and *dependability* and *earning your keep.* Had he meant those things, or was that just something you told yourself when you couldn't find a *soft gig*?

This soft gig would pay double her Burrito Barn salary, and though the prospect of extra fun money and free time was titillating, Cherry was still uncomfortable. She'd rather Ardelia had just asked her as a friend.

On the subject of friendship: Cherry wasn't sure she and Ardelia *were* actually friends, now that Ardelia was, for a few hours a week at least, her employer. It surprised her to think this way at all, since from the beginning she'd told herself she didn't care what Ardelia thought of her, that they were passing acquaintances at best, that Ardelia was maybe surprisingly cooler than her mega-glam lifestyle would suggest, and that Cherry was a little more comfortable in her presence than she'd expected to be. But spending more time with Ardelia—structured, *professional* time—Cherry wondered whether Ardelia actually *liked* her, or if Cherry was just a local curiosity, like a cheap Red Sox cap you wore around a few days as a joke, then threw away.

Then, just before lunch on Friday, the last official day of Cherry's suspension, Ardelia called. Cherry was in the Spider, driving back from BJ's Wholesale with a pallet of Chunky Chicken Noodle and a five-pound tub of peanut butter. Being suspended, Cherry was living in a weird dimension populated by housewives and old people. It was strange how the world just kept going during school hours, with cheaper movie tickets and early bird specials and all the super-shiny chatty daytime TV. Cherry felt like the youngest, newest member of a secret club: the Daytime Ladies.

Her cell jingled Ardelia's special ring: "Rich" by the Yeah Yeah Yeahs. She hesitated, cradling the cell to her ear. The light turned green, and Cherry accelerated onto busy Sturbridge Street. Maybe with her new paycheck she could buy a headset.

"Hello?"

"Hello! Hi. So, you mentioned you run." Ardelia sounded breathless, like she'd just been working out. "My usual running buddy's twisted her ankle, and, good

Lord, in every scene they've got me eating petits fours or tea sandwiches, or today it was wedding cake. Wedding cake! Six takes! I feel like an orca."

Cherry changed lanes, switched the phone to her other ear. She didn't ask the obvious question, which was, *Don't you have anyone else?*

"Uh, sure."

"Fabulous! What are you doing right now?"

Red and blue lights throbbed in the rearview. A siren squawked. "Right now? Getting pulled over for talking on my cell."

"Oh, no! Call me back!"

"Okay."

"And I'll see you in a few hours!"

"Wait—!" The line went dead. Cherry pulled over.

The cop took his sweet time. Finally he sidled up to her window, knocked on the glass.

"This your car?"

"Believe it or not."

"Bet you get a lot of tickets in this baby."

"First one," said Cherry through clenched teeth. The cop handed her the cell-phone violation. Half a week's pay. Gone. *Poof.*

Two hours later, Cherry found herself running her usual loop with Ardelia. It was odd to see this route after sunrise. In the light of day, everything seemed cheap and colorized, saturated and filthy. It all seemed so . . .

impoverished—a word she'd only ever heard in social studies, usually coupled with *nations*. At least it all seemed that way compared to Ardelia, who, in her running gear, was like a visitor from a cleaner, more advanced planet. While Cherry ran in sneakers, track shorts, and a tattered SpongeBob T-shirt, Ardelia sported a matching jet-black tank and shorts, sleek white running shoes, a baseball cap, wraparound sunglasses, a pulse monitor, and a hip clip for her BlackBerry. She even had a silver water bottle on a lanyard to "keep hydrated," which was ridiculous, since they were just running a few miles and for God's sake, they could just have a drink when they got back.

"How much does all that stuff cost?"

Ardelia shrugged. "You don't know how good it feels to get away from the set," she said, her chatter punctuated by their footfalls. "I. Just. Love. It."

They jogged up Route 9, the least-attractive stretch, the trucks belching fumes and tossing dust. Workers from the bottling plant waited in line at the food cart and ate their lunches at plastic tables. They looked harried, wrapping themselves around their limp sandwiches and $2.99 empanadas.

"I love this time of year," Ardelia went on. "I want my baby born in spring. They say spring babies are happier."

They came to the bridge over Sweet Creek, just beyond the trailer park. Per tradition, Cherry paused to look over the water. She leaned against the cement barrier, stretching out her calves.

"Why do you want a baby?" Cherry asked. The question had been riding her for days. She hadn't asked because she assumed the answer should be obvious. But it wasn't.

Ardelia was quiet.

"I mean, you don't have a boyfriend, which I guess means you don't want one. But you *do* want a baby. Around here, being a single mom is something girls try to avoid, you know? Around here, being a mom is tied up with, I don't know, husbands and houses and cars and groceries and a whole life. But that's not what you're looking for, I don't think."

Ardelia gazed over the water the way she had stared at the painting in Maxwell's hotel room. She took a long breath, as if testing the flavor of her words before sharing them.

"I have a theory. Certain things are easy to like. Like candy." She smiled, seizing an example they both could relate to. "It's sweet. It's available. Who doesn't like candy? But you don't meet many people who *love* candy. I mean, are *passionate* about candy. Would actually truly *die* for it."

"No, I guess not," said Cherry, not sure where this was going.

"The things that you *love*—well, they're not always something you *like* at first. I mean, take this film I'm in. It's based on this big, thick, heavy book that takes *forever* to get started, and the characters are cruel, and all the sentences are ten pages long. It's not very *likable*. But"—her face softened—"I *love* it, Cherry. I think it's *beautiful*. It took me a while, but the more time I spend with it, the more I *love* it."

"Okay." Cherry wasn't sure she could think of an example in her own life of something unlikable that she loved. She loved Lucas, and Lucas was very likable.

"I guess what I'm saying is, I am like candy. I'm nice, I'm rich, I'm famous, and I'm not . . . bad-looking." She shrugged. "It's easy to like me. But I don't think anybody loves me. I don't think anybody could."

"Jesus," said Cherry. "That's a terrible thing to feel."

"I want to be important to someone," Ardelia said, turning her eyes to the lake. "I want to be meaningful to someone. Not just sweet."

"You want to be a mom."

"Exactly."

"And you really can't have a baby yourself?"

Ardelia smiled sadly.

A duck settled on the pond. It ruffled its feathers, poked its beak into the dead, sweet water, saw there was nothing to eat, and took off again.

No, Cherry didn't believe that it was hard to love what you liked, or like what you loved. She loved and liked this pond, her family, her friends, her Lucas. And suddenly it hit her—there were things Cherry had in abundance that Ardelia didn't even know she was missing. And all at once, Cherry felt that maybe she actually did know a thing or two that Ardelia Deen didn't.

She put her hand on Ardelia's tummy. "What's the deal, womb? Huh? Stop being so lame."

Ardelia laughed, sounding relieved. "So, you'll help me?"

"I said I would."

"Yes, but you were still thinking about it."

She *had* been thinking about it. Because she hated charity and hadn't known what she had to offer in exchange for Ardelia's wages. But now she did.

Anyone can roll a burrito.

"Dude," Cherry said, opening her arms for a hug, "we're gonna find you a baby mama, no problem."

Chapter Twenty-one

The Hot Seat

Saturday morning, Cherry drove downtown to the "historic" Four Hills Theater, where the crew had been filming all night. Spanner was waiting outside Ardelia's trailer dressed in a smart jacket and skirt. One ankle was sheathed in a black brace that somehow managed to look stylish. She was texting.

"So . . ." Cherry tried. Spanner put up a finger, finished her text, and pocketed her phone. She gave Cherry a once-over.

"Now that you're on the payroll, dress a little more professionally."

Cherry had meant to look professional. She'd worn jeans, not cutoffs, and a black tank top—her only shirt without writing on it.

"Didn't know there was a dress code."

"You look like a stagehand."

"You look like a super-villain."

Spanner's lips twitched, a possible smirk. "Come on."

Ardelia's filming schedule necessitated conducting interviews between scenes. Today she was in full costume—or, rather, half costume, having exchanged her hoop skirt and bustle for jeans. Above the waist she wore a high-necked corseted top with poofy shoulders, hair in the same wavy 'do as last time, cheeks powdered and rouged. She seemed frazzled.

"Don't say it. I look ridiculous. I've been up all night. Scene thirty-five, 'The Grand Theater.' Some of this dialogue is absolutely awful. All about moons and trifles and treetops."

At least Ardelia worked hard for her money.

Spanner and Cherry flanked their boss on the couch, facing the raspberry love seat where Cherry and Lucas had sat earlier that week. The whole situation was rigid and bizarre. Spanner checked a binder, clicked a pen. What did binders and pens have to do with making babies? Why did they all have to be sitting on the same couch? Would the candidates dress *professionally* or like mommies in high-waisted jeans and baggy kitty-cat sweatshirts? For a horrible instant, Cherry worried there might be a physical-examination component. Would the candidates have to undress? No, that was stupid. Wasn't it?

"They're not going to, like, get naked, are they?"

Spanner and Ardelia looked around at her slowly.

"Why would they be *nude*?" Spanner said.

"I don't know, for, like, a physical examination?"

"A doctor does that, luv," said Ardelia. "We've got their medical histories right here." She gestured to Spanner's binder. Each of the twenty-two candidates had her own file, complete with height, weight, and age. Also every skinned knee, booster shot, wart removal, and root canal. There were photographs, too. Smiling girls between the ages of eighteen and twenty-six, oozing sunshine, dependability, and availability. It was a Mommy Catalog.

This model also available in taupe!

"So what's left to interview them about?"

Spanner seemed to be waiting for this question and pounced. "I've devised a twenty-seven-point personality test, the results of which, when tabulated, will give us an excellent picture of the subject's fitness. One," she said, ticking the numbers off with her fingers, "is the candidate a flight risk, i.e., is she likely to run away with the baby? Two, is the candidate psychologically fit to be a carrier, i.e., does she have a history of violence, criminal activity, or drug use, which may not appear in her medical record? And three, is she a liar, i.e., is she lying about being healthy and mentally fit?"

She closed the binder with a satisfied slap.

"Span is very scientific." Ardelia made a serious pout.

She was poking fun a little. "Now *I,* on the other hand, like to trust my instincts. I'm intuitive by nature and can get an excellent sense of a person just by spending a little time with them."

"Well, *some* of us," Spanner interjected, her gaze lingering on Cherry, "prefer to have all the data before we make a judgment."

Cherry met Spanner's look. "But you just said people lie on their records. So how do you know they're not going to lie to *you*?"

Spanner rolled her eyes. "Well, *obviously* that's part of the —"

But before she could finish, someone knocked at the trailer door. Their first candidate had arrived.

"Okay," Ardelia said, squeezing the other girls' hands. "Here we go!"

Cassie Warren, age twenty-six, was mousy and waifish. Cherry couldn't imagine her frame supporting a big tummy. She was nervous, fidgeting on the love seat, twiddling her beaded necklace. Her grin was airtight.

"So," Ardelia said, offering the girl a water, "let's get to know each other."

"Okay."

Cherry couldn't tell if the girl's eyes were naturally wide or if the sight of Ardelia in her fused-woman outfit was freaking her out.

"Why don't you tell us a little bit about yourself?"

"Okay." They waited while she thought of her answer. "I'm twenty-six. Sagittarius. I'm a teacher's assistant in Newton, but I also volunteer part-time at the Nature Conservancy. Um . . . I'm very healthy! I'm a vegan, but I still get a lot of protein."

And *bam*—Cherry was bored. Hippies were boring.

"I like to crochet. And bake—I'm a very good baker."

Yawn.

"I like to go kayaking with my boyfriend—"

"Wait." Cherry sat up. "You have a boyfriend?"

Spanner and Ardelia looked startled, like they'd forgotten she was there.

For the first time, Cassie's grin touched her eyes. "Uh-huh. His name's Steve."

"Your boyfriend's okay with you renting out your womb?"

"Oh, yeah, he's fine with it. He's great. He's a nature guide. You know, for kids?"

Spanner opened the binder. "May we proceed? Ms. Warren's time is valuable."

Cherry sat back. "All yours."

Spanner launched into her interview. The questions seemed designed to root out unstable people. *Do you ever feel depressed? Have you ever been violent?* Cherry could answer yes to both of those. She felt down sometimes, like she was shouting herself hoarse in a big pit with no one listening. And she'd been violent, sure. She once punched a hole through the Sheetrock in her bedroom, the time Stew accidentally threw away the old family photo album.

How do you manage stress?

See answers to one and two.

Ask the right questions, and everyone seemed nuts. Cherry couldn't think of a single person who wasn't a little unstable, except maybe Lucas, and he got depressed sometimes, too.

"Have you had a baby before?" Spanner asked.

"No."

"Have you ever done drugs?"

"No."

Cherry snorted. It just came out. In her boredom, she'd only been half listening. But . . . *come on.*

Everyone was staring at her.

"Sorry," she said. "But I mean, you've *never* done drugs. Not once?"

"No!" Cassie's fine eyebrows stitched.

Cassie the Hippie didn't seem like a liar, but Cherry knew a pothead when she saw one. She looked to Spanner, expecting the cynical one to back her up at least, but both women just stared.

"Cherry," Ardelia admonished in a soft tone, "we're not here to accuse. If she said she doesn't, she doesn't."

160

Cherry withered. Maybe she wasn't supposed to talk *at all* during the interview. (*Demonstrates severe impulse-control problems.*)

Still, though.

"But there was that *one time,* right? Everyone tokes up once. Even tight-ass over here." She jerked a thumb at Spanner. Cassie laughed a little, then checked herself. Spanner clucked her disapproval. "My brother likes to smoke in the morning," Cherry offered. "Wake and bake."

"Steve smokes, too," the girl said sympathetically.

Cherry felt the others straighten. "My first boyfriend was a pothead," Cherry said. "Oh, man, *every* time it was all, *Oh, everything feels better when you're stoned. You're so tense.* Know what I mean?"

There was a light of recognition in Cassie's eyes. She eased forward. "It's true! It's, like, that's not me. Why do I have to smoke, too?"

"I hear ya," said Cherry. "And sometimes, *God,* you just take a pull, just to shut him up, you know?"

"Yeah, and then you feel—"

Cassie's face fell, the sunshine washed from her features. Her lips moved, trying to re-spindle the words, but it was too late. She glanced at Ardelia, then back at Cherry. "I mean, I haven't, or I barely *ever*—not anymore, not in years. That's not *me.*"

"Totally," Cherry said, folding her arms. She cast Spanner an *I told you so* look.

Cassie burst into tears. Eyes jammed shut, gagging on her sobs, her tiny body shaking in its loose-fitting sundress. She rushed out of the trailer, one hand to her face, the other raised in self-defense.

The three on the couch were frozen.

"Oh, my God, I'm sorry," Cherry said at last.

"That was . . . impressive," said Spanner.

"Oh, shit. Oh, shit." Cherry stood. Ardelia stared up at her, mouth open, blinking her false lashes.

Burning with guilt, Cherry rushed after Cassie. The girl hurried away from the trailer in mad little steps, hugging herself. Cherry called out, and she turned.

"So?" The force of her tone stopped Cherry in her tracks. "So I get stoned every once in a while. Is that so bad?"

"No!" Cherry said. Her throat constricted. She'd just wanted to prove she was right, to prove she belonged there. She hadn't meant to wreck this girl's chances. It hadn't occurred to her that being an occasional pothead would blow Cassie's chances — though, of course it would. With so many candidates, how could Ardelia settle for anything less than perfection?

I Don't Think.

"I really needed this! I really, really needed this! I would have quit weed, I swear! I don't know what I'm gonna do!" She searched the ground for a solution. "Do you think I *want* to carry someone else's baby?"

Cherry didn't know what to say. She'd thought, *Yes, Cassie* had *wanted to carry the baby.* If not, what was the point of the interview?

"You know what? Fuck you!" Cassie surprised them both. The curse didn't quite fit in her mouth. Her eyes widened, then narrowed again. She savored the words this time. "*Fuck. You.* You're rich! You don't know what it's like!"

Before Cherry could respond, Cassie climbed into a rust-spotted Volvo and slammed the door. She leaned her forehead against the wheel, her shoulders quaking. She sat like that for a while.

When Cherry came back into the trailer, Spanner was scribbling a check. She handed it to her with a flick of the wrist.

"What's this?"

Ardelia put a hand on Cherry's shoulder. "Darling, I'm clearly not paying you enough."

Chapter Twenty-two

The Ideal Woman

Monday, Wednesday, Friday, and Sunday evenings, from four until eight. Wombs on parade. Girls of different heights, weights, and shapes took their turn on the raspberry love seat while Spanner quizzed, Ardelia smiled, and Cherry watched like a judge on *America's Next Top Mommy*.

At first she'd counted the minutes until quitting time, until she could run home to Lucas. But the more she paid attention, the more time seemed to fly as it never had in school or at her old job. This was more interesting than rolling burritos, and she was better at it than school. When the guilt over Cassie the Hippie had faded, Cherry remembered she was *protecting* Ardelia. She was guarding her friend against a bad match, against the lying, greedy, unstable rent-a-moms of the world. She felt like Sherlock Holmes, deducing what Spanner's personality test couldn't, simply by watching. Cherry judged and was confident in her judgments.

She learned a lot from their clothes.

Some candidates dressed professionally, as if they were applying for a job at a bank. Others were deliberately casual, in jeans, shorts, or heavy Earth Mother dresses that fell to the ankle but barely covered their planetary cleavage. And some were in between, like the redhead Cherry saw pull up on a bike, walk halfway to the trailer, remove her blazer, untuck her blouse, and muss her hair. Cherry, who would have worn the same sweats every day for the rest of her life if it were socially acceptable, had never realized how much clothes said about a person. The girls chatted on, answering Spanner's questions, while their outfits whispered subliminal messages: *I'm reliable. I'm spiritual. I'm relaxed. I don't care what you think.*

After Spanner rejected her first work outfit, Cherry took herself on a little shopping spree. It was her first day back at school, and Vi was eager to hang out, but this was something Cherry wanted to do alone. It was shameful, somehow, passing over the thrifty stores like ShagaRelics and Beater Tees and heading instead for Jennifer Walters and Fwoi!, where the mannequins leaned on invisible pianos and held invisible cigarettes in their delicate fingers. She ventured into Raich and Ems, and a salesgirl in a perfect white blouse and mile-high heels trapped Cherry in her tractor-beam smile. Cherry panicked. She pressed her phone to her ear, pretending she'd received a call, and ran out.

After a hellish hour, she came home exhausted, dumping her bags on the bed. She considered herself in the full-length mirror. What did Cherry's clothes say about her? *Fun!* said her Daisy Dukes. *Sporty!* said the mesh tank top. *Laid-back!* said the busted Chuck Taylors with the laces so old they were like cardboard. Working beside Spanner's checklist had introduced some new words into Cherry's regular rotation. Words like *unreliable, unprofessional, unkempt, disinterested, disrespectful.*

Dumb, thought Cherry, and stripped off her old clothes. She rolled on new thigh-high stockings (whoops, a little shorter than she thought they'd be), stepped into the new heels (*Jesus,* they were higher than she'd realized), and shrugged on the simple black skirt and top. There was a band of exposed skin around her thighs where the hem of her skirt didn't quite reach the top of her stockings. Oh, well. She completed the look with some new Ravishing Ruby lipstick and Ennui eye shadow. Apparently the point of makeup was to make you look exciting yet bored.

"All right," said the New Cherry in the mirror. "Okay, then."

Pop whistled when she came into the kitchen. "Looking snazzy."

Stew looked up from the TV. "Damn, Cherr. Way to class it up."

She peeked at her reflection in the kitchen window. "It's just for work."

That evening the crew was shooting on location, just a few blocks away at the bottling plant. Walking over, she passed dozens of reflective surfaces: the shop windows along Hope Ave., all the tinted windshields and rearview mirrors. She tried to catch herself, to see what she looked like to others, but in each reflection she looked stiff, her eyes flicking back and forth, like someone trying not to look like she was looking at herself.

It was impossible to see herself and be herself at the same time.

The Star Haulers were lined up along Route 9. The craft service guys whistled as she passed, toasting her with steaming Styrofoam cups of coffee. Cherry knocked on Ardelia's trailer door. Spanner answered. Her eyes bulged.

"*No.*"

Cherry flinched, pulled at the hem of her skirt. "Whaddya mean *no*?"

Ardelia appeared over Spanner's shoulder. "Oh, dear." She covered her mouth, stifling a laugh. "Oh, honey."

"Come inside," Spanner said, "before someone thinks we're soliciting a prostitute."

From then on, Cherry's work outfits were selected and vetted by her employer.

She watched how the girls fidgeted. She watched how they spoke with their hands. She watched where their eyes went when they listened. Cherry had never examined *anything* this closely, let alone a stranger, and the long periods of concentration felt funny, like a warm spot between her temples.

She learned a lot watching girls walk from their cars to the trailer. She had a good view from the trailer's rear window and felt like a spy. Out there, the girls were more themselves, still girls, not *candidates*. They twirled their key rings, adjusted their clothes. One girl with black curls and red cheeks halted halfway, ran back to her car, and drove off, never to be heard from again.

The flighty ones forgot something on the passenger seat, the nervous ones tripled-checked their locks. Some gave themselves psych-up speeches in their makeup mirrors. One girl crossed herself. Another took a sip from a flask. These women had nothing in common, except they all wanted to carry Ardelia Deen's baby. They all wanted the money: $250,000 (the number was so large, Cherry couldn't wrap her mind around it). Which meant, on some level, they were all greedy.

Which was maybe why Cherry didn't like a single one.

"Thoughts?" Ardelia asked after a promising applicant had gone.

"She'll drive you crazy," Cherry said.

"She seems like an excellent fit," said Spanner, lifting her binder by way of argument.

"I thought she was nice," said Ardelia.

"She's vain," said Cherry with absolute certainty. "No one wears big honking granny glasses like that unless they're (A) epically uncool or (B) think they're way hot and can pull it off. Besides, she kept checking herself out in the window."

"Well, a little vanity isn't so—" Ardelia started with a smile.

"Dude, she's used to being the hottest thing in the room. Did you see the way she tightened up when she saw you? Girl could crack walnuts with her ass cheeks."

As often happened, Ardelia and Spanner met Cherry's appraisals with stunned silence.

"This is ridiculous," Spanner said at last.

"No," said Ardelia. "You know, I did get an envious vibe off her."

Vibe was a Cherry word, and it was cool to hear it with an English lilt.

"I'm telling you," said Cherry. "It's like that Streets song. *'Fit but you know it.'*"

And so Hot Girl with Glasses, whose name Cherry had already forgotten, was struck off the list.

Driving to the set early Friday evening, Cherry spotted Lucas walking up the street toward Sweet Creek. He was dressed for his shift at Willie's, black stain-resistant pants, orange striped vest over one shoulder. He looked like an out-of-work clown.

She slowed, trolling along beside him. "Hey, stranger."

Lucas kept pace, bending to peer in the window. "Is that Ardelia Deen in that car?"

"Hop in, I'll give you a ride."

He climbed into the passenger seat, and Cherry headed for the highway.

"How's work?"

She made an exasperated noise. "Skags and tight-asses."

"Wh-whoa." He laughed it out.

"No, I mean . . ." She sighed. "They're nice, really. They're fine. I'm sure they're good people. It just fucks with your head. All these girls trying to seem impressive. And these *clothes.*" She tugged at her skirt. She was wearing an Ardelia-approved outfit tonight, a Jennifer Walters ensemble. Trim, clean, professional. "I feel like a lawyer."

"Well, I think you look very nice."

"Well, thank you."

She turned up Route 9, toward Willie's towering neon sign hailing commuters and vacationing families off the highway for a $3.99 baked potato or the Delux Steakums BBQ Combo. The strip mall was always crowded on Fridays, mostly with kids hanging out after school, soaking up the pre-weekend sunshine, the best kind of sunshine there is. A security guard waved some skaters off the sidewalk. They flipped him off and rolled off toward the other end of the mall.

Cherry pulled into a free spot outside of Sal's Liquors. Lucas climbed out and came around the driver's-side window. He rested his arms on the door, leaning in. He smelled like hazelnut coffee and wood polish.

"Call me after your shift?" she said.

"Won't be too late?"

"Never too late."

The security guard was crossing back toward his little go-cart. The sight of Lucas leaning in her window made him adjust his course. He sauntered their way, and Cherry saw him coming.

"Uh-oh. Am I in trouble?"

"Maybe this is a no-drop-off zone," Lucas said.

The guard gave a little half-assed salute, one hand on his belt. "Evening."

Lucas straightened up. "Hey."

The guard ignored him and nodded at Cherry.

"Ma'am, is this gentleman bothering you?"

Cherry looked around, looking for the gentleman in question. She didn't realize he meant Lucas.

"Him?" she said. "This is my boyfriend."

"Hi." Lucas did a lame little wave.

The guard nodded and started to turn away. "All right, then."

Cherry stiffened. "What do you mean by that? Why would you think that?" The guard either didn't hear or pretended not to. She leaned out her window. "Hey! Fucking . . . Barney Fife! I'm talking to you!"

The guard didn't look and kept walking.

"Jeez, Cherr, don't swear at men with nightsticks," Lucas said, forcing a laugh.

"*Fuck* him." She slammed herself back into the seat. Her neck felt hot, and she knew she was flush — and not just from anger. She felt humiliated, though about what, or in front of whom, she couldn't say exactly. "So, you see a black kid leaning on a white girl's car, and suddenly it's a mugging?"

"Well, you do look pretty mug-worthy with the nice clothes and shiny car." Lucas was smiling. Lucas was the cool one. "Maybe he saw the way I was leering at you."

"Yeah, maybe."

"I'll call you, okay?"

"Yeah."

"Okay?"

Her jaw was set. She drummed her fingers on the

steering wheel, just to keep them from trembling. "Just . . . sometimes this town is so . . . small. You know?"

He leaned in the window and kissed her forehead. *"She-Hulk angry."*

Cherry smirked. *"She-Hulk smash stupid security guard."*

"Another *no*," Ardelia said when the last girl had gone on Sunday evening. She checked the clock on the trailer's microwave. "Care to do dinner?"

"I have the thing with your publicist at eight thirty," Spanner said, closing her binder. Ardelia turned to her.

"Oh, you can come, too, Span. If you want."

Spanner's cheeks mustered a little color. Cherry could hear her teeth grinding. "No, you two enjoy yourselves." She stood and hobbled out the door on her sprained ankle, mumbling something Cherry couldn't quite hear about *the sooner, the better.*

"I should get home," Cherry said. She had vague plans to watch *The Hangover* with Lucas on his tiny bedroom TV.

"Oh, come *on*." Ardelia gripped Cherry's hands, bouncing them on her lap. "I haven't had a night off in *two weeks*. I need to get away from this town." She dropped Cherry's hands and clapped. "Oh! I know what let's do! Let's go to Ascot. Have you been to Ascot?"

"Ascot?" It sounded like a standardized test.

"The owner's a friend of mine. I love his places in London. I wanted to give the U.S. version a try. Can we go, *please*?"

There was reheated Stouffer's waiting for her at home. And about a million German verbs to conjugate.

"All right, fine. But, seriously, I can't be out all night."

"Early night, I promise." Ardelia squealed. "Oh, this is so exciting. You don't know how I've been craving food that isn't deep fried."

Chapter Twenty-three

The Ascot Scene

Ascot was a fashionable restaurant on the top floor of a waterfront high-rise. Floor-to-ceiling windows encircled the large, blindingly white room, and Cherry felt like she'd stepped onto the bridge of a posh spaceship. A girl in a suit stood behind the front podium and smiled as they approached. She was about to welcome them when a fussy man with helmet hair brushed past her with open arms.

"My fair ladies! How are you?" He executed a low bow. "Ardy, darling. How nice of you to grace us."

"Alan! What are you doing in the States?"

"Making the semiannual rounds to all my American restaurants." He bobbed as he spoke, rolling back on his heels. "And this is not Spanner, is it? Or is it?"

"Alan, this is my friend Cherry."

"Ah!" Alan was overwhelmed with delight, clutching his heart. He shook Cherry's hand. "My second favorite berry. Judith!" He whirled on the girl behind the booth. Her name tag said KATE. "The best table in the house." Judith or Kate flipped through her register, but Alan had a better plan. "*Arrêtez-vous!* Ridiculous!" He bobbed in their direction, hands folded. "Chef's table?"

"Delightful!" said Ardelia.

"Follow me, please."

Alan led them through the dining room. From movies, Cherry'd expected the patrons of a fancy restaurant to be straight-backed senior citizens with little spectacles on sticks, blue hair, and yappy lapdogs. The crowd at Ascot was younger and lively. The men wore shiny shirts. The women were all beautiful, with pale necks and sparkling ears. Everyone seemed to be laughing, toasting each other, as quiet girls in gray aprons tended to the tables like bees pollinating flowers. They refilled glasses, removed half-empty plates just in time for new ones to arrive; everyone seemed perfectly in sync, diners and staff, as if they'd all learned the steps and been rehearsing.

Ardelia slipped effortlessly into the flow, sashaying behind Alan, waving when someone called her name. Cherry was in everybody's way. She knocked into a waitress carrying a tray of oysters. A woman at a nearby table laughed at something, her eyes happening past Cherry and darkening in confusion, as if to say, *Who let* you *in?* Cherry concentrated on placing one foot in front of the other. What was it about people watching that made you forget how to walk?

At last they passed through a pair of swinging doors into the kitchen, and here she was much more at home. The glistening ranges, the rubber mats on the floor, the heat and noise of men and women in spattered whites calling out to each other in two languages. It reminded her of a little Burrito Barn and Pop's garage. All work spaces have the same matter-of-fact ugliness. They were built to stain, and she liked that.

"This way." Alan gestured toward a leather booth in the corner, a dollop of luxury amid the chaos. The girls sat. Alan raised a finger, said, *"Un moment,"* and disappeared.

"I've never seen a booth in the kitchen before," said Cherry. "Aren't we in their way?"

"I thought you'd like to see the geniuses at work," Ardelia said.

Alan materialized with some meats and cheeses on a wooden slab.

"A *petite charcuterie* to begin."

"We didn't order anything yet," said Cherry.

"We will," said Ardelia. "This is just a little . . . present."

"Will we have to pay for it?" Cherry asked.

Ardelia ignored her question and turned to Alan. "What do we have today?"

Alan named the slices, arrayed in a fan pattern. The only word Cherry recognized was *salami.* There were also yellow, gray, and green lumps identified as cheese, which was ridiculous because cheese, as everyone knew, was *orange,* unless it was way past its expiration date. Ardelia held a squishy lump under Cherry's nose. "Try this."

Cherry recoiled. "It smells like gym socks."

"Camembert," Alan corrected. "An *earthy* aroma."

What was wrong with these people?

"This. Has. Gone. Bad."

Ardelia's brow settled into a furrow, really hunkered in there like it wanted to spend the winter. "We need to work on your palate."

"My what?" Cherry said.

"Darling, Marshmallow Circus Peanuts are fine, but you've got to expand your repertoire if you want to enjoy the finer things in life. You'll thank me, I promise."

"I don't *like* fancy food," Cherry said. She turned to Alan. "Do you have, like, chicken tenders?"

Ardelia touched her arm. "You don't *know* what you like. You haven't *tried* anything."

Cherry wanted to protest but in the spirit of fairness conceded. After all, Ardelia hadn't turned up her nose at 7-Eleven. At the starlet's instruction, Alan produced a sampler of tiny platters, which he referred to as "the major food groups."

Ardelia handed her a small bowl with anonymous black chunks. "Try this. And *smell* first."

Cherry sniffed her food. "Smells like . . . nuts. And dirt?"

"*Now* taste."

She chewed. It *tasted* like dirt. Worse, it tasted like dirt mixed with old coffee grounds. She spit into her napkin. "What *is* that?"

Ardelia laughed behind her hand. "Chocolate!"

"You lie."

"It's pure. No milk and very little sugar. It's divine, once you get used to it."

Cherry wiped her mouth. Even dark chocolate M&M's weren't *that* bitter. "Moving on. What are those bubble things?"

"Try them. They're salty."

She scraped a few off the plate and put them on her tongue.

"Some kind of fruit?"

"Caviar," said Ardelia. "Fish eggs."

Cherry reached for her napkin, but Ardelia stopped her hand.

"Give them a chance!"

"This tastes like . . ." The thought was too dirty to utter in front of Alan. She forced down the caviar and shuddered. "Gross."

"This you will love." Ardelia handed Cherry a small bowl with jam. It was thick and dark red, almost black. "Try it."

She did. It was rich and sweet, melting in her mouth.

"This is amazing! What is it?"

"Cherry purée," said Alan.

"Bullshit. That's not what cherries taste like." She thought of cherry cola's sharp, syrupy flavor. The purée was mellow, round, and soft. She swallowed another mouthful. "I guess I never tasted real cherries before."

"Only the finest in my kitchen," said Alan. "Everything fresh and unsullied by chemicals and sweeteners. Good, pure food."

"Leave the chocolate," said Cherry. "It'll go good with the purée."

Ardelia grinned. "You see, Alan? We have a convert."

Cherry tried the chocolate again. "This stuff must be pricey as hell."

Ardelia spooned some caviar onto a wafer of flatbread. "It's not all fast cars and fancy dresses."

Cherry stumbled from the Escalade, waved to the driver, and started around to the back of the trailer. The fence was a little trickier to get over tonight, and she tore the hem of her shirt a little. She felt marvelous. She felt like a king.

What was the name of the wine? La Lluvia, from Spain. She hadn't been able to pronounce it.

She rapped on Lucas's window. It was dark in there. She knocked again.

"Open up! It's the cops! We got a report a vandal lives here."

There was movement in the room. Lucas climbed out of bed and opened the window. He cleared his throat, his voice thick with sleep. "Hey, I thought you were gonna be home early tonight."

"I *loooove* you." Cherry leaned into the word, draping herself on the windowsill.

"Are you drunk?"

"I'm *tipsy*. There's a difference. Did you know that? Did you know that British people say *pissed* instead of *drunk*? Ardelia got a little pissed, but not me." She bugged her eyes at him. "Did you know wine coolers don't taste *anything* like real wine? Real wine is sooo different. We had wine from *Spain*."

"Your mouth is purple."

"It tastes good. Want to try?" She stood on tiptoes to kiss him. It was a little sloppy. Then she lay her head down on the sill and closed her eyes. "I'm sleepy."

"Go to bed," said Lucas. "It's late."

Cherry jerked up. "Are you mad at me?"

"Why would I be mad at you?"

"Because I'm drunk. I mean tipsy." She whispered loudly behind her hand, *"Actually, I'm drunk."*

Lucas didn't laugh. Maybe he was just tired. It occurred to her that this may not have been the best idea.

"Drink some water before you go to bed, okay?"

"Okay." Cherry nodded. And nodded again. "Okay."

She stumbled to the fence, then turned and pointed to him with both fingers. "You complete me!"

"Uh-huh. Okay, wino."

"You do," she said, a little softer, and began the process of pulling herself over the fence. It took her two tries, but she got there.

Chapter Twenty-four

Crossing the Rubicon

There was no auditorium at Aubrey Public, just the gymnasium. For the all-senior assembly, the folding chairs had been arranged in the center, and the wobbly dais, which after today would be packed up until graduation, clapped together at the front. Principal Girder took to the podium and the squealing, unruly microphone (ice picks stabbing Cherry's brain), while the nudging, chattering mass of seniors waited to hear his annual "Make It Last" speech. Every April, about six weeks before commencement, Principal Girder called the matriculating class into the gym for a heart-to-heart. It was the only time anyone saw the guy display any real emotion, and it was always a little unsettling, like the live sparks leaping from the ancient, dusty PA system.

Girder cleared his throat and moved on to page two.

"Do not dismiss the time you have left here. These are your last days as high-school seniors. For some of you, your last days as students. *Savor them.*"

Cherry and Vi were near the back. Cherry had hoped to sit with Lucas, but he'd come in early to help set up the dais and so had to sit near the front. If Cherry strained, she could just see the top of his head. That morning she'd woken in a panic, worried she'd pissed him off with her stupid drunken visit. But when she came into the kitchen, there was her boyfriend, sitting at the breakfast table with Pop and Stew. He'd brought her one of those big twenty-ouncers of Gatorade.

"Thought you might need a few extra electrolytes this morning."

Why the hell was she so lucky?

She was double lucky with this assembly, since Girder's speech interrupted European history, for which she had totally neglected to do the assignment. She was buried under makeup work from her suspension, and doing all that thinking and analyzing with Ardelia night after night sapped her mental mojo. And school-work all seemed so stupid. Even more stupid than usual. Normandies and Utrechts and Rubicons. She knew how dumb and immature it was to say, *Who cares about school?*, but really, *Who the* hell *cares about school?*

"I mean, I see him in homeroom, right?" Vi was saying. "But that's the only time I really have to see him."

She meant Neil. This was another topic Cherry didn't have the energy for. She could feel her friend wobbling on the whole Neil thing. She'd seen Vi do this before, make a good decision—like dumping Neil's sorry ass—then go back on it. She was like one of those inflatable punching dolls that kept bobbling back into place, no matter how hard you hit them.

"But you guys are, like, *done,* right?" Cherry whispered back.

"Yeeeahh . . . I think so."

"Vi, *no.* Now's your chance to break free."

"I guess. And I mean, I'm *not* going to college with a boyfriend. *That's* for sure."

"Your life after school is long," Girder droned on. "Far longer than the four years you've spent here. It will come soon enough. For now . . ."

"Seriously, though," Vi whispered. "Soon as they hand me my diploma, I'll be all, *Suck it, fools!* I'm going to run out that door and not stop until I hit Rutgers."

A girl sitting ahead of them turned in her seat. "Um, you know they don't hand you your actual diploma, right? They mail it to you later. So people don't pull stunts like that."

"Hey," Cherry whispered back. "I've got a question that maybe you could answer? And the question is, *Who the fuck* asked *you?*"

The girl scowled. Cherry recalled some vaguely

annoying detail about her, like how she was going to film school or something. She had the black coffee-shop fingernails you'd expect from a girl going to film school.

"Flash forward three years, and there's Cherry Kerrigan in line at the ShopRite with two kids and stretch marks," the girl said. "Taking night classes and scarfing her kid's Ritalin prescription. . . ."

Cherry made a jerk-off motion.

"Ladies?"

Shit. They'd been spotted. Principal Girder somehow managed to look at them over his spectacles, despite being up on the dais. The surrounding chatter stilled as all eyes turned their way.

"Ms. Fernwire, turn around in your seat. Ms. Kerrigan, need I remind you you're still on probation?"

"No," said Cherry.

She glanced in Lucas's direction. He gave her a smirk like *typical you.* She winked at him.

Girder resumed his talk, and the seat-level chatter started up again.

Cherry leaned forward so her mouth was inches from Ms. Goth Nail Polish's ear. "The best part about this town is that all the shitheads *leave.*" She leaned back and saw that Vi had heard her. "Except for you, obviously," she whispered.

Vi looped her arm around Cherry's and smiled. It was supposed to be an *apology accepted* smile.

Nah, Cherry heard her mommy-evaluating self whisper, *that was totally a* pity *smile.*

After assembly it was lunch, and the seniors were herded through the rear double doors into the cafeteria. A few peeled off into the parking lot, which wasn't strictly allowed, but assembly days were a little different and you could get away with stuff like that. Even a few teachers were out there, smoking.

Mrs. Ruppert, Cherry's history teacher, gave her one of those *I'm watching you* hand signals.

Double shit.

"You know what sucks?" said Cherry. "*Not* being suspended."

"I'll take your word for it," said Vi.

"There's Lucas." She spotted him exiting the cafeteria. He was scanning the crowd, looking for her. "I'll be right back, okay?"

She jogged over. They kissed under the birch tree. Some girls went, *"Ooohhhh."*

"I got free period next," Cherry said. "Want to walk the track with me?"

"Nah, they're bumping third period back to after lunch."

"What? Damn it." Cherry glanced over her shoulder at Mrs. Ruppert stubbing out a cigarette. "I'm about to get my ass handed to me."

"The history assignment?" Lucas knew Cherry's homework woes. "You have time now. You want to use Dad's office?"

Cherry bit her lip, watching Ruppert shuffle back inside in her sensible red Easy Spirits and frowsy beige pant suit. *I'm serious. I'm academic. I'm tough.* She thought of Mrs. Ruppert's car, her sad little Yugo with the bumper sticker reading: THINK EDUCATION IS EXPENSIVE? TRY IGNORANCE.

She was probably a cries-in-the-car type.

"Nah," said Cherry. "It doesn't matter."

Lucas stuck his hand in her back pocket. "Suit yourself. You hanging with Vi tonight?"

"Maybe." She spotted Vi in the crowd. She was talking to that nail-polish chick. Vi was laughing. Cherry could hear the laugh all the way across the lot. Would Vi start wearing hipster flannel shirts and dark nail polish at Rutgers? She wondered if they had a film program.

Lucas started to remove his hand, but she held it there. "Don't," she said. "Just hold on for a second."

Chapter Twenty-five

Mostly Harmless

Thursday night Cherry and Vi went to ShagaRelics, a campy thrift store downtown in what almost definitely used to be a Pizza Hut. It was different from the Salvation Army, since the owner actually curated the selection for cool or weird clothes, and there wasn't the same rustling, resigned quiet. It was one of Vi's favorite places to shop, and occasionally Cherry found the odd funky T-shirt she liked. Even better, ShagaRelics was open late on Mondays, when the owner spun a big disco ball and played dance music from the '70s.

"What are you eating?" Vi asked, shrugging out of a too-small pleather jacket.

"Chocolate," said Cherry. She plucked another black wafer from the wax paper bag.

"Where'd you get it?"

"The store."

Vi snatched the bag away. "I've never seen this before. Which store?"

"Sunflowers." Cherry swallowed. "It's an organic market."

Vi read the label. *"Chocolate morsels. Eighty-five percent kow-kow-ah."*

She put one of the black wafers on her tongue and shuddered. Her face bent into a grimace. It was a look that said, *I trusted you!*

"This is fucking *terrible*. Why are you eating this?" Her eyes narrowed. "Wait, is this an Ardelia thing?"

"I just like 'em."

"It is. It's an Ardelia thing." She handed the package back.

"Well, so what if it is?"

"Whatever. They're your taste buds."

"Yeah, they are. And they know what's good."

Vi bristled. "I know what's good."

"You should expand your repartee," Cherry said, not certain she'd used the right word.

"You should get your head examined," said Vi.

Cherry's pocket hummed. Her cell sang, *"Rich, rich, rich!"*

"Oh," said Cherry, reading the text.

"What is it?"

"It's nothing."

"What nothing?"

It was from Ardelia. The text read:

> You. Me. Boston. Whatever you want. Let's
> be crazy. Tonight. Call me!

"Don't you see her enough already? I thought it was your night off," said Vi. "Also, what time is it? It's like nine o'clock already. On a school night."

Cherry pocketed her cell. "Yeah."

Vi held a skirt to her hips, draping the fabric over one knee and admiring herself in the three-way mirror. There was a small stain on the hem and some loose threads.

"What do you think?"

"It's cute," said Cherry. It really was cute.

Vi met her eyes in the mirror and followed their gaze to the stain, the frayed hem. She returned the skirt to the rack. There was a long pause, the kind usually filled with Vi chatter. The thump of disco music took its place. A sign over the changing rooms read: ONE PERSON AT A TIME!—a rule she and Vi had flagrantly ignored since grade school, squeezing together in the little plywood phone booth, Cherry zipping up Vi's skirts, Vi re-angling Cherry's caps. Now that she thought of it, they hadn't done that in such a long time. It probably wouldn't be the same now if they tried.

"I should get going," Cherry said at last. "I got a lot of stuff to do."

"Oh. Okay, sure." Vi looked as if she wanted to say something more. Instead she smiled brightly and went, "Let's go!"

"You don't mind? I'll drive you home."

"Course not." Vi set the other items she'd selected on the rack.

"You're not going to get any of those?" Cherry said. The pink top had been super-cool, if a little grungy.

"Nah, none of these are good enough," Vi said. She squinted, *thinking,* the worst fake thinker in the world. "You know, this place isn't really my thing anymore."

"No?"

"It's kind of played out."

Another *thumpa-thumpa* pause. Cherry felt as if she'd swallowed a coat hanger.

"Yeah," she managed. Her voice crackled. "This place is kind of played out."

"Night off, night off, night off!" Ardelia twirled Cherry through the hall outside her Parcae suite, her voice tumbling up to a trilling falsetto. "It's my night ooooooofff!"

"Wow. You go for the sixteen-ounce Red Bull today or what?"

Ardelia was freshly scrubbed, her skin bright without

makeup, hair still damp from the shower. She smelled like spring.

"What do you want to do?" She squeezed Cherry's hands. "We could do dinner in the big spinny restaurant upstairs. Or—oh! There's this club that just opened—Maxwell was telling me about it—where they fill the room with *bubbles*. No, actually, wait." She tapped her chin, a frantic tapping. "Let's go to the park. It's *such* a gorgeous night."

Cherry laughed. She couldn't help herself. Ardelia's energy was better than caffeine. As they waited for the elevator, watching the floors illuminate in succession, Cherry imagined a countdown to launch. It was a Thursday night, and she was leaving earth behind.

The Boston Common seemed to stretch on forever, like a series of green lily pads strung through the great river of stone and asphalt. At this hour, Aubrey Park was empty and for good reason. The bright lights of Boston, the lamps along the walkway, everything seemed sleepless, restless, and alive. Sure, there were a few sketchy dudes here and there, the smell of weed floating from the public bathrooms, but mostly it was stumbling groups of drunken college kids, couples clinging tightly to each other despite the unseasonably warm night air, and the smell of late-night hot dog vendors and pretzel guys. White apparitions the size of cars loomed through one stand of trees, and as they walked around a bend, Cherry saw that they were gigantic wooden swans, clustered under a bridge. Sure, why not giant wooden swans? Why not anything at all? With Ardelia, anything seemed possible.

"Maybe I'll move to Boston," Cherry said. "It's not *so* far from home, but it's like a different planet."

"Hmm," Ardelia said. "Sure. Hey, you want to be a little crazy?"

"Sure," Cherry said. Ardelia could have asked her to jump for the moon, and she would have.

They were turning onto a stretch of path running along an open sports field. Floodlights turned the grass pale gray and cast dagger-like shadows from the couples crossing the grass. A few outbuildings dotted the path.

"I've got an idea. You see that kid in the sweatshirt?"

The nerd in question was walking and reading a paperback. He might have been cute without the acne and little-boy haircut. She guessed he was her age or maybe a college freshman. His sweatshirt said *42* on it, but she doubted he was actually on a sports team.

"Go talk to him," Ardelia said.

"Why?"

"This will be hilarious. Trust me."

Without explaining further, she disappeared behind one of the outbuildings, like grown-up hide-and-seek.

Cherry considered chasing her, but the dork was getting close, moving slowly, like a sleepwalker.

"Uh, hey," said Cherry.

No response. She tried again in a more friendly tone. "Hi. Hey there."

The kid looked up, perplexed that a girl was speaking to him.

"Hey." He smiled. He had good teeth. At least that was something.

"Do you know this area?" Cherry tried. "I'm uh, a little lost."

The kid shrugged. "Yeah. Where you trying to go?"

"I'm looking for the . . . burger . . . place." What was Ardelia *doing* back there? Filing her nails?

The kid looked suspicious. "Which one? There are a few."

"Oh. I guess the uh . . ." *Shit,* she didn't know any burger places in Boston. "The big one?"

"Big Bang Burger Bar?"

"Yeah," said Cherry. "That one."

The kid tucked his paperback in his sweatshirt pocket and began to point out the way. Cherry pretended to listen, but some movement near the shed caught her eye. Ardelia floated around the corner like a ninja assassin. She was literally on tiptoe, biting back a grin. She swept up behind the dork and tapped his shoulder with a dainty pointed fingernail. He turned, and Ardelia pounced. She pressed her lips to his, not just a peck but a deep blockbuster kiss, turning her face and draping her arms around his shoulders. Her victim was stupefied, eyebrows backpedaling up to his hairline as he recognized the crazy famous person assaulting him in the park. Then, grinning wickedly, Ardelia made a mystical pass with her hand, waggling her fingertips before his eyes.

"And no one will *ever* believe you."

Ardelia whirled, all swirling skirt and bouncing curls, and grabbed Cherry's hand. They ran for the trees, leaving the stunned kid to pull himself together, alone on the walkway.

"Oh, my *God.*" Cherry's face ached from laughing. "That was *epic.*"

"Mmm." Ardelia ran her tongue over her teeth. "Tasted like cinnamon gum."

They were hidden now behind some elms and a length of wire fence. Ardelia rested against a tree, tipping her face toward the stars.

"I wish I'd taken a picture of the guy's face," Cherry said. "I think you gave him a stroke."

Ardelia laughed, breathless. "Sometimes it's even better. One guy actually fell over."

"Wait, have you done that before?"

"Once or twice." She shrugged. "Who knows? Maybe someone will start a website. A bunch of online conspiracy theorists. *Does Ardelia Deen* really *kiss strange boys in the night?*"

Cherry shook her head. "You're like the tooth fairy, except for make-outs." She looked over her shoulder to where they'd left him, imagining the kid still standing there, mouth hanging open, smeared with Ardelia's lipstick. "Jesus. I almost feel a little sorry for him."

"Oh, who cares?" Ardelia reached for Cherry's hand. "Come on, I can't sit still."

A while later they lounged on a park bench, each with an ice-cream cone from the snack stand near the gate. It was the first truly warm night of the year. Voices carried over the park, other couples on other benches, a little kid screaming and laughing, despite the late hour, and somewhere someone playing a boom box. The park and the air and the cold ice cream on her tongue — it all felt too special to be real. They were only missing fireworks and a picnic blanket.

Ardelia sniffed. Her nose was running a lot tonight. She dabbed it with a paper napkin.

"You get allergies?" Cherry asked, catching a rogue dribble of mint chocolate chip.

Ardelia tipped her face toward the sky, blinking. "Sure." She sniffed again.

"Vi was making fun of me earlier." Cherry caught another dribble as it raced down her waffle cone. She was judging the perfect moment to bite off the bottom and slurp out the remaining ice cream, just like old times. She hadn't changed *that* much. "She was ragging on me because I bought these fancy chocolates from the organic market."

"Oh?" Ardelia seemed distracted. She looked up the walkway toward the park entrance, sniffed again. "Sounds like reverse snobbery to me."

"What's that?"

"What? Oh, you know, it's like the regular variety, except in reverse. It's when you think someone must be uptight, condescending, stuffy—what have you—simply because they have a little more money than you do."

"Huh." She'd never known there was a word for it. It felt weightier with a word. She felt a little stab of guilt, wondering how much of Cherry's reverse snobbery Ardelia had sensed in the beginning.

"You know?" Ardelia said suddenly. "Fuck her, right? You're trying new things. And what's she doing? Making fun of you for it."

"I guess. . . ." Cherry focused on Ardelia's red eyes, her running nose, her twitching knee, which was frankly two twitches away from driving Cherry absolutely bonkers.

"Sorry," Ardelia said, and laughed at herself. "Don't know where that came from."

An errant drip slid off her cone and planted itself in Cherry's lap.

"Wait, are you *on* something?" Cherry asked.

Ardelia bit her lip. She smiled guiltily. "Maybe."

Cherry was scandalized. She'd never seen anyone on drugs, other than weed, and that didn't count. Ardelia seemed twisted on something exotic. And exhausting.

"What? What is it?"

"*No.* I'm not telling you," Ardelia said, a little of her manic cheer returning. "Don't do drugs. *Don't do drugs, Cherry.* I don't want that for you. I'm responsible for you."

Cherry laughed. "I didn't say I wanted any."

"*Good.* Do as I say, not as I do. Okay? Okay?" She pressed her forehead to Cherry's. "Okay?"

"Yeah, okay." Cherry couldn't stop laughing. Was this what they called a *contact high?*

"Come on." Ardelia stood and tossed the remainder of her cone into the trash. "We can't stop now, or it'll just be too depressing."

They were out a long time. Walking, talking. Cherry could barely keep up with Ardelia. And then, after ordering milk shakes at a twenty-four-hour diner not far from the harbor, Ardelia decided she had to be taken home. The Spider zipped quietly through the vacant back streets, the wheels bobbling over the cobblestone avenues. It was that too-late or too-early hour of the night when the city was most empty. Cherry could smell baking bread.

Ardelia wiped her cheeks. They were sparkly in the low light of the dash.

"Are you crying?"

"My eyes are just raw." Her voice was hoarse, that of a much older woman. Ardelia seemed to have aged ten years since the park. She curled up her knees and rested her cheek against the seat. She put her hand on Cherry's knee. "Thank you."

Cherry squeezed her friend's hand, not sure what she was being thanked for. By the next stoplight, Ardelia was asleep. She looked roughed up, her hair frizzed from the night's humidity, her lips dry and cracked. It was the first time Cherry had seen her look frayed, frail, and she couldn't decide if this was the kind of raw that comes after a workout — the used-up, good-for-you kind — or the beat-down look of someone who's just had the shit kicked out of them.

Without Ardelia's infectious energy, the late hour pulled on Cherry like a lead coat. She felt beat-up herself. She thought *they'd* been having fun, but, really, Ardelia was having fun with herself. Cherry was an accessory, an add-on. She thought of the kid in the park and the warm air and the ice cream — and it took the sweetness out of everything.

But it was also — sort of, a bit — *exciting.* And it *had* been pretty funny, pretty ridiculous, the look on the guy's face. Jesus. She felt so *different.* Even the exhaustion, the fact she'd have to sneak in through her window so Pop wouldn't know she'd been out all night, and the knowledge that tomorrow she'd be wrecked for school were good things. She felt stretched, sore like a muscle that didn't get much exercise, used for the first time.

She yawned, guiding the Spider toward Ardelia's hotel, through the orange and empty streets. The sun was rising in a city, and look how she'd been out all night, and look at the color of the sky, a color you could drive into forever.

Chapter Twenty-six

Fugu

Next morning wasn't pretty. In homeroom Cherry clutched her thermos of coffee, taking tiny, trembling sips. First period was biology, which Cherry usually enjoyed, mostly because she liked Mrs. Polino. Mrs. Polino had a sense of humor. You could tell she used to be a dumb kid from the way she joked around with the dumb kids and didn't take any shit from the smarties. Mrs. Polino was tough. A chalk thrower. Which was why Cherry should have known better than to fall asleep in her class.

A terrible bleat like an air-raid siren jerked Cherry awake. Her knees hit the underside of her desk, nearly toppling her. The class was in hysterics. Polino stood a few feet away, brandishing the air horn she used to snap unruly students to attention.

"Oh, I'm sorry," Mrs. Polino said. "Did I interrupt your nap?"

"I wasn't—" Cherry started. Polino squeezed the horn again. Kids were convulsed with laughter, in *tears*.

"See me after class, Kerrigan."

Everyone went, *"Oohhhh."*

Cherry stayed seated until the last student filed out and she and Polino were alone. Polino leaned against the teacher's desk, arms crossed, and indicated that Cherry should sit closer by kicking out the nearest chair. Cherry moved to the front row.

Polino glowered, letting her stew, studying her.

"Are you on drugs?"

"What?"

"Smack. Dope. Grass."

"Grass?"

"Cherry."

"I'm not on drugs, Mrs. P. What makes you think I'm on drugs?"

Polino opened a folder on her desk. "Your academic record's never been stellar, Kerrigan. But lately it's *atrocious*. There's a smell coming off this thing." She waved the file in the air. "It smells like deadbeat." Cherry tried not to smile. Polino was funny even when she was ripping you a new one. "Then there was your suspension—"

"That was for a good cause! Vi—"

Polino stopped her with a raised hand. "I admire your motives. But you didn't make up *any* of the work you missed. You didn't even try. Look." She moved from her desk to the seat next to Cherry. "I'll let you in on a little secret. In case you can't tell, your teachers like you. *I* like you. Boy, if I could have given it to that punk Neil . . ." Polino entertained that fantasy for a moment, then refocused. "You are dauntless, Cherry Kerrigan. But lately you've been *stupid*. What's going on?"

Cherry studied her hands. She trusted Mrs. Polino. There weren't many teachers you could talk to about real shit. "I'm going through some changes."

"Uh-oh."

"Not like that! I'm not preggers. It's just . . . Have you ever been certain you wanted one thing, just this regular, normal, wonderful thing? And then you try something a little more . . . I don't know, *exotic*? And suddenly you're not so sure?"

"Okay," Polino said, taking this in. "You know a lot of girls experiment—"

"Oh, for Jesus." Cherry covered her ears. "I'm not *gay*. That's not . . . Forget it." She stood. "Thanks for the talk. I mean it. Let's just chalk this up to senior-itis."

Polino looked up, frowning but not angry. "You know the puffer-fish thing?"

"No. What's that?"

"Puffer fish live at these great depths, down where the pressure is so intense it would crush a human to a pulp."

Cherry laughed. "I know that feeling."

"Well, these puffer fish, when you bring them up to the surface, where there isn't so much pressure, you know what happens?"

"They go, *Why the hell didn't I do this earlier? It's way nicer up here?*"

"They explode," said Polino. "Their bodies aren't used to it, like the fish who were born near the surface. The puffer fish burst."

Cherry shifted her weight. "This is a metaphor."

"I teach biology, kid," said Polino. "English lit is down the hall."

Chapter Twenty-seven

Cold Cuts and the Queen's English

That evening Ardelia took Cherry to dinner again, this time at the craft service table on set. Morale was low. Today's session was cut short, with one cancellation and a no-show. The girls who'd kept their appointments were hardly stellar mommy material. They were nearing the bottom of Ardelia's list, and Cherry wondered whether they'd been too harsh on the earlier candidates. A snotty attitude or slight gambling problem didn't seem so bad compared to a manic-depressive or a girl with a stutter who'd stormed out calling Ardelia a *p-p-pretentious bitch*.

The evening's shoot was a crowd scene, and dozens of extras milled around under a large tent, waiting for costumes. Cherry thought she recognized a few kids from school. They were like cattle, cordoned off in numbered sections. She followed Ardelia past the tent, toward the spread of eats labeled PRINCIPALS ONLY. The extras nearest stared with envy. *Starving* cattle.

"I'm getting a little discouraged," Ardelia said, piling her plate with fruit. Cherry had tried to detect any lingering effects from last night's chemical freak-out, but Ardelia seemed undamaged, if a little maudlin. "We're two-thirds through the list, and every candidate seems like a disaster. I suppose we could go through another agency, but I'm not sure I have the energy for it."

"It only takes one," Cherry said, turning her back to the hungry-looking extras.

"That's true."

She couldn't believe the bounty on the craft table. In addition to picnic-style crackers and cold cuts, there were cookies, cake, pastas warming in chafing dishes, chicken wings, skewered meats, and coolers full of different sodas and bubbly water.

"Jesus, next time I'll bring a shopping bag."

"I know, it's meager. They're cutting costs," Ardelia said.

They took their eats to a nearby table, out of sight of the extras. Cherry picked at her cold cuts and looked up to see Ardelia studying her.

"What?"

"I think you'd look nice with your original color, that's all. Wouldn't Cherry look nice with dark hair?"

Ardelia asked someone over Cherry's shoulder. She caught a whiff of scented shampoo as Maxwell dropped beside her.

"Stunning," Maxwell said, helping himself to one of Cherry's French fries. "Of course, you really can't top Ardelia's Bride of Frankenstein look."

Ardelia modeled her tower of hair. "There're three support rods in this thing. I don't know how ladies did it back then."

"How goes Mommy Quest 2013?"

"Miserably," Ardelia said. "Maxwell, won't *you* carry the baby?"

"Can't. No babies. It's in my contract."

"Poo."

"Hey," said Cherry, "wouldn't Spanner do it? Seems like she'd do anything for you."

"I asked. She said no," Ardelia said.

"She said no? To you?" Cherry couldn't believe it. "I know it's a big decision, but I can't picture her turning you down."

Ardelia twirled some cold sesame noodles around her fork and shrugged.

"Too bad Cherry's only seventeen," said Maxwell. "She could carry it for you."

"How do you know how old I am?" Cherry said.

Ardelia smirked. "Maxwell's taken quite the interest in you."

He took another fry. "Careful, Deen."

"He checks your Facebook page."

Cherry turned to him. "You do?"

Maxwell glared like he was trying to incinerate Ardelia on the spot. "Is it so wrong to take an interest in the girl who saved my friend's life?"

"Are you stalking me?" said Cherry.

"Yes, Maxwell!" Ardelia planted her palms on the table. "Are you Cherry's stalker? Are you *obsessed* with her?"

"I mean, I am pretty fabulous," Cherry said. "You wouldn't be the first man I've broken."

"Har-har. This is why I eat lunch alone." Maxwell stood. "Now, if you'll excuse me, I'm due in makeup."

"I've got to run, too," Cherry said, clearing her plate.

The girls hugged good-bye, and soon Cherry found herself walking in the same direction as Maxwell. She didn't get nervous around boys. Even with Lucas, her first feelings had been fluttery but never edgy. Now she found herself searching for something to say. All she could think of were references to his movies, which seemed dumb.

Maxwell spoke first. "She adores you, you know."

"I adore her," Cherry said. As usual, the thinking happened after the talking. Cherry realized it was true — she adored Ardelia.

"She hasn't taken to anyone like this since Spanner."

As if conjured by her name, Spanner emerged from the director's tent a few yards away, doing her best not to hobble on her ankle brace. She looked furious.

"She sprained it falling out of bed," said Maxwell. He didn't explain further, and Cherry didn't ask. They watched Spanner signal a hapless PA, waving the doomed boy over.

"That's why she hates you, you know," Maxwell said. "You remind her of herself."

"Her?" Cherry raised an eyebrow so high it hurt. "Oh, yeah, we're total soul twins."

"You wouldn't know it, but Spanner's from humble beginnings," said Maxwell. "They met when Ardelia was filming *The Rented Girl* in a tiny village in the West Midlands. Spanner was cast as a child circus performer." Maxwell chuckled. "Ardelia says that girl spoke with the thickest backcountry accent you've ever heard. Almost unintelligible. I suppose she's what you'd call British trailer trash."

"*Spanner?* But she's so . . . polished."

"*Spanner* was her last name," Maxwell corrected. "*Gracie Spanner.* She changed it to *Spanner Grace* a few years later, around the time she started speaking the Queen's English and buying designer clothes. Quite the Eliza Doolittle." Maxwell smirked. "You can always spot a social climber. They know the *proper* way better than the ones born rich."

Spanner harangued the PA. Her voice reached them across the lot, the distance robbing it of coherence, leaving only its sharpness.

"Why are you telling me this?" Cherry asked.

"Just thought you should know what's possible," said Maxwell. "In life. You could have what she has, if you want it." His eye met hers for the first time, and the force of their blue was like a physical shove. Cherry felt something stir in her center — and squashed it.

"I don't want what she has. Thanks."

Maxwell shrugged. "The way Ardelia's been grooming you, you may not have a choice soon."

"*Grooming* me?"

He didn't seem to hear her. His thoughts had wandered elsewhere. "I was thinking of exploring your town tonight," he said, his conspiratorial tone gone. "Anything here to do besides throw cans off the bridge?"

"There's a club," Cherry said. "Shabooms."

Maxwell considered this. "Sounds interesting. I think I'll check it out. *Ciao,* my dear."

Before she could react, he kissed her on both cheeks. She knew from television this was how Europeans said good-bye, but that didn't stop her turning red. And then she was staring at his back as he sauntered away.

"Hey," Lucas said. He was right there all of a sudden, like he'd teleported in straddling his tiny trick bicycle.

"Jesus! You scared me," she said. "Why aren't you at work?"

"I'm going in at nine," he said. "I thought I'd visit you."

"Security let you past the gate?" It sounded terrible. It sounded exactly how she didn't want it to sound. Lucas shrugged.

"It's not exactly Fort Knox. Who was the guy giving you Frenchy cheek kisses?"

Cherry winced. "You saw that, huh?"

"Yep."

"That was Maxwell Silver." She flipped her hair, making a joke of it.

Lucas looked to where Maxwell was still crossing the lot, hands in his pockets. "The pirate?"

"Well, in this one he's a nineteenth-century business tycoon with TB, but yeah. Same guy."

"He was hitting on you?"

Cherry didn't know the answer to this question, so she said, "You jealous?"

Lucas's eyes hadn't left Maxwell's back. "No, but I'm not into movie stars kissing my boo."

"He was just being . . . *foreign*. Don't worry about him. He's not into me." She didn't believe it. She wanted to believe it.

Together they walked Lucas's bike to the parking lot. Cherry unlocked the Spider.

"Wait. Your bike won't fit."

"Oh," said Lucas. The vintage car's trunk was big enough for picnic lunches and maybe a carton of cigarettes. Cherry winced at the thought of muddy tires on the leather interior — and hated herself for it.

"I'll just bike back," he said. "I'll meet you at my place in thirty, okay?"

Before she could respond, Lucas pedaled off, wobbling over the uneven pavement. He'd biked two miles to see her, and now he'd bike all the way back. She watched him go, part of herself going with him, stretching like Silly Putty, until she might snap.

"Lucas, wait!"

He braked and waited as she jogged over. "Fuck the car. Can I still fit on the handlebars?"

"Considering you're the same size you were in eighth grade, yes."

She punched his shoulder. "Come on, then, muscle man. Gimme a ride."

She climbed on, steadying herself, and lurched as he kicked off. The bike swerved, and Cherry yelped with joy, nearly losing her balance. The road teetered with the seasick bobble of the bike, straightening as they picked up speed. She felt elevated, like a kid on her father's shoulders. It was fun and scary to see the world from an artificial height, and part of the fun was knowing it wouldn't last, and soon your feet would touch boring old earth.

For now, she squeezed the handlebars, the front wheel zipping between her knees.

She could still feel the spots on her cheeks where they'd been kissed. She shut her eyes and let the spots tingle.

Chapter Twenty-eight

Teenage Mutant Ninja Freud

They made it to Sweet Creek before a private path through the trees enticed them off the road. Twenty minutes later, Cherry was brushing a mud stain from her slacks, and Lucas searched for his shoe in the bushes.

"You have leaves in your hair," he said.

"I have leaves *everywhere*." She felt like a wild woods girl, a sprite. She wanted to climb into the nearest oak and fall asleep. She stretched, felt an ache in her jaw, and winced.

"You okay?"

"Yeah, fine. You were . . . vigorous." She grinned evilly. "Maybe I should let you see me flirting with Euro dudes every day."

He turned his back and pulled on his shirt. When she saw his face, it wasn't what she wanted it to be.

"Sorry. I won't tease."

"I'm not a jealous guy," he said. Compared to some, this was true. But he *was* jealous now. Cherry knew the difference between horny kissing and jealous kissing. Horny kissing didn't make your jaw hurt. Or leave bite marks.

"I know," she said. "I'm just being a dick."

"Just . . ." He pulled away, only slightly. "I have to hear you say it. You wouldn't ever, right?"

"Lucas, I would never, *ever* cheat on you. The thought would not cross my mind."

He thanked her, but there was still a little air pocket between them. Other people—Vi, for instance— sometimes accused Lucas of being cold, but Cherry never interpreted his silences that way. He was a thinker, a listener. He thought about what he said before he said it. Now, though, she wished he'd say *something*. She'd apologized; she'd promised. Wasn't it his turn to comfort *her*?

They came to Cherry's trailer, and she lowered herself off the handlebars. Gravity pulled extra hard today.

"I'll text you later?" he said.

"Damn right you will." She put his hand on her ass, earning a smile at least. She went in through the garage and found Pop getting ready to leave, the keys to the tow truck in his fist.

"You've got a leaf in your hair," Pop said.

"How bizarre." She plucked it out and cleared her throat. "What's up?"

"I need you to stay in tonight."

"What? I did my time!"

Pop pulled on his leather jacket, reflexively patting the breast pocket—a habit left over from his smoking days. "I'm going up to Hanover to see about a winch replacement. I'll be back tomorrow morning. You've got to watch your brother."

"He's sixteen."

"He's grounded."

"Ooh!" She rubbed her hands together. *"What he do?"*

"Caught him smoking behind the shop." Pop didn't say *cigarettes,* but Cherry assumed. If it were weed Pop caught him with, Stew wouldn't be grounded. He'd be dead.

"I'll be back before you get up." He kissed her forehead. "How was work?"

"Weird," said Cherry. "As usual."

"Well, keep it up. Maybe if you do a good job, she'll give you another car."

She felt a twitch of guilt for abandoning the Spider but decided it was all in the service of being a good girlfriend. Though didn't quite feel like that, either. She would put extra gusto into being a good big sister, though. That she was always good at.

Stew was on the couch reading a magazine. She came up behind him and dug a knuckle into his shoulder. He screeched and batted her with the December issue of *Front*. She dropped next to him and helped herself to his box of Cheez-Its.

"He gone?" Stew asked.

"Solid gone."

"Finally!" He turned on the television and leaned back, folding his hands behind his head. (Super Big Sister. Letting the kid watch TV when he wasn't supposed to.)

"Wanna order a pizza?" Stew asked.

"Sure. Let's get Giovanni's," said Cherry.

"The froofy place? What's wrong with Domino's?"

"I'm sick of Domino's."

"Whatever," said Stew. "Nothing fancy, though. No olives or gold leaf or whatever the hell they do over there."

She went to order online and found the browser open. Stew had been tagging Facebook pictures. In one Stew lay in a grassy field with a curly-haired girl's head on his stomach. Both squinted up at the camera, Stew flipping the bird.

"That Tori?"

"Who?" Stew said, leaning over her shoulder. "That's Jessica."

"What happened to Tori?"

"Don't hate the player; hate the game."

"You're such a man-whore."

"Just because I'm not Molly Monogamy."

"Uh, hello. I had boyfriends before Lucas."

Stew tipped back onto the couch with a *thump*. "Yeah. One. Who you dated for, like, a month."

"That's because Deke was a dick," Cherry said.

"Very true. It's also because you're anal."

"Excuse me?"

Stew sighed dramatically. "I mean like anal-retentive. You're uptight. It's from psychology."

Cherry looked at her stoner brother in his Mario Bros. beanie and unspeakably filthy sneakers. "Since when do you know psychology?"

Stew shrugged. "I've been reading this book. On Freud and stuff. It's interesting."

"For school?"

He shrugged again.

"Can I see it?"

He reached over his head, pulled a paperback Cherry had never noticed from the clutter on the end table, and tossed it to her. The cover was boring and brown with the words *The Ego and the Id*. It was thick, the pages musty and dog-eared, a plastic slot from the Aubrey Public Library pasted to the back cover.

"What's it about?"

"You know. The brain."

"I'm not stupid," she snapped.

He sat up with mock exasperation and hugged his knees. Cherry had a sudden flashback to Stew as a little kid, sitting on his bed in footie pj's in the same position, guiltily telling her he'd accidentally thrown out the family photo album.

"Well, you got the id, right? And the id's like . . . The id's like what you *want* to do. Like smoke and eat cake and do it. All the fun stuff. The id's like Michelangelo from the Teenage Mutant Ninja Turtles. Dude just wants to party and eat pizza."

Cherry laughed. "All right. Michelangelo."

"But there's also this part of your brain called the super-ego. That's the part that knows right and wrong and kinda keeps the id in check."

"Like Shredder? The bad guy?"

Stew made a so-so gesture. "More like the rat, Splinter. The super-ego's a good thing. But you need both to stay sane, you know?"

Cherry turned the book over. It was heavy. She flipped through the pages packed with minuscule type.

"Would you wanna be a psycho . . . psycho-anal-yst?"

Stew turned back to the TV. "I don't know. Maybe. I like trying to figure out why people do what they do." There was a pause while the show faded out and was replaced by a commercial. "I mean, I'm not gonna work in Pop's garage until I die, that's for sure."

A monotone version of "Superb Ass" jingled in Cherry's pocket. She went into her room to answer.

"I feel like we've been weird," Vi said straight off. "You and me. Have we been weird?"

Cherry dropped onto her bed, shoving aside magazines and a takeout carton, letting it all slide to the floor. "Yeah, maybe a little."

"What's up with that?"

"I don't know," Cherry said. "Maybe it's like you're sad you're leaving for school while I'm staying here?"

"I was thinking maybe *you* were like that. Sad about me leaving."

"I don't know." She retrieved the takeout carton from the floor. "Maybe."

"Well, let's not be sad," said Vi. "Let's be awesome."

Cherry laughed. "That's usually my line."

"Yeah, well, I learned from the best." Cherry heard the *tsssk!* of a Diet Coke being opened and Vi swallowing. "So, let's be awesome together tonight. Let's do something fun."

"Wanna come over? I'm babysitting."

"No, you're not!" Stew called from the living room.

"Um, *no*," said Vi. "Come out. Stew can take care of himself."

"And do what?"

"Well, I heard about this place, Technodrome? I guess they do nineties remixes on Friday nights. I know you're all into Boston lately, so—"

Cherry sat up in bed. A shiver shot through her core, like swallowing a slug of ice. It had been a crazy week for trying crazy things. *Shit.* Was she really doing this?

Why not?

"Actually," she heard herself say. "Clubbing could be fun. But why don't we go to Shabooms?"

"Whoa, really? You never want to go to Shabooms!"

"I'm in a dancing mood."

"Sweet!"

"I'll call you when I'm ready," said Cherry.

She went back out and kicked Stew's shoe. Leaving him was still being a Super Big Sis. He didn't want to be stuck with her all night. She was being nicer this way, really.

"I'm going out."

He looked up. "I thought we were getting pizza."

"I'll leave you some cash," she said. "You can get whatever you want."

He shrugged, turning back to the TV. "Okay."

"But you have to *promise* to stay home. And no girls over."

"Yeah, yeah."

"*Seriously,* dickhead. If Pop comes home to find you Greek wrestling, my life is over." She grabbed a pressure point on his knee and twisted. "And so is yours."

"Ow! Jesus! Okay!"

Cherry went to change, hesitating over her wardrobe

choices. She considered one of the pricey black tops Ardelia approved for interviews. It was modest, but pop a few buttons and it could be . . . fun. She weighed it against her Blow Pop T-shirt and decided on the fancier look, wondering whether it was her id or super-ego that made her do it. She selected the shorter of her two "professional" skirts.

She paused again in front of the bathroom mirror, fluttering her eyelashes, making a pout. She imagined her hair re-ravened. No, it was too weird to even think about. She rummaged through the medicine cabinet and found some Maybelline eye shadow, purchased for last Halloween's zombie cheerleader costume. After a few false starts, she managed to dust the area around her eyelids. She liked the effect. Her eyes looked smoky and mysterious.

"You look nice," Stew said when she came back into the living room. He was brazenly packing his pipe on the coffee table, crumbs spilling from a plastic bag. Ironically, this put her at ease. At least stoned he was more likely to sit there and stay out of trouble.

"*Please* behave yourself."

Stew clicked his lighter. "Hey, I'm not the one who got suspended."

Chapter Twenty-nine

FemBrats

What partyers there were in Aubrey bottlenecked at Shabooms on Saturday nights. The under-eighteen policy only applied to Thursdays, so the line on this Friday was mostly college kids from Worcester. Cherry scanned the crowd as they drove past. She recognized a few PAs from the set. Some seniors who were either over eighteen or, like Cherry and Vi, hoped to squeeze under the bar waited anxiously near the door, craning to see what kind of mood Bernie the Bouncer was in.

They drove on, looking for parking, and Cherry craned her neck, scanning the crowd again.

"What is the *point* of a fancy car if you just leave it lying around?" Vi was saying. "It would have been sweet to buzz the club in *your* car is all I'm saying. Instead of my piece o' shit."

They parked Vi's Mitsubishi across the street and waited at the crosswalk.

Vi's cell buzzed. She looked at it and huffed. "Neil."

Cherry snatched the phone away and hit Ignore.

"I wasn't going to pick up," said Vi.

"Good," said Cherry.

"Girls' night," said Vi, taking Cherry's hand.

"Girls' night."

She scanned the crowd a third time.

"Are you looking for somebody?"

"No. Who would I be looking for?"

"I dunno, but if you pivot your head any more, it might fall off. Oh, God . . ." Vi's tone rose an octave. "Oh, my God, is that who I think it is?"

It was. Maxwell approached the club on the other side of the street, a pair of sparkling girls in his wake. He cupped his hands around his mouth and shouted Cherry's name. People looked over. They looked at Maxwell, recognized him, and looked back at her. She clutched at the open collar of her shirt.

This was a mistake.

"This was a mistake," said Cherry. Vi was catatonic. Cherry tugged her friend's sleeve. "Let's just go to Mel's, okay? I'm serious. I don't want to do this anymore."

Vi's paralysis broke, and she whirled on Cherry.

"Are you *insane*? Maxwell Silver is calling your

name. He's calling *your name!* You can't just ignore him. *Come on.*"

She dragged Cherry forward into oncoming traffic. They crossed against the light, Vi holding the cars at bay with an outstretched hand.

"Evening," Maxwell said as they came over. "I decided to take your suggestion." His dates hovered over his shoulder like pilot fish, looking slightly dazed, as if being gorgeous left no energy for speaking or moving.

"Yeah, well." She tried to marshal herself. She had not come here to see him. She hadn't. She didn't want to *be* here at all. "I should have mentioned—they don't allow foreigners. You should probably just go home."

Maxwell chuckled. "Who's your friend?"

"This is Vi."

Vi looked shell-shocked. "I . . . like the way you talk."

"You should visit Liverpool. We all talk this way."

"Well," said Cherry. "See you in there."

Maxwell frowned. "Don't wait in line—come in with us."

"We're cool. This is more of a girls' night out." She looked to Vi for confirmation. "Right?"

"You don't have to join us," Maxwell said. "Just let us get you in the door."

Cherry felt a pinch in her side.

"The line sucks," hissed Vi, not taking her eyes from

Maxwell. She happened to be right. The line extended all the way to Mel's.

"Fine," said Cherry, addressing Maxwell. "Thanks."

"Our pleasure." He gestured for them to lead the way.

Bernie let them through without trouble. Past the "velvet rope" (really a chintzy plastic chain), the club was dark and close, like an undersea cave. Colored lights swam across the walls. It was smaller than Cherry expected: a few booths, a long bar with illuminated bottles, and a crammed dance floor. A DJ pressed one earphone to his head and nodded to the beat.

"You are released," Maxwell said. "See you on set!"

Cherry watched him go with a twinge, feeling a little abandoned on the top step and more than a little watched. Everyone had turned to look when Maxwell Silver entered, and now they were staring at the girls he'd left at the door.

"Okay, that was pretty much the coolest thing that's ever happened," Vi said, breathless. "You think they'll let us drink, since we came in with Max?"

"Now he's *Max*?"

"Whatever, hater. You know you want him."

"I never said that. I mean, I don't. Want him." Cherry took Vi's hand. "Come on, let's dance."

They found a space and started to move to the music. It was mostly girls dancing. The few boys remained still as fire poles while their dates slithered around them. Vi watched Maxwell's table over Cherry's shoulder, making her sexy pouty face, the one that made her look like a duck. Cherry tried to focus on the beat. It was the new track by FemBrat, but the DJ had ruined it, speeding it up. It was supposed to be a sad song; now it just sounded hysterical. Fem was halfway through the second verse, Cherry's favorite, about *"tell her you've found somebody new,"* when Vi put her arm around her waist and rode her knee up between Cherry's legs.

Cherry recoiled.

"What are you doing?"

"Dancing," said Vi.

"Molesting, more like."

"Come on, don't be weird." Her eyes were over Cherry's shoulder again. She draped her arms around her friend's neck. Cherry removed them.

"Would you relax? Guys like it when girls dance like this," Vi said.

"If you were a guy, I'd kick you in the balls."

"Whatever. He's not watching us, anyway." She dropped back and straightened her skirt. "I need to pee."

They cut through the crowd and waited in line for the ladies' room, then waited in line again to check their makeup at the vanity. Cherry liked the way she looked. The other girls were gaudy, a child's drawing, colored outside the lines. Compared to them, Cherry looked refined, adult. Sophisticated.

"You're starting to look like her," said Vi.

"Who?"

"Ardelia."

"That's stupid. We don't look anything like each other."

Vi studied Cherry's reflection. "I don't know. It's, like, how you're standing or something. It's weird." She let it drop, reapplying her lipstick. "So, Maxwell seems cool."

The girl next to Cherry reapplied her eyeliner, pretending not to listen.

"Ignore him," said Cherry.

"Don't you like him?"

"No, I do. I mean, I don't *like* him like him. He's nice. It's just, he's also kind of a sleaze? You know how he and Ardelia were a thing?"

"Hello, I'm the one who *told* you about that."

"Yeah, well, I think he slept with her friend. The bitchy one. Spanner."

"While they were still together?"

"No, but . . ."

Vi shrugged. "Seems okay to me."

"So, you'd be fine with me hooking up with Neil?"

"That's different."

"How?"

"Neil's not a movie star."

They returned to the dance floor, and Cherry let the full wattage of her ire radiate at Vi's back. She'd forgotten about Single Vi, who was even more flirtatious and petty than Attached Vi. At Mel's they could just be friends, but at the club they were competitors, even if Cherry wasn't trying to *win* anything. *She* wasn't competing. But she hated the way Vi just *assumed* Maxwell would be checking *her* out and not Cherry. Vi so wasn't his type. If anyone was —

Cherry dropped back into a corner and texted Lucas. *Clubbing w. Vi. Huge disaster. Wish I was with u.*

She waited a beat, hoping for the friendly buzz and glow of a return text, then remembered that Lucas turned his phone off at work.

Vi emerged from the crowd, grinning and flush.

"Come on. Maxwell's waving us over."

"Vi, no —!"

Her wrist in Vi's robo grip, Cherry was yanked across the floor to Maxwell's booth. He was tucked into the leather half-moon with his dates on either side. As Vi toddled over, he gently pushed one of them out and gestured for the girls to slide in.

"Have a drink with us."

"No —"

"Yes!" said Vi. "We'd love that, thanks."

Maxwell leaned in so only Cherry could hear. "*Please* save me from these two. I swear they've got one brain between them, and they left it in the car."

Maxwell's dates were staring blankly in the same direction. Cherry laughed.

"Fine. One drink. One."

Cherry slid in beside the other girls, Vi next, with Maxwell at the end. This made a speedy escape impossible. She felt claustrophobic. Maxwell's dates bobbed to the music. The nearest looked familiar.

"Are you an actress?" said Cherry. The girl smiled. Her breath was spearminty.

"Kendra!" she shouted over the music.

"Cherry."

Kendra pointed to her friend. "Kendra!"

"You're both Kendra?"

Kendra nodded.

"Can you say anything other than *Kendra*?"

"What?"

"Never mind."

Vi was leaning on Maxwell, using the noise as an excuse to bring her face close to his. "I'm a big fan."

"Then you must really blow," said Maxwell.

Vi squinted, then shoved his arm. "You're teasing me."

"I never tease."

"He's a scoundrel," said Cherry. "Don't trust him."

"Scoundrel," said Vi in a British accent. "He's a scoundrel, *dahling*."

Maxwell raised a finger, and a waitress appeared with a bottle and a tray of glasses.

"You know we're underage," Cherry said.

"Not in London," said Maxwell. "The drinking age is eighteen—"

"We're seventeen," Cherry put in.

"And that's why there's less bingeing back home," Maxwell finished.

"That is so *cultural*," said Vi.

Cherry rolled her eyes. Trapped between Ditzy and Desperate.

She sampled her drink, remembering how much she'd enjoyed Alan's wine at Ascot, and how it made her feel happy, dopey, sleepy—the best three dwarves. Whatever it was that Maxwell had ordered shot down her throat like molten lead.

Cherry wheezed. *"Ay, caramba."*

"Grappa," said Maxwell. "The peasants' drink."

"Drink what?" said Vi.

"My dad drinks this," said the other Kendra.

Vi pounded her glass and poured another.

"Easy," said Cherry.

"She's right," said Maxwell. "This is a man's drink."

He leaned in as he said it, setting his glass on the table beside Vi's so their rims were just kissing. He placed his hand on Vi's knee, her best friend's knee, his smile in Cherry's face like something obscene. The grappa flash-boiled in her stomach. A movie star in a small town with four girls at his table.

And she was one of them.

"What does *that* mean?"

"Hmm?" Vi had whispered something in Maxwell's ear, and he'd lost the thread. He blinked. "What does what mean?"

"What does that mean?" Cherry repeated. "*Man's* drink?"

"I just mean it's strong."

"So men's drinks are strong and women's aren't?"

Vi slouched into the booth. *"Here we go."*

"Chemically, men have a higher tolerance for alcohol," said Maxwell. "It's science."

"It's bullshit," said Cherry. "Next you're gonna say men are better at sports."

Maxwell zipped his lip and threw away the key. "Well, I mean . . . they *are,* though."

"Uh-oh," said Vi.

"Oh, *really*?" said Cherry. "So, you think, scientifically speaking, that *you* are a better athlete than *me*?"

Maxwell shifted, looking sheepish. "I can see I've kicked the hornets' nest."

"So, you're not saying that?"

"I'm not saying . . . What I'm saying is . . . Well,

yes. I'm reasonably certain I could best you in any athletic arena."

"How about a push-up contest?" said Cherry.

Maxwell tried to laugh. "Wait. You're serious?"

"Yep."

"Here?"

"Parking lot," said Cherry. "Unless you're afraid to get your ass whupped by a girl."

"Excuse me, sweetheart. There is *no* question I would win." He stated this as an obvious if somewhat lamentable fact of life.

"Then let's go," said Cherry.

People at the nearby booths were starting to pay attention. It was clear from Cherry's body language that a conflict had arisen, and the gawkers leaned in.

"This is exciting," said one of the Kendras, and hiccuped.

"Well . . ." said Maxwell, glancing at his audience. "A gentleman never competes with a lady when it comes to physical prowess. It wouldn't be sporting."

"So, you're chicken?"

"That's not what I —"

"It's okay," said Cherry, patting his shoulder. "You're chicken. It's not a big deal."

Lightning forked in Maxwell's eyes. "Lady, you're on."

Chapter Thirty

The Contest

The lot beside Shabooms was a flurry, the crowd circling, camera phones flashing, the *clitter-clatter* of texting thumbs. Maxwell stripped off his jacket. He winked at Vi.

"Ready to be impressed?"

Vi wrinkled her nose. The grappa had done its work. "You're going to lose."

In the center of the ring, Cherry hopped, stretched her arms, cracked her neck. This wasn't just for personal pride. This was for Female Honor. This was for Womankind.

Maxwell gestured to the asphalt. "Shall we?"

Cherry pointed at the sky. "Count 'er off, Vi."

"On your marks! Get set! Go!"

Cherry dropped to the ground and executed three perfect reps before Maxwell had completed his first. Soon they were in sync, the crowd counting along, *"Sixteen!*

Seventeen! Eighteen!" Maxwell puffed, face reddening. Cherry was expressionless, eyes closed, in a state of Zen flow.

"Thirty-three!" the crowd shouted, drawing out the words as the combatants' pace slowed. "Thirty-fouuuur!"

Maxwell tried showing off, going up on one arm, clapping his hands at the zenith, but Cherry couldn't be baited. He glanced her way, the fear starting to show in his eyes, until at last, with a wet cough, Maxwell collapsed, turning onto his back, blinking, gasping.

"We have a winner!" Vi held Cherry's fist in the air like a prizefighter's. The crowd was hysterical. Maxwell, on his feet at last, held out a hand. Cherry looked at it warily.

"I know when I've been bested."

They shook. "Don't feel too bad. You never had a chance."

Maxwell's smile strained. He turned to Vi and the Kendras. "What do you say to a victory lap in the limo? There's room enough for five."

The Kendras squealed. Vi raised her eyebrows at Cherry. "What do you think?"

Aglow with the pride of victory, Cherry shrugged. "Fuck it."

"Excellent," said Maxwell.

He offered his elbow, but just as Cherry moved to

accept it he pivoted oh-so-slightly, and it was Vi who walked arm and arm with him to the limo.

Cherry followed behind.

She had been in a limo once. Junior prom. Vi's mom had sprung for a rental, with cigarette burns in the carpet and the stink of stale beer. The interior of Maxwell's stretch was like a mini-nightclub, LEDs along the floor and an illuminated bar that glittered and rang. An opaque window hid the driver, who could be contacted by pressing an intercom switch. Despite the spacious interior, the passengers were pressed in on each other, legs interweaving in the well between the long leather seats. Cherry sat between the Kendras on one side; Vi sat with Maxwell on the other.

"I just got out of a relationship," Vi said.

"My boyfriend thinks I'm studying for the SATs," said one of the Kendras. This seemed directed at Cherry, so she nodded. "What about Lucas?"

"Sorry?" said Cherry.

"How's Lucas? Your boyfriend?"

It hit her: the Kendras were students at Aubrey Public. Her year. She hadn't recognized them in their fancy clothes. She'd assumed they were older.

"He's . . . fine," she said, trying to recover. She glanced at Maxwell. Vi was chatting in his ear. Cherry couldn't hear her words over the music, and Maxwell didn't seem to be listening, either. He was watching Cherry, his gaze at once guilty and brazen. His eyes rested on her a moment, then he turned to Vi . . .

"You want some?" Kendra was asking. "They're Maxwell's." She held out her cupped palm. Three lavender smiley faces beamed up at Cherry. It took a moment to register what she was looking at. Her mind felt sluggish, lagging behind the others', the last to get the joke. Maybe it was the booze plus push-ups. The muscles in her arms twitched and jumped.

Kendra popped one of the pills in her mouth.

"Oh, Cherry won't," Vi said. "She's a prude."

"No, I'm not. Why does everyone keep saying that?"

"Oh, I don't know," said Maxwell. "She seems pretty bold to me."

She groped for a way to defuse the situation without saying something dorky. Like, *I don't do drugs.* An old Bugs Bunny anti-drug campaign popped into her head. *Just Say No, Doc!* Cherry felt childish. A little kid in a car full of adults. She took a pill from Kendra and swallowed it, grimacing as it went down dry.

"Who's a prude now?"

Vi raised her eyebrows. "Wow."

She expected to feel different. She didn't feel anything. At least, not physically. But something clapped shut inside her. First times, large or small, were one-way doors. Once you moved through them, there was no going back. They split your life into *before* and *after*. She didn't like this feeling of finality, of irreparability. She wanted to reach into her throat and pluck the pill out, undo the decision. She wasn't sure whether she regretted it; just *making the choice* felt wrong. Oddly, this made her think of sex, and why she was glad she and Lucas were waiting until marriage. She was proud of that. Of waiting. That felt good. It felt really good.

She was *thrilled* about how good that felt.

Now that she thought about it, *everything* felt good.

"Whoa," said Cherry.

Kendra grinned. "Right?"

Chapter Thirty-one

Chartreuse Is a Funny Word

The limo sped along a dark stretch of highway, streetlamps blipping like a heart monitor. Cherry was a hovercraft. She floated above her seat on a cushion of glee. She glanced at the Kendra who'd taken the pill, to see how she was acting. Kendra was playing with Cherry's hair.

Panic in a joy blanket. Her heart was a toxic seed encased in sweet, soft fruit.

"We should go," she said, leaning forward to touch Vi's knee. "Home. We should go home."

She wanted only to go home. She imagined the glory of her bed. The sheets. How good would those sheets feel? So good.

Maxwell put his hand over Cherry's, her fingertips dissolving with the warm contact on both sides.

"We're almost there," Maxwell said.

Cherry tried to focus. "You're trouble. Blue eyes."

Maxwell removed Cherry's hand from Vi's knee and gently pushed her back into her seat.

"Be nice," Vi was saying, though Cherry wasn't sure which of them she was addressing.

Kendra twirled her finger in Cherry's hair.

"How do you feel?" she asked.

"Chartreuse," said Cherry.

The limo dropped them someplace bright. Cherry recognized the doorman's gold frogging. This was Maxwell's hotel. They were in Boston. This was a disaster, but Cherry could not make herself feel bad about it. That one-way-door image occurred to her again, only this time all the doors were blown open, and she could go wherever she wanted and do whatever she wanted. She walked around to the back of the limo and puked in the street. The pill made her feel nauseated, but the nausea was weirdly disembodied. Someone else was sick. Someone else was scared.

She rejoined the group, dragging her finger along the black, beveled limo, liking the way it *squealed*.

There were already people in Maxwell's suite, and at first Cherry thought, *We're already here.* They were men and women she didn't recognize. They had also returned from a night of clubbing, their skinny ties low-slung, high heels kicked off. They raised their glasses and offered Maxwell and company drinks, and Cherry moved away from their warm little circle toward the piano. There

241

were scuff marks on top from somebody's shoes. Ardelia's shoes. No, Cherry's shoes, which Ardelia wore when she stood on the piano, a thousand years ago. She traced the streaks with her fingertips.

Maxwell was at her elbow.

"You turn up in funny places," Cherry said dreamily. "Like my car keys."

"Do you want to go home?"

Vi's laughter rang across the room. She was perched on the bar, chatting with a man in a blazer.

"I can't leave her."

"You look after her, don't you?"

"I worry a lot. About people."

"Who worries about you?" he asked.

And then she began to cry. She couldn't remember the last time she'd cried. One of her internal trapdoors had been holding it in, and now the feeling surged up from the basement and overwhelmed her. She wiped her eyes, not too far gone to be embarrassed, and couldn't stop her shoulders from shaking. When she composed herself, he was there, shielding her from the room, so the others wouldn't see.

"What do you want to do?" he said.

"Come on."

She led him into the small room with the painting on the wall, the one of the woman in the movie theater.

She washed her face in the private bathroom and drank some water from the faucet. When she came out again, Maxwell was standing by the window.

"Feel better?"

Cherry sat on the bed. "A bit, yes."

He was watching her.

"What are you looking at?" she said.

"You."

"Can you see my orange stripe?"

"I don't know what you mean," he said.

She held out her hand, and he came over. He sat beside her, his weight on the mattress pressing her toward him. His hand was on her back now. His fingers pressed on her skin. He kissed her. She kissed him back. It was happening. What was she doing? A little flame of panic licked her insides. But, no, it was okay. She could venture out. Just a little. Just a tiny exploration. She wanted to see the show. All the doors were open, and she could just see what it was like. What *she* was like. And then she could come safely back to herself, and it would be okay.

You don't know what you like. You haven't tried anything.

He was a good kisser. He was really very wonderful. Maxwell's hand was under her shirt, his palm on her rib cage. That was okay, too. She wanted that. Another hand slid south. The pressure of his palm, his insistent fingers, the bite of his nails into the flesh of her stomach.

She adjusted. She moved his hand away, but it kept pushing. Then both his hands were on her shoulders, and he shoved her back.

And all of a sudden, she wasn't safe at all.

She was on her back, and he was climbing on top of her. This wasn't what she wanted. He was pushing up her skirt and tugging at her underwear and simultaneously unclasping his belt. The thought of him flopping out of his pants. *No, no, no.* Suddenly this was all very serious and grown-up and wrong, and what had she done? What was she *doing*? This wasn't what she'd meant; this wasn't what she wanted.

"Stop."

Maxwell stopped. She pushed him away. His face showed stupid, stupid surprise.

"What's wrong?"

She wormed her way out from under him. "What are you *doing*?"

He studied her, not angry, just confused. He smacked his lips and blinked.

"I thought you wanted to fuck."

The word was like a slap in the face. She used it a million times a day, but it didn't mean anything. Not really. Certainly not *that*. It wasn't really attached to anything real. But for him it was. They were staring at each other across a great gulf of experience. And Cherry was suddenly alone in a man's bedroom. Not only did she not want to fuck — she wanted to undo all the things she'd already done, which were not okay, which were not safe. She wanted to undo it all.

She couldn't undo any of it.

Lucas.

"I'm sorry." The words fell like two pennies, plopping on the duvet, so soft.

Maxwell's eyes searched her, semi-drunken, red. *"Jesus,"* he hissed, and dragged himself from the bed. He stood at the window a moment, deciding what to do. Then he went to the door.

"Lock this after me. Who knows what might stumble through it."

Then he left her, sealing her in the dark with herself.

Chapter Thirty-two

One-Way Doors

When she woke, the clock read 4:30. Outside the window, the streetlights were an angry orange. The streets were empty. No reasonable person was up at this hour. Somewhere a car alarm whooped and sighed. She gathered her things, pulled on her shoes.

She went into the living room. Someone was asleep on the foldout. She thought a tangle of blond hair might be Vi's, but Vi was curled in an armchair, asleep.

Cherry picked up the room phone.

"Front desk."

"I need . . ." What did she need? She squeezed her keys. "I need a car."

"Certainly. Would you like a call when it's ready?"

"No," said Cherry. "No, I'll come down now. I'll wait in the lobby."

She thought of leaving quietly. Without Vi. Vi might ask what happened, which meant thinking about what happened, and Cherry didn't want that. She shook Vi's shoulder.

"We have to go."

Vi blinked, her gaze lingering on the couple on the foldout. She looked disappointed.

"Okay?"

"Okay."

The lobby was bright and empty, except for a family just arriving at the front desk, a little girl asleep on her father's shoulder. Cherry tried to remember the last time she'd fallen asleep like that. When the car was ready, she gave the driver Vi's address. Cherry watched the passing streets, the anemic buildings. Vi was either asleep again or pretending. Cherry wondered if she might like this city better in the daylight.

She must have fallen asleep, too, because all at once they were in Vi's driveway. The girls exchanged a half-articulated good-bye, and Cherry gave the driver the second address. It was after six when they reached the parking lot across from the bottling plant. The sky was beginning to turn pale. The film crew had gone, taking all their equipment. Food wrappers tumbled through the lot like an abandoned carnival site. The Spider waited under an elm tree, seedpods littering the soft top and piled in the wiper well. It was in bad need of a wash, grime fanned across the doors, the windshield spattered and streaky. It looked as if it had been waiting for her a hundred years.

Cherry took out her wallet.

"No need for that, miss," the driver said. "All taken care of."

"No, it isn't." She had a twenty in her wallet. She held it out.

"I really can't, miss," the driver said.

"Take it! Just take it!" She jabbed the bill at him. She would scream if he didn't take it. She could see his eyes in the rearview mirror. He took it.

The Spider's cabin was freezing. She cranked up the heater, turned on the radio, and pulled out onto the empty avenue. Despite the dry heated air, she was shivering. Tiny dots danced before her eyes, and she felt sick. There was a horrible soreness in her shoulders. She wanted a shower. She wanted her bed. She wanted to lock the door forever. And more than anything, she wanted to see Lucas. She imagined him curled up under his checkered blanket.

No, she couldn't even think about him.

What came to mind instead was Ardelia. Ardelia singing and dancing on the piano. Ardelia inviting her to Maxwell's party. Ardelia kissing the strange boy in the park. Ardelia tossing her the car keys. She was like an infection, spreading into every cell of Cherry's life. And now Cherry felt diseased. Something stank. A dead smell, a polished smell. It was the smell of the car. Expensive leather. Chrome. She hated it. It climbed up her nostrils and clung to her brain. She rolled down the window, but the stink got worse. Chlorophyll. The smell of money.

Instinctively, like swatting an insect, Cherry jerked the wheel. The streetlights pitched. Rubber squealed as the car skidded, swerving at a right angle to the road. The wheel spun free of Cherry's hands. Weightless silence. Then the passenger side smashed the concrete divider. Lightning flash, double flash. Cherry had a vision of yellow and green and colored confetti. There was a rattle of broken glass and the slice of the seat belt across her chest. And then quiet.

The car rocked, settled. Something hissed. Something clicked. Grunting, Cherry unbuckled and climbed out of the wounded car. She took a step back to examine her handiwork. The Spider was facing the wrong way in the breakdown lane, the passenger side crushed against the barrier, both windows shattered on that side. Long smoky skid marks chased each other across the pavement. Something was leaking from the engine block, and the hood had buckled down the center. There was glass everywhere. The car was dead. She knew a dead car when she saw one.

Feeling the nauseous sense of satisfaction that came

with yanking a loose tooth, Cherry started on foot toward the trailer park. The dawn air was crisp and cleaned the sweat from her skin. Her eyes stung; her limbs twitched. Her chest burned where the seat belt had dug in. Good. She deserved pain. She hoped it would get worse. She hoped it would bruise. She hoped her eyes would burn for days. She liked the ringing in her ears, which made thinking impossible.

She knew something was wrong before she reached the end of the bridge to Sugar Village. She sensed movement at the end of the street. Then she saw Lucas. He was coming toward her out of the shadows, and for a hallucination he seemed awfully solid. He was running toward her, calling her name.

Cherry stopped, not sure what to do. She braced herself, her knees going weak. He knew. Somehow he knew everything about Maxwell. So this was it, the end of them. Would she cry? Would he yell? Whatever her immediate punishment, nothing could be worse than losing him. As he got closer, she saw his expression — something unfamiliar that frightened her more. He threw his arms around her and squeezed.

"I'm so sorry," he said, his words thick, almost drunken. "I'm so sorry."

"W-what?"

"It's gone. It's gone, baby."

He looked at her beseechingly. He shook his head,

but Cherry pushed past him, running toward the end of the street, where she now saw the slow sweep of red and yellow lights and heard voices. Somewhere water pattered on the ground. Mrs. Budzenia watched from her door in a bathrobe. Other neighbors peered from their windows.

Her trailer was a twisted black hulk. The roof had arched and caved like the convolutions of a roller coaster. The walls had come away in sections and lay on the scorched lawn. She could make out the cooked nub of the refrigerator, the chalky outline of the rooms. Everything was black and wet. Fire hoses crisscrossed on what used to be the driveway. And that was it. There was nothing else. The fire had taken everything.

"Cherry!"

Stew wore a starchy blanket around his shoulders, his face streaked with gray ash. He'd been crying.

"You the sister?" a fireman asked.

Something clicked in Cherry's brain. "Where's Pop?"

"We've reached your father. He's on his way."

Stew was holding her, his face pressed into her shoulder so hard it hurt.

"It's my fault. It's my fault! It's my fault!"

There was a little circle around Cherry now. The fireman, Lucas, and her brother. They were waiting for her to say something, waiting to see what she'd do. Everyone was frozen.

And then all at once, she knew what to do. The pain in her head and joints vanished.

She held Stew away. "It's not your fault. It was an accident. You hear me?" Stew sniffed. He didn't seem so sure. She held his ears like she was about to rip them off. "You *hear* me?"

He nodded.

"You all right? You hurt?"

He shook his head.

"Then everything's okay. Everything's fine." She turned to Lucas. "Can we stay with you tonight?"

"Yeah, of course," he said. "I'll tell Dad."

"Go with Lucas," she told her brother. "Take a shower. I'll wait for Pop."

Stew wanted to protest, but Cherry's tone left no room for argument.

"Thank you," she said to the fireman. "We'll be fine. Thank you."

The fireman touched his helmet and then motioned to the others.

"Hey," Lucas said.

She looked at him in the pulsing lights of the fire trucks. She noticed he was barefoot, dressed in his sleeping shorts and tee. He didn't want to leave her, but he would if she said to. Her guilt didn't matter now. All that mattered was Taking Care of Things.

"Make sure he drinks water," she said to Lucas. It seemed like the right thing to say.

He kissed her forehead, then put his arm around Stew and led him around the bend, toward his trailer.

The firefighters were packing up. There was nothing more for them to do. Cherry watched their careful efficiency, rolling the hoses, climbing onto the chassis, serious but not indifferent. The siren bleated once, and the two trucks pulled away. Mrs. Budzenia had gone back inside, and the neighbors' windows were dark now. The sun had just breached the tree line, and long shadows fell across Cherry's street. It was about time for her morning run.

Cherry turned back toward the wreckage of her home. She could see straight through to Lucas's bedroom window, where the light was on. A morning bird chirped its two-note song. It was Saturday.

Cherry sat down on the curb and waited for her father.

A little after ten in the morning, Cherry went into Lucas's room. The shades were drawn. He was awake, lying on his side. He held up the covers so she could slide in. She pulled off her skirt and the crumpled black top. She'd washed her face in the DuBoises' bathroom, and her skin tingled where it was still wet. She tucked in beside him, warming herself against his thighs. Nothing had ever felt so good. It was the first time they'd been in a bed together since kindergarten.

"Everything's going to work out," he said.

She'd always been confident this was true. Life's trampoline could bend only so low before rocketing you back up again. Now she wasn't sure things would work out. It seemed likely they wouldn't. Things would get worse, and keep on getting worse, until there was nothing left. But she didn't say any of this.

"Say something," Lucas said.

He thought she was in shock. And maybe she was. She didn't deserve his pity, because she was a cheater. A traitor. She could still feel Maxwell's lips on hers. She couldn't confess, because if she did, his anger would be dampened by how sorry he felt for her. He'd forgive her because she'd lost everything and because he was a good person.

So that was her punishment. Having to keep the secret. Never getting to be a good person again. She'd stepped out into the cold, because she was curious, because she was covetous, and now she could never, ever get back in.

"I'm homeless," said Cherry.

Chapter Thirty-three

Circling the Wagons

A trailer is too small for three people. With three people, spaces overlap, single rooms split into mini-rooms, shelves in the medicine cabinet subdivide into a tic-tac-toe of his razor, her shampoo, the other's toothbrush, the shared floss. With the DuBois trailer now supporting five, there was no such thing as personal space.

They lived like refugees. Stew slept on the living-room floor, Lucas on the couch. Pop had a camper bed in Mr. DuBois's bedroom—"Just like the army," Mr. DuBois joked—but usually fell asleep in Leroy's armchair. Because she was a girl, Cherry had Lucas's room to herself, and on most nights Lucas would climb over her brother asleep on the floor, using the crackle of the TV to muffle his footsteps, and climb in beside her. His bed was a single. They both had to learn to sleep totally still, in spoon position, the edge of the mattress inches away.

Cherry found it hard to keep still while he lifted the sheets and wrapped himself around her. She pretended to sleep. If he thought she was awake, they might end up talking, and if they talked at night, for that four or five hours they were actually alone, she might tell him what she'd done.

In the mornings, everyone was cheerful. It was a little like camping. Cherry made coffee and eggs, Stew put away the blankets and sleeping bag. Mr. DuBois read aloud from the *Aubrey Times,* and Pop would crack jokes about the stupidity of this politician or that coach. Stew teased Lucas about his snoring, and Lucas would make cracks about Stew's toxic foot odor. They were double the family in half the space, something super-dense, like a collapsing star, and the only things light enough to escape were jokes.

Cherry kept an eye on her father. His initial reaction had been to just stand there in the ashy puddle of their lawn, hanging off himself like a wet winter coat on a rickety stand. When the shock wore off, he was almost relieved, as if the world were lighter without the trailer in it. He hugged her and Stew a little tighter now and a little more often. He spoke softer and moved more delicately, and it worried her. She worried and worried. There was more hair in the drain than usual—long, dyed-blond strands.

Cherry hoped school would at least feel normal, but

no such luck. She was a celebrity again, but for worse reasons. Instead of envy, she got pity—sticky, sweet, and synthetic, like the syrup on the cafeteria flapjacks. Kids she'd never met said things like, *If there's anything I can do . . .* which was meaningless. Still, she couldn't blame them. If *their* homes burned down, Cherry would have felt the same vague pity and unease, as if a burned-down house were contagious, like chicken pox or VD.

And it did seem like misfortune had cursed her, what with the trailer *and* her beautiful car destroyed. It was hard for people to wrap their minds around both incidents at once. The two didn't fit into a logical relationship. Had she crashed the car *into* the trailer, causing the fire? No. Had she seen the fire from the highway and lost control of the vehicle in a state of shock? No. The destruction of both trailer and Spider were simply unrelated tragedies, two awful things for the girl who'd rescued Ardelia Deen. It was so odd, most people had nothing at all to say about it.

The Monday after the fire, Principal Girder called Cherry down to his office and proposed a food drive for her family.

"Our trailer burned down, not the grocery store."

"Well, then." Girder straightened his pencil, aligning it with the edge of his blotter. "Maybe something else. Perhaps a charity fund-raiser?"

"We're fine," said Cherry. "We'll be fine."

Fine was all she said anymore. When Coach White asked her if she wasn't feeling up to running laps, she said, "It's fine." When Mr. Sackov asked if she needed an extension on her paper, it was also *fine,* even though she'd desperately needed an extension *before* the fire. It was like the fire was an excuse to get all the slack a normal person needed just to get through senior year. Maybe if everyone's house burned down, kids wouldn't be so stressed.

The only person who didn't ask her how she was doing was Lucas. They ate lunch together on the bleachers, which was against the rules. They got away with it, though, and this was the extent of the charity Cherry was willing to accept.

"Someone tried to flush a hat in the second-floor girls' room," Lucas said, opening a can of soda. It fizzed everywhere.

"Who wears a hat?"

"Who tries to *flush* a hat?" Lucas said. They watched a flock of geese land on the field, readying a fresh barrage of grass-killing shit. The geese squawked at one another. Cherry decided she hated geese.

"Is this what it's gonna be like?" Lucas said. "When we're married, I mean. Living together." He thought this over, chewing his roast beef sandwich. "I guess we won't see each other during the day."

"Not unless we work at the same place," said Cherry.

"You want a janitor job?"

Cherry shrugged. She wanted to make a dirty joke about riding the floor buffer but didn't have the energy.

She had to make do with only the clothes she'd been wearing the night of the fire and an ancient Minnie Mouse T-shirt she'd left at Lucas's a million years ago. Her old photo albums, favorite DVDs, everything she'd ever owned was gone. She couldn't begin to catalog it. The little trailer had held *so much.* Now everything was reduced, scarce. The Gremlin, made with love, had burned up, along with the attached garage. With no car, her whole world had shrunk to a slim hourglass, with Sugar Village and Aubrey High conjoined by a narrow path she walked every morning with Lucas. Chunks of herself, her *life,* had burned away.

During study period, Olyvya Dunrey approached Cherry in the library. She was sans entourage this time, her messed-up teeth hidden behind a pout. "Saw you on the news," she said. "Again."

Cherry didn't look up from her textbook. "Yep."

"I'm so sorry about your trailer. *House.* Trailer home. Whatever." She seemed unglued, nervous. Cherry took a little pleasure in that.

"Thanks."

"It's not fair," Olyvya said a little louder. Cherry looked up. Olyvya's face was puffy and pink, like she'd swallowed something hot she was trying to keep down. "I just mean, you save someone's life, and then this stupid, awful thing happens to you. It's not fair."

Cherry was stunned. Olyvya seemed genuinely upset. "Are you okay?"

"It's just not fair." She took a calming breath and handed Cherry a piece of construction paper with glitter. "I made you a little cheer-up card. I asked Vi to give it to you, but she doesn't like me."

"Thanks." She took the card. It was heavy with glue and stick-on stars. It looked like a child had made it.

"Anyway, you just seem really tough, you know? I just wanted to say, I don't know how you do it." Olyvya shrugged. "Anyway, if you need anything . . ."

Cherry started to roll her eyes.

"I noticed we have the same brand of phone, and I thought maybe your charger got burned up, and I have an extra one, so you can have it." She pulled a knotted black cord from her clutch and placed it on the table. "I don't know if it'll work with yours since mine is newer. But, anyway."

Cherry stared at the cord. She did need a new cord, actually. It was the first practical thing anyone at school had done.

"Shit. Uh, thank you."

Olyvya shrugged again. It was almost a twitch. "Anyway, see you around."

And then she hurried away, a total surprise.

Cherry dreaded seeing Ardelia. She had ignored the movie star's calls immediately after the fire, texting back, *I'm fine, see you on Monday.* By then the crew had decamped to a stately home on the other side of town, where Ardelia's death scene was to be filmed. The trailers were circled like wagons on the back lawn, the home's rear patio artificially arbored in gaffing and stage lights. Ardelia sat under the hot lights in a wicker rocking chair, a blanket over her lap, face caked with ashen powder to make her look sickly. When she saw Cherry, she leaped up, miracle-healed, and rushed to her side.

"You poor angel!" She wrapped her arms around Cherry. Cherry's arms hung limp at her sides; she was too drained to hug. "Ten minutes!" Ardelia called to the exasperated-looking director of photography.

Cherry, Ardelia, and Spanner gathered in Ardelia's trailer.

"I saw the whole thing on the local news. I tried to call you! And no one was hurt?"

Cherry retold the night's events, editing out any mention of Maxwell or the Spider (now interred behind Pop's garage).

"And it was a cigarette that did it?"

"A 'cigarette.'" Cherry put the word in air quotes. "My brother fell asleep with a joint. The couch and the carpet are all polyester. The place was a death trap. He got out of there before the walls went up."

"How horrifying," said Ardelia.

Spanner was at the kitchenette and Ardelia on the couch, leaning forward to clasp Cherry's hands like a daytime talk-show host.

"So, where are you staying now? With family or . . . ?"

"We're crashing at Lucas's," said Cherry. "We don't really have family in the area."

"Doesn't Lucas also live in a trailer?"

"Yeah. It's a tight squeeze. But it's okay. After that, I'm not sure."

Ardelia was shaking her head, denying the whole horrible mess. "No, no, no, that simply is not acceptable. Spanner!" She clicked her fingers at the slim black booklet on the kitchenette counter: the checkbook.

"Thanks," said Cherry. "For my paycheck."

Ardelia looked confused. "Your what?"

"My *paycheck*. Thanks for giving it to me a little early this week. I appreciate that."

Ardelia's face was pained. Her fingertips twitched. She wanted (*needed,* maybe) to be generous. And Cherry was asking her not to be. Refusing the money made Cherry feel like her old self again, for a moment. It was the kind of thing the old Cherry—before limos and drugs and Maxwell—would have done. It let her feel good about herself, for a moment, and that was worth more than money, in a way.

"Thank you," she said. "I mean it."

"Of course." Ardelia fumbled the pen from her purse and wrote Cherry a check for her weekly salary, not a penny more.

They talked awhile longer. Ardelia was trying to be supportive, but her worry and compassion were suffocating. She wanted to wallow in the horror of it all, to *be there* for Cherry, but Cherry didn't feel like being there herself. She didn't want to talk about it, didn't want a shoulder to cry on. She told Ardelia she appreciated the night off but needed to be alone.

"Of course. Call me if you need anything," Ardelia said, looking hurt. "I'm here."

Spanner followed Cherry out. They walked along together toward the main road. When they reached the gate, Spanner spoke at last.

"What are you going to do?"

Her tone had none of its usual venom, but there was no pity, either. Cherry appreciated that.

"I honestly have no idea." An odd thought struck her. "What would you do?"

Spanner blinked. "Me?"

Cherry could see her weighing a snarky response

against an honest one. When she spoke, it was in an unironic tone Cherry wasn't used to hearing from her. And Spanner clearly wasn't used to using it.

"I would leave. I'd take my savings and go. Usually you've got to burn your own bridges to escape. Someone burned them for you. Also"—Spanner nodded over her shoulder to Ardelia's Star Hauler—"I would have taken the bloody money."

Like his son, Mr. Dubois worked a second job on the weekends. He cleaned public libraries with three Hispanic men, roving from town to town after dark in a van they shared, vacuums and wet mops piled in the rear. On these nights the Kerrigans were in the odd position of being alone in someone else's home. Cherry noticed the change in Pop and Stew, who moved delicately now, practically on tiptoe, and cleaned up after themselves as they went, reminding Cherry of the dog in *Alice in Wonderland* with a broom for its head and tail. Without Leroy and Lucas to joke with, they were cowed, ashamed of their need, embarrassed by their own presence. It was these nights that Pop got grouchy, snapping at Stew and Cherry for the slightest indiscretion: turning up the TV too loud or neglecting to wash a dish. Stew and Cherry bickered in the evenings, elbowing for space on the couch. It was as if they couldn't stand the sight of one another.

The DuBoises didn't act put out by the Kerrigans, so the Kerrigans were put out on their behalf.

To get away, Cherry did what she hadn't done since grade school: climbed the elm tree and hid in its branches. The buds on the Kerrigan side were singed away, and the bark on that side was blackened, maybe forever. From her branch she could see the tracing-paper outline of their old trailer. The debris had been mostly cleared, but she could still feel the kitchen, the skinny hall, the thin divider wall between her room and Stew's, like an indent in the carpet left by a piece of furniture moved for the first time in decades.

Saturday night, in the tree, she called Vi.

"You should stay with me," Vi said. "I don't know if we could put up your dad and Stew, but at least you'd have a little more privacy over here. You could stay in Beth's old room. She won't be back until summer break."

"That's probably a good idea," Cherry said, having no intention of leaving her family. That was something Vi, way out in the sticks, wouldn't understand. People like the Kerrigans and the DuBoises huddled closer together in times of crisis. *Circling the wagons,* Pop called it. She couldn't run away to Vi's big ranch house now, even though she sort of wanted to.

"Still, must be nice getting to sleep with Lucas every night," Vi was saying. "God, I miss having a boyfriend."

"It's okay," said Cherry.

"I mean, I guess you guys can't really do anything, 'cause the walls are so thin."

"Yeah."

She wanted to tell Vi about Maxwell. The words were right there at the back of her throat, but she choked them down again and again. She told herself Vi might blab, not to Lucas but to *someone,* who might blab to someone else, and down the daisy chain it would go until some asshole went, *Hey, Lucas, I hate to be the one to tell you* . . . But when she was honest with herself, Cherry knew she couldn't tell Vi. Because she was ashamed. She wasn't who she thought she was. She was a monster, a traitor. She was no better than her mother, who had left them all.

That night when Mr. DuBois's pickup pulled into the driveway and he and Lucas came inside, suddenly the DuBoises' trailer was bright and full of voices, the men and the boys joking with one another, the tiny tribe banding together. At last something had brought them all together, tied them to one another securely. And here was Cherry, exactly where she deserved to be: alone, in a tree, in the dark.

Chapter Thirty-four

Franken-Girl

The bell rang for last period, signaling the end of her second Monday since the fire. Cherry was the last to leave her seat. The halls were nearly cleared by the time she reached her locker. Vi was waiting for her.

"I'm going to my cousin's. This weekend," said Vi.

"Okay."

"You are officially invited." Vi did a little bow, sweeping her arm as though an invite to Shelley Ravir's cottage in Falmouth was a royal summons.

"I don't think I should." Cherry closed her locker, trying not to slam it.

Vi huffed. She seemed torn between genuine frustration and an obligation to be sympathetic. "But . . . *come on*. I thought you'd want to get away from Camp DuBois for a few days. You know, clear your head?"

They stepped into the parking lot. It was nearly May and felt like it. The air was bright and warm. Windshield and chrome sparkled. Cherry scanned the lines of cars for the Spider, then remembered it was gone. *Oh, right.* She kept forgetting. Just like occasionally, for a second or two, she felt normal, like the pre-everything Cherry. They were little delicious moments of forgetfulness, like marshmallows in her mushy cereal life.

Vi touched her shoulder, squinting toward the lot exit.

"Isn't that Ardelia?"

One of the studio's Escalades idled by the curb. The rear windows were lowered, and Ardelia sat in back. She held her cell to her ear.

"She looks like a spy," Vi said.

Cherry's phone buzzed. She answered it, saying, "I'm looking at you."

Ardelia swiveled. "Where are you? Oh!" She waved them over. Cherry couldn't tell if her outfit was a costume or just weird fashion: she wore a long white jacket that buttoned to the collar and matching white mad-scientist gloves. "How are you holding up?"

"Fine," said Cherry.

"Good. I have something for you." It was a blue-and-gold envelope, heavy and expensive looking.

"What's this?"

"An invitation. The studio's throwing a little soiree

for your town. The mayor, city council members, that kind of thing. Our way of saying thank you for letting us stop traffic for the last six weeks."

The card was embossed. *You Are Cordially . . .*

"Wait. The movie's finished?" said Cherry.

"We finish shooting on Thursday. Maxwell and Cyrus have more scenes in the Netherlands, but that's it for me." She snapped her fingers. *"Finito!"*

"You're leaving," said Cherry.

"Back home for a little R & R, yes."

"But wait a second." Her mind was rushing to catch up with Ardelia's words. She felt like she'd just been fired. Maybe she had. "What will you do? I mean, about a baby?"

Ardelia managed to sigh and smile at the same time, something only starlets can do. "I suppose we'll start again with a new batch back home. These things take time. I'll find the right match eventually. I'll miss your input." She took off her sunglasses and smiled at Cherry. "I'll miss you."

"I'll miss you, too," said Cherry. "Shit."

"What's wrong?"

"I can't believe you're leaving." She shook her head. It was so sudden. Just, *So long!* from the backseat of an Escalade and then—*poof*—she'd be gone. They weren't even saying good-bye in private. "I knew you would go eventually. Just not . . . not right now."

"Well, you'll probably be glad to get back to your normal life," said Ardelia. "And I'll see you at the soiree. Both of you. Promise me you'll be there."

"Are you kidding?" Vi said, snatching the invite. "Free food? We're so there."

"Cherry, promise."

"I promise."

Ardelia pointed a manicured nail at Vi. "Make sure she goes." She gave them a million-dollar grin. "It should be a night to remember."

For days Cherry's attire had consisted of her only surviving skirt and black top (the ones she'd worn clubbing), the old Minnie Mouse tee, and a few items borrowed from Vi. It was a weird fused-woman outfit, posh on the bottom and cheap on top. She didn't have much cash for new clothes. She'd spent her latest paycheck on toiletries and underwear, and couldn't, under the circumstances, ask Pop for money to buy evening wear for Ardelia's soiree. So Thursday afternoon she hiked to the Salvation Army and rummaged for an hour, looking for something that wasn't retro or ironic or freakish—just *nice*. Her definition of fashion was permanently mutated thanks to Ardelia, and she passed over items that she would have found totally acceptable a few months ago: a darted sweater, striped Beetlejuice shorts, a spread-collared shirt printed with skulls. These didn't seem funky or cool anymore, just *tacky*—an Ardelia word. Cherry didn't want to think this way, but she couldn't help it now.

She settled on a red faux-silk dress with a broken shoulder strap.

On the walk back, she passed the organic market, imagining the orgasmic dark chocolate wafers she could no longer afford. Spanner had been right, way back at Maxwell's party. Ardelia was leaving, and Cherry's life was snapping back into place. Except, it wasn't. Nothing was returning to *normal*. If Cherry were a rubber band, she'd lost her spring. She'd been stretched permanently out of shape.

Friday evening she stood before the bathroom mirror. Her tiny makeup collection had gone down with the trailer, so she'd have to go *au naturale*. Some fabric was needed to repair the broken strap. She snipped a section from the sleeve of her Minnie Mouse tee, and with a little needle-and-thread work was able to make a patch. She could fasten the strap now, but there was no way to hide the ugly strip of T-shirt material. It was a Franken-dress.

Hating herself, hating Franken-Dress, Cherry wandered outside to find a wildflower for her hair. Pop was standing in the side yard, drinking a beer.

"You look like spring," he said. He looked beer warmed and, maybe, happy.

"What are you doing out here?"

"Watching the sunset." He gestured toward the horizon. "Got sick of TV."

She stood by him and let him put his arm around her shoulder. She always felt tiny and protected in Pop's arms. How did kids with skinny dads ever feel safe?

"That is a beautiful sight," said Pop. "Better'n HD."

"You're in a good mood."

"I guess I am. Huh." He sipped his beer. "I dunno, Snack Pack. Insurance won't cover the cost of a new trailer, which means we might need to sell the auto shop or at least refinance it all to hell. The situation ain't great. But we got to make the best of it. Everything's got to change now. And we can roll with it or get stuck." He puffed out his mustache.

"I shouldn't have left Stew alone."

Pop took another draw from his tall boy. "Yep. Wish you hadn't done that." He squeezed her tighter. "Accidents happen. I'm just glad we're safe. And together."

They were silent awhile, watching the blues deepen to oranges and reds in the sky.

"You don't hate me?"

He kissed her forehead. "I could never."

Chapter Thirty-five

The Grand Theater

She didn't mind walking to the theater. It was a short trek across Aubrey Park, the field a little soggy from the morning's rain. Some kids were shooting hoops, and the slap of the ball echoed across the grass and made Cherry think of summer. She passed the darkened gazebo, which she now thought of as hers and Lucas's. The floodlights were busted. A sign hung on the gate reading:

CLOSED FOR REPAIRS
NO TRESPASSING
AUBREY PARKS COUNCIL

The Four Hills Theater was all lit up, the lot jammed with cars. She'd never seen it so packed. The theater was Aubrey's half-assed attempt at a cultural center. On New Year's Eve, the town held First Night celebrations here, and sometimes the high school's proms were in the basement all-purpose room. It was a hideous monstrosity, tarted up with fake plaster moldings and peel-away frescoes. Tonight the brass railings and ashtrays were dusted off for the big Paramount thank-you party, and all the local Important People — council members, business owners, basically anyone who owned a tux — had turned up in their minivans and station wagons for a rare night of glamour.

There was a bar in the theater lobby, and Cherry waited in line for a free ginger ale. She stood by an urn of fake roses, nervously fiddling with her wildflower. Soon there would be no more nights like this. She wasn't sure if she was relieved or disappointed. She certainly wanted no more parties, no more drugs, no more skanky limousines. She thought of pictures she'd seen of towns destroyed by tornadoes, the path of devastated homes cutting through the otherwise untouched landscape. The storm was moving on, and she was left behind to rebuild.

The revolving doors blinked, and Lucas entered the lobby. She waved to him, and he crossed the plush carpet, sidestepping waiters with trays of nibbles. He'd worn his funeral suit and a dark-green shirt.

"Hey," she said, adjusting his tie. "Looking snazzy."

"I couldn't find the right shoes." He looked her over. "You look incredible." He threaded his fingers through hers and squeezed. "I like your flower."

"Cherry!" Vi trotted up, her gargantuan purse clinking as she moved. "Isn't this *amazing*?" She patted her bag. "I snuck some of my mom's wine coolers in case it gets boring."

"*Vi,* this is supposed to be a classy affair."

Her best friend and fiancé glanced at each other, then at her.

"What?"

"Since when do you care about *classy*?" Lucas chuckled.

"Or call things 'affairs'?" said Vi.

Cherry ruffled. "Fuck it," she said, doing a crack imitation of herself. "Let's get our seats."

"You go ahead, Vi," said Lucas. "We'll be right behind you."

"All right, but if you guys ditch me to hook up in the parking lot or whatever, I'm gonna be pissed."

Vi tottered toward the theater, rattling as she went.

The lobby was clearing out, and soon they were alone.

"What's up?"

He searched for the right words. "Is everything okay? You seem different lately."

"Well, my house *did* burn down."

"Yeah. No, I mean, you seem sort of *distant*. Like you're all up inside yourself, looking out."

"I've had a lot on my mind, Lucas. You know?"

"I know!" He touched her arm, trying to avoid offense. "I just wanted to make sure *we* were okay. I don't want you to feel . . . if things have changed for you, I mean . . . we don't have to."

She didn't know what to say. She wasn't sure what he was saying. "What do you mean? What are you even saying?"

He looked away, pushing his breath out. "Nothing. Never mind. This is stupid."

"No! What is it?" She jerked away from his touch. Why was she suddenly so pissed off? So terrified? "You brought it up."

"Fine," he said. "It's just, I thought when you and Ardelia started hanging out, there was no way the whole movie-star lifestyle would interest you, because you're Cherry and you don't give a shit about glamour and clothes and money. But now it kinda seems like it *does* interest you. And I can't understand how you could be friends with a person like Ardelia"—he took a breath, readying himself—"and want to marry a person like me."

"Fuck . . . *what*?" Suddenly she was holding back tears. "I mean . . . where the fuck is this coming from?"

Lucas's voice was even, but his hands were trembling. "Does that mean I'm right?"

She was stunned. She'd had no idea he felt this way. How long had he been holding this in? What kind of girlfriend was she, not to notice? It was like lowering binoculars and being startled to discover how far away everything really was. The great gulf, the great space you cannot fathom, inside the person you love.

"You're not right!" She held his fingers, squeezed them, pulled him back to her. "Listen. This has been the most insane month of my life. But it's over now. These people are leaving, and it's just you and me. Whatever happened while they were here, it doesn't change anything, okay? It doesn't change anything about you and me."

He wanted to believe it. She could see it stirring inside him. "You sure? Because if you want to call it off . . ."

She kissed him. "I wanna marry you, you dick."

And suddenly it seemed doable. Things *could* go back to normal. Maybe she *could* forget about what had happened with Maxwell. In fact, she promised herself she *would*. She was moving on. She was rolling with it. She wasn't a different person. And to prove it to herself, she grabbed her boyfriend by the hand and yanked him down the stairs, through the revolving doors, and out into the warm evening air. A few stragglers were coming up from the parking lot, and Cherry and Lucas raced past them, two kids up to no good.

"We're totally gonna get caught," Lucas said when they reached the gazebo. It was dark, eerie, private. Their gazebo.

"I don't care." She pulled him down, hiding them both behind the gazebo's whitewashed fence. The concrete was gritty and cold, but she didn't feel it. She just felt the warmth of him, his fingers pressed into her wrists, her thighs, drawing on her, marking her as forever his. She didn't know if the world was vibrating or if she was. This was happening, this was happening. And, yes, this was exactly what she wanted, here in a familiar place, with his familiar smell and familiar touch, at home, at home, at home. He wrapped his arms around her from behind, his green sleeves and her red dress — *in and up, in and up,* just like the poster said.

She couldn't breathe. He was saving her life.

Vi had saved them seats in the back row. Onstage a man in a flannel suit was droning *thank-you*s.

"Where have you been? This has been *so boring.* There was a speech from the mayor, and then the arts council, and then . . ." Vi's eyes went wide. She looked Cherry up and down as if she were glowing green from head to foot. "Oh, my God! *Oh, my God!* You guys were just doing it, weren't you?"

Someone shushed them.

"*Shut up,*" Cherry hissed, trying not to giggle. She was soaring. She was *stratospheric.* Lucas looked away to hide his face. He was shaking with laughter.

"Holy shit!" Vi squeezed Cherry's hands. "You totally just lost your V-card. It's all over your face, you *slut*."

The guy who'd shushed them turned around in his seat.

"Will you please be quiet?"

"What's that?" Cherry said as loudly as she could, putting a hand to her ear. The man scowled and turned back as Lucas and Vi melted with laughter.

"Classic Cherry," said Vi, stifling her own laughter.

"Yeah," said Cherry. *Classic me.*

It felt so good to be Classic Cherry again. How could doing something for the first time make you feel like your old self?

She held Lucas's hand, feeling warm and sore and elated.

The director introduced his "Olive and Stewart," and Ardelia entered stage left in a voluminous green gown. Trailing in its wake was Maxwell in a shark-skin suit. The sleaze. Cherry felt impervious now. And as for Ardelia, she felt only affection. The movie stars glimmered distantly like details from a dream. Ardelia was where she belonged, onstage, and Cherry belonged here, in the back row, with the troublemakers, the trailer trash.

"Can you believe we partied with *him*?" said Vi.

"Look at that suit," said Cherry. "He's so cheesy."

Vi thought, then chuckled. "Yeah, he *is* kind of cheesy."

Cherry felt a tap on her shoulder. Spanner stood in the aisle. She looked like an overdressed usher, holding a clipboard and wearing a headset with an orange stripe across the earpiece.

"Do you *ever* get a night off?" Cherry said.

"Ardelia wants to see you."

She glanced at the others. She didn't want to leave the protective halo of their company. "Now?"

Spanner scowled. "Of course not now. They're about to play a clip. You can meet her backstage while it's rolling."

"Where?"

"There's a stage door there." She pointed to a small black panel in the corner.

"How will I . . . ?" started Cherry, but Spanner swept back up the aisle, as if escaping a horrible smell.

The lights dimmed, and the crowd clapped. Cherry glanced up the gloomy aisle toward the back of the theater. She looked to Lucas, squeezing his hand.

"Go!" he said. "Maybe she wants to give you a good-bye present."

"Yeah, and try not to crash this one," said Vi.

"All right, all right. I'm going."

Cherry made her way down the red carpet toward the tiny black door. There was no knob, only a round hole where it had once been. She pushed against the black panel, into the dark. Her eyes adjusted. She heard the scrape of feet, the zip and shuffle of curtains. Someone rushed past her. She saw what looked like a chintzy replica of Aubrey. These were sets from a recent production, pasteboard housefronts and a phony train station, a length of white picket fence made of Styrofoam. A sign read:

UTILITY ACCESS ONLY
NO ADMITTANCE

"Cherry!" a voice called.

"Where are you?"

"Over here."

Ardelia stood against a wall lined with pulleys and ropes for controlling the curtains. More phony fencing was stacked on the scaffolding above her, reminding Cherry of railroad struts. They were cramped together in the tiny cave of scaffolding and rigging. Ardelia spoke in a whisper. "Listen, I've got something I need to say to you."

"Okay."

A bright panel began to flicker above. They were starting the clip. Ardelia's breath was warm on her cheek.

"I've been thinking it over."

An enormous, flip-side Ardelia spoke on-screen in a bogus southern accent. *"Stewart, my dear. It is not for love of Robert that I hesitate. But what shall become of you, should I . . . should we . . . ?"*

"This may be a bit surprising, what I'm about to say," the real Ardelia went on, "but I want you to think about it, and don't answer now."

"Okay . . ."

"I cannot begin to comprehend the consequences, my love. For the angle of the moon is but a trifle in a treetop, but when that silvery orb is reached, hundreds of miles make the difference . . ."

"Cherry," said Ardelia, cupping her hand around the other girl's ear. Cherry smelled lavender and saw the white flash of teeth in the reverse movie light.

"Yes?" she said, breathless.

"I want you . . ."

"What shall we do?"

"I want you to have my baby."

The lights cracked off. The house erupted in applause.

282

Baby

Chapter Thirty-six

Expecting

The Batman T-shirt was stretched to its limit, Robin looking all bloated. Cherry ran her hands over the bulge, studying her reflection in the door mirror. She cast a big-bellied shadow on the wall. Her eyes were killing her. She was exhausted from several nights of fitful sleep brought on by constant sugar crashes. She'd been eating chocolate like crazy, the good bitter stuff.

Her cell rang for the nth time. Cherry sighed, tugged the basketball from under her T-shirt, and dropped it in the open suitcase on Lucas's bed. Vi's number flashed on-screen.

"I'm just calling to say I'm not speaking to you."

"Vi."

"You won't come to Cape Cod with me, but you'll go to *England* with Ardelia?"

"It's different and you know it. This is like . . ." Cherry tried to think of what it was like. It wasn't like anything. "We need the money."

"So you're definitely going to have the baby?"

Cherry tugged off the Batman tee, folded it, and dropped it in the suitcase. What did you pack for a week in the English countryside? Sweaters? A pith helmet? It was supposed to rain a lot in England, so she'd bring her new boots from the Salvation Army and the 7-Eleven mini-umbrella.

Lucas popped his head in. "Will I need a bathing suit?"

Cherry covered the receiver with her hand. "I don't know. Yes. Ardelia said there's a pool."

"She has a pool!" Vi bellowed on the other end of the line.

"I'll leave you two alone." Lucas made a face and disappeared.

She put the phone to her ear. "He's excited."

"Of course he's excited. It's *insanely* exciting." Vi's shouts crackled through the tiny speaker. "I don't see why he gets to go and I don't."

"Because he's my fiancé, and at the moment my womb is . . . well, not like his *property,* but he's got a say in what I do with it. And Ardelia said I could bring Lucas and one family member, but Pop won't go and I'm sure as shit not bringing Stew. He'd probably get busted at customs for having weed sewn into the waistband of his boxers."

"*I'm* family," Vi whined. "Or are you forgetting eighth grade when we did blood sisters?"

Cherry ignored this, staring down at her near-empty suitcase. Everything she owned fit inside, with enough room left over for a small person. "Maybe I could smuggle you in my luggage."

"You know what really hurts?" Vi said.

"No, but I'm sure you'll tell me."

"You care more about what *she* thinks than what *I* think. *I'm* your best friend, you know, in case you've forgotten."

Cherry sighed and sat on the bed. She rubbed the temple that didn't have a phone pressed to it. "Vi, this isn't about *friendship.* It's about money. And if I say yes, I get a lot." Vi was quiet. Cherry said it again for emphasis. *"A lot."*

"I know," Vi mumbled. "How much is it again?"

"Two hundred and fifty thousand dollars." She'd said it so often to herself that the rhythm was like a nursery rhyme. *Two HUNdred and FIFty THOUsand DOLlars.* No matter how many times she said it or wrote it out, the number had no real meaning. She'd tried breaking it down into fathomable terms. Two hundred and fifty-thousand cell phone minutes. Eight thousand gallons of gas. Three thousand Mel's Lumberjack Specials. Five top-of-the-line mobile homes. It was more than enough to resettle Pop, get Stew an apartment when he graduated, and put a down payment on a place for her and Lucas.

"Well, buy me a pool when you get back," said Vi. "Wait, you are coming back, right? You aren't just going to stay there and get preggers?"

"If I decide yes, I'll live with Ardelia in England," Cherry said, reciting the terms she'd conveyed to dozens of young hopefuls on Ardelia's raspberry love seat. "But either way, I'll come home for graduation."

"Like school even matters with that kind of scratch. Are you freaked out about . . . you know . . . having a baby?"

"Jesus, Vi. I haven't decided yet."

"Yeah, but if you *do* . . ."

Lucas passed by in the hall, whistling. They'd been up every night, talking about the decision. He refused to weigh in on whether she should carry the baby, but he definitely thought she should take Ardelia's offer to think it over for a week at her estate outside London. And that was *before* he knew he was invited. As to what happened next, her swelling belly, some other man's baby stuff (and another woman's, in fact) inside her, the nine months and change she'd be away from home . . . Lucas was too good a guy to mention the downsides. He knew they already loomed large in Cherry's mind.

What he didn't know was that one could worry without really *thinking*. You could freak out without actually weighing the options. You could panic, blindly, without coming anywhere near a decision.

"I'm not thinking about that yet," said Cherry. "This is just a vacation."

As far as freaking out was concerned, no small part of her recent sleeplessness and worry-eating had to do with the six-hour flight she'd be taking from Logan Airport to London. Six hours of airborne travel, miles and miles above the ground . . . or, actually, the *ocean*. Cherry didn't like climbing to the top of the *bleachers*. She spread the DuBoises' world atlas on the kitchen counter and calculated the distance with a ruler. Pop was under the sink, fixing their congested garbage disposal.

"Three thousand three hundred miles," she said aloud. "That's like ten times farther from home than I've ever been."

"Not sure about your math," said Pop. "But it's far, all right."

She took a long breath, letting her ruler clatter on the tabletop. "Is this insane? Should I not go?"

Pop grunted and leaned against the cabinet. He wore a red handkerchief around his neck, and his hands were spotty with grease. Her father never looked so at home as when he was under something, fixing it.

"I don't know what to say, Snack Pack. Of course, I want you to go. Little nest egg like that handled right? You'd be set for years. Maybe life." He wiped his forehead, leaving a brown-and-black smudge. "But I don't know if I could do it. Carry someone else's baby, I mean."

Cherry chuckled. "You *couldn't* do it, Poppa. You don't have the parts."

"You know what I mean. . . ." He rummaged through Mr. DuBois's toolbox. There were girlie pictures taped inside. "Goddamn it, Leroy, what self-respecting janitor doesn't have a Phillips head?" He sighed. "Listen, kiddo, I always wanted you to get out of this town, see the world, meet fascinating people. This wasn't exactly how I pictured it, but beggars can't be choosers."

"Is that what we are? Beggars?"

It was a rare moment alone, just the two of them. Lucas and his father were at work, and Stew was off with a new girlfriend. Pop thought. What he said next, he said slowly, like the words were fine mechanical parts he was carefully reassembling.

"I know you don't want to be like your mother. But you're not running off. If you do this, it'll be for the right reasons. The truth is"—he stared at his hands—"I envy her, getting to pick up and go. I couldn't last a minute away from you kids, but if I could have taken you with me, shown you something other than the inside of a goddamned auto garage, I would have."

Cherry said nothing. She'd never thought her pop's life might not be entirely his first choice. He was a grumpy guy, but not unhappy.

"Do you wish you never had kids?"

He didn't answer immediately. He was thinking about it.

"No," he said. "If I didn't have you two, I might be okay. But I'd have no idea what I was missing." His eyes drifted to the toolbox. "Fucking thank Christ. *There* it is." He brandished the screwdriver. "This thing looks like it's never been used. No wonder that school of yours is falling apart."

Sunday afternoon, a town car arrived to carry Lucas and Cherry to the airport. Mr. DuBois, Stewart, and Pop saw them off. Vi was there, too. She'd recovered from her disappointment.

"Remember," she said. "Over there, *poofter* is a gay guy, and *banger* is a sausage."

"You learned that from *Arrested Development*," Cherry said.

"Yeah, but it's true, I think."

Cherry hugged her best friend, realizing mid-squeeze she didn't want to let her go.

"I'm gonna miss you." Vi's voice was thick with tears.

"It's just a week," said Cherry, surprised at the lump in her throat.

"Yeah," said Vi. "Sort of."

"Keep an eye on her," Pop was telling Lucas. "Anything goes wrong, I'm holding you personally responsible, DuBois."

"I know," said Lucas.

"I mean it. I've talked it over with your dad, and he's okay with me killing you."

"O-okay," said Lucas, trying and entirely failing to smile.

"Send me a postcard," said Stew. "I can't believe how fucking lucky you are."

"This is for all of us," said Cherry. She leaned in close and said low in his ear, "And no smoking while I'm gone, or you won't see a *penny* of this cash."

Stew laughed. "Wait, seriously?"

"Seriously. Straight edge, or you're living off your garage salary."

She left Stew blinking over his future. Cherry hugged her father.

"Remember how you used to cry at the end of *The Wizard of Oz*?" he said.

"That was *you*, you pansy."

"Oh, that's right." He held her shoulders. "You have everything? Passport? Got your rape whistle?"

"I'm *fine*, Pop."

"Good, because I feel like I'm gonna have a heart attack."

She kissed his cheek.

In the limo, she held Lucas's hand and watched Sugar Village slip away.

"Where to?" the driver asked.

"Logan Airport," said Cherry. "British Airways. Private flights gate."

The driver glanced in the mirror. "You kids win some kind of contest?"

"Yeah," they said together, and left it at that.

Chapter Thirty-seven

Stratospheric

Ardelia met them at the gate. She was in full Ardelia mode, kissing their cheeks, squeezing their hands, fluttering on about *Jolly Old England* and how they were just going to *love* it. Spanner was there as well, dressed for comfort in black track pants and flats.

"You're short without heels," said Cherry.

"You're freakishly tall *with* them."

Cherry smiled.

"What's funny?"

At this point Spanner's bitchiness was just kind of comforting. Like a favorite scratchy blanket. "Nothing," said Cherry.

Ardelia motioned for them to follow. "Come along, my little chicks. Time to check our bags."

Instead of passing through security with the rest of the beleaguered masses, they were led to a private line with men in suits and women in expensive casual wear. Pearls, diamonds, and gold watches were dropped into a plastic pan, and a female security guard asked Cherry if she had anything metal on her person.

"Like piercings?"

The security guard looked exhausted. Her name tag read JOAN. "Step this way, please."

Joan passed a wand over Cherry's entire body, which was humiliating, especially when it whistled at her crotch. After removing her belt and shoes, Cherry was allowed through. The guards gave Lucas a weird look, due to his shit-kicker boots and Thug Life sweatshirt. She wished he hadn't worn it. The guards asked if they could open his bag.

"Sure," said Lucas.

"What's all this?" Joan the guard held up his pencil case. "You got any razors in here, son?"

"They're pencils," said Lucas.

"He's an artist," Cherry said from the end of the line. The black guard closest to her smiled.

"Brother," he said to Lucas, "I don't know what you're up to, but keep it up."

Their chartered jet waited on the tarmac, all alone, its tail emblazoned with a British flag.

"It's like an Austin Powers plane," Lucas said.

Cherry was terrified. She'd never been *terrified* before. All the other times she might have used the word, she'd been wrong. She'd been *afraid* of dying, like the time she and Vi saw a rabid dog in the woods behind Vi's house. Now she was *certain*. Her knees started to wobble as they approached the mobile stairs leading to the hatch. She made sure to step across the threshold with her right foot first, for luck.

Once she was inside, Cherry's terror was momentarily muffled. She'd never been on a jet, but this looked nothing like the cramped, baby-squalling coaches she'd seen in the movies. The cabin was tiny with plush seats turned toward the center, a little like a limo and a little like someone's living room. The windows were curtained. A screen set into the far wall played an undersea documentary.

"Fish are calming," Ardelia explained.

Lucas dug his toe into the plush carpeting. "This must be a bitch to clean."

Ardelia nodded, frowning. "It must. I wonder do they take the carpet out or . . . ?"

"Don't pretend to be interested," said Spanner. She moved past them into the cabin and took the farthest seat. She extracted a magazine from a basket and hid behind it. *SkyMall.* "Oh, look: air-conditioned golf clubs."

A flight attendant with a Union Jack uniform appeared. "If you'd like to take your seats, we're nearly ready for departure."

Ardelia ordered food and drink as if she'd just been

handed a menu. "Cucumber sandwiches, please. And Perrier. And does anyone want something stronger?" She leaned on Cherry's elbow confidentially. "I like a little champagne on a long flight. Makes it go faster."

"Champagne? Really?" Lucas checked with Cherry and shrugged. "Sounds pretty sweet."

"Open the Veuve Clicquot," Ardelia told the flight attendant. "Four glasses."

They took their seats. Cherry made sure that Lucas sat closer to the window, though no matter where she looked, blue ovals of sky stared blindly back at her. Knowing the tarmac was only a few feet below didn't make her feel any safer.

"Will there be . . . ? Is it going to be bumpy?" she asked the flight attendant.

"We're expecting a little weather, but nothing to worry about." She smiled. "First time flying?"

"It's that obvious?"

"I personally guarantee a smooth ride," she said. "My name's Maleficent, if you need anything."

She turned to Lucas when the flight attendant had gone. "She's the witch from *Sleeping Beauty*!"

"What?"

"Maleficent! That's the witch from *Sleeping Beauty*!"

"You've gone totally nuts."

"Yes. Yes, I have."

"I'm right here." He squeezed her hand. "Dad and I

used to fly to New Orleans to see Uncle Joe, remember? Flying's easy."

Cherry glared in the direction of the kitchenette. "She's gonna turn into a dragon. I just know it."

As the plane taxied, Maleficent came around with flutes of champagne. Cherry didn't touch hers.

"I don't always do this, you know," Ardelia said. "I usually fly public, to save. But I thought this would be more fun."

"Fun," Cherry murmured. She spied another plane through the window. Its enormous bulk floated into the air, just coming loose from the ground, as if by accident. It looked like CGI. She couldn't believe it.

"Of course, flying will be a no-no once you're pregnant," Ardelia continued. "Bad for the fetus, I've read. But once you see the house, you won't want to leave, trust me."

Spanner peered over her magazine. "Are you all right, Cherry? You look a little under-ripe."

"I've never flown before," said Cherry.

She was experiencing a kind of cosmic claustrophobia. On the map, England seemed impossibly far away. Now the planet felt so *small*. "The farthest I've ever been from home is Boston, and my first time was with you."

"Well, this is *doubly* exciting," Ardelia grinned.

Cherry wanted to smack her. "I think my head's going to explode."

"Are your ears popping already?" Ardelia said. "Try going like this. *Muh-muh-muh . . .*"

The pilot announced that they were clear for take-off. Cherry checked that her seat belt was safely fastened, then rechecked, then triple-checked. Jesus, what was the point of seat belts on airplanes? If they went down, seat belts sure as shit weren't going to save them.

The engines roared, a whistling, pissed-off howl.

"Are they supposed to make that noise?"

Lucas was grinning like an idiot. Why was everyone smiling? They were going to burn alive.

Cherry was pressed into her chair. Then suddenly they were airborne. The ground peeled away, and Cherry shut her eyes. She pressed her feet into the carpet, trying to push them back to earth, trying not to think of all the mechanical parts, all the little fixable, breakable, fallible things working together to keep them aloft. She felt the world wobble. Her tummy wobbled, too, like a washing machine off its casters. She tasted burritos and bile.

"Cherry, you have to see this," Lucas was saying. "You can see the whole city!"

She shook her head, phosphenes dancing on the backs of her eyelids. She felt someone touch her hand. She peeked just enough to see Ardelia looking worried. The girl had no setting between Thrilled and Concerned.

"Do you want a Somnol?" She rattled a bottle of pills like a cat toy.

"No!" said Cherry. "No pills."

"She doesn't like pills," said Spanner, flipping a page. "I wonder why."

Cherry jerked around to meet Spanner's gaze, then shut her eyes again as the jet banked right, threatening to slide them off their cushion of air into the ocean. Through the cloud of her terror, a new worry began to flash and crackle. Spanner couldn't have meant what Cherry thought she meant. She couldn't know about Maxwell. Could she?

The floor seemed to roll, undulating like a wave. Again her lunch visited the back of her throat. She couldn't take it anymore. She clawed off her seat belt and somehow *fell* to her feet. Her insides were doing barrel rolls.

"Cherry?" Lucas said.

She yanked back the little curtain separating the cabin from the kitchenette, surprising Maleficent, who was strapped into a little jumper seat.

"I'll need you to return —"

She made it to the bathroom just in time. The toilet was a metal salad bowl with blue Kool-Aid at the bottom. Up came her burrito. Could you get sucked out an airplane toilet? A headline leaped to mind: "TEEN FALLS TO DEATH OVER ATLANTIC, BARFING."

Soon it was over, but the wibble-wobble of the plane ensured there'd be more to come. Better to stay close to the toilet, forearms on the cool metal. She hadn't felt this bad since junior prom, when Vi'd spiked the Mountain Dew with Everclear.

A shadow fell over her shoulder. Not the Grim Reaper, unfortunately, but one of the other passengers. She'd forgotten to close the bathroom door behind her.

"Occupied," Cherry managed.

She felt someone's knees press against her back and heard the little door close. A light went on overhead.

"We need to talk," said Spanner.

Cherry swallowed. "You really wanna see this?"

"Now."

She struggled to her feet, ignoring Spanner's offered hand. She pressed the spigot and splashed water on her face. Her hands were shaking.

"If you want to join the mile-high club, you're barking up the wrong—"

Another lurch. Cherry steadied herself against the sink. Spanner handed her a box of green Tic Tacs. She took one.

"Okay," Cherry said finally. "What is it?"

Spanner folded her arms. "When we met, I thought you were stupid. I don't think you're stupid anymore."

"I thought you were a stuck-up bitch." Cherry let that line linger.

"I was willing to tolerate and maybe even respect you back in Shitpot, U.S.A., but this has gone too far."

She pressed a pencil-thin finger into Cherry's sternum. "*I should be carrying the baby. Not you.*"

"I don't even know if I'm going to say yes. Besides," Cherry said, "Ardelia asked you, and you said no."

"Is that what she told you?" The plane dipped, and the girls fell into each other. Both girls stiffened, backing as far from the other as the tiny space allowed. "You'll say yes. Of course you will. You *have* to. What else are you going to do with your life?"

Cherry felt vomit rising again and swallowed.

"Why do you want to do it, anyway?" Cherry asked. "You're already rich."

For the first time, Spanner's gaze broke from Cherry's. She studied the inch of space between them. "It's not about the money."

"What, then? Are you that much of a control freak?"

The Death Mask snapped back on.

"You're so bloody ignorant," Spanner growled. "You don't know half of what's going on here."

"I know she doesn't trust you." *Because you sleep with her exes,* she almost finished.

"Oh? And should she trust *you*?"

For an instant, she really thought the floor had given out beneath her.

"What are you inferring?"

"*Implying,*" said Spanner. She smiled, Grinch-like.

"Look," Cherry started, "I don't know what you think you know . . ."

"I think there's something you're not telling Ardelia," Spanner said. "And you and I both know what it is."

"You don't know shit," Cherry said.

"Maybe I do; maybe I don't." The smirk carbonized into a sneer. "All I'm saying is, watch your back, Daisy Duke. I could make things *very* uncomfortable for you." Spanner opened the door and stepped out into the kitchenette. "You've got sick on your shirt."

Cherry waited a moment, until she felt steady enough to make her way back to her seat.

"You feeling any better?" Lucas asked.

She buckled in, hands trembling. Her eyes met Spanner's across the cabin. She swallowed.

"No," she said. "Much worse."

Chapter Thirty-eight

Both Sides Now

Thanks to Ardelia's eye mask and earphones, Cherry was finally able to sleep. She woke to the last track on Ardelia's iPod, some Joni Mitchell tune. Lucas was asleep beside her. She risked a glance out the window. Something was odd. The view appeared upside down, and as she blinked sleep from her eyes she saw why. They were flying above the clouds, where, Cherry realized, the sky was always clear. The sun was low in the window, turning everything below into a rippling sea of pink. It all looked so still and so large. It was always like this up here, whether there were people below or not, whether those people were happy or not, whether they were good or bad, loyal or not. It made sense that people thought of heaven like this.

The cabin was dark and quiet. Everyone was asleep. Spanner snored softly. The engines seemed to snore themselves, like giant cats. Only Ardelia was awake, watching her.

"I'm glad you're awake for this," she said. "We're making the sun rise."

Cherry wondered how this could be, then understood: they were traveling east, into the daylight. It was an early sunrise on the other side of the clouds. Cherry felt like saying something that even in her head sounded silly. But they were alone, and everything was so quiet, she didn't mind saying it.

"I feel like I won't be the same now."

"That's why I travel. It changes you."

Lucas smacked his lips and turned toward the window, and Cherry felt wobbly again. She looked around the opulent cabin. Her champagne had gone flat.

"Listen, Ardelia—"

"You look cold."

She offered Cherry her tiny blanket. It *was* cold. Cherry tucked it around her shoulders. Ardelia hugged herself. There was gooseflesh on her arms.

Lucas's chest rose and fell in the steady rhythm of sleep. He looked perfect. She wanted to seal him in a steel box and bury him under the ocean, where nothing could get to him and nothing could hurt him, not even her mistakes.

"I really have to tell you something."

"I have to tell you something, too," Ardelia said.

Cherry turned to her, surprised. The other girl's face was pinched, her eyes searching the cloud cover. She shook her head, a tiny, decisive, almost imperceptible movement. "Though not yet."

"But—"

"And whatever it is," Ardelia said, "we'll forgive each other, won't we?"

Cherry didn't know what to say. Ardelia held her hand across the aisle, and she took it. The sun had climbed a little higher. It was just the two of them, awake in the sky. Far away.

Somewhere, underneath the clouds, was everything.

Chapter Thirty-nine
Maison des Liaisons

The hilltop town of Orchard—with its view, remote location, and sterling local cuisine—had turned a sleepy village into a retreat for the super-rich. Beyond the small main street with its antiques, farmers' markets, and other shops flourishing on the easy dollars of movie stars, the town was mostly scattered manor houses lurking behind old-growth firs, some new and stylish, but mostly rambling mansions older than the advent of the automobile. Cherry glimpsed a few as they drove down a quiet back road. Some appeared to be crumbling, as if struck by falling rocks.

Ardelia Deen was not rich because she was a movie star. Her family had money going back generations, which, much to Cherry's confusion, didn't seem to *come* from anywhere. Rich people in America worked for big companies or had parents who worked for big companies.

But in England you were just *rich,* the way some people were just tall or agoraphobic.

Cherry felt relieved. She was in a storybook world, or at least some movie based on a Jane Austen novel. The thrill of the new place, plus the joy at being on solid ground again, made her giddy, almost drunk.

The Deens' house, Liddell Manor (that was the other odd thing about England: houses had names), was at the highest point of the hill, near a cherry grove in full bloom. The upper stories were scalloped with cloud-like balconies, and rooftop garrets formed a mini–mountain range. The long road they'd been riding on turned out to be a private drive, Liddell Way, with a gate at the end.

Cherry whistled as they pulled onto the property.

"Oh, man. It's like the house from Clue," she said. "Are there secret passages?"

"Two, actually," said Ardelia. "There's a maintenance tunnel connecting the basement and the pool house, and another running from the master bedroom to several of the guest rooms. In architecture it's known as a *Galerie des Liaisons.*"

"What's that mean?"

"Well, *galerie* is a kind of hallway, and *liaison* is, well, a liaison." She turned to address Spanner, who had been relegated to the backseat. "How would you describe it?"

"It's so the master of the house can have affairs with

the help, without being spotted leaving his room," said Spanner.

"A hook-up hall," suggested Cherry.

"Brilliant," said Spanner. For the first time since the airport, she removed her sunglasses. She gazed over Cherry's shoulder, at the house growing larger in the windshield. "It's nice to be home, anyway."

It had started to rain, and there was a mad dash from the cars into the massive foyer. The guests dripped on the marble floor.

"Your rooms are straight up the back," said Ardelia. Cherry raised an eyebrow. "Your father made me promise that you and Lucas would have separate accommodations. Do what you like, but there are two rooms if you need them."

Cherry took off through the archway and jogged up the stairs. Rain and lightning shimmered through slim windows that were like chinks in a castle wall. Only the frilly tops of cherry trees were visible, trembling in the wind.

She came to the third floor and turned a corner into a long, empty hallway. The rooms were cavernous, with vaulted ceilings and large bay windows where Peter Pan would have felt at home. She heard Lucas thumping up behind her. Shivering, she peeled off her wet top and took a sweater from her bag. She was pulling it on when Lucas came in.

"Aww, I missed the show."

"Good things come to those who wait," Cherry said in her best British accent. She was getting good at it.

Lucas swept her up and carried her to the immense canopy bed. He climbed on top of her, but she fended him off with her foot. "Easy, easy! I'm crampy."

His shoulders fell. The look of pure misery on his face made Cherry laugh.

"You're not on your period, are you?"

"Any day now," she said. "Can't you tell I've been PMS-ing like crazy?"

"I couldn't tell if that was PMS or just regular Cherry crazy."

She kicked him, hard. "You're not getting *anything* with that attitude."

He grinned and rolled to the floor, jumping up and heading into the private bathroom. "Oh, man, is this a Jacuzzi tub?" He gave her a come-hither look. "Wanna take a bath?"

"Later," she said. "You go ahead. I'll unpack."

"Suit yourself."

Steam was rolling out of the bathroom when Ardelia knocked on the door.

"Getting settled?"

Cherry closed the bathroom door, feeling a little silly and prudish. *Whatever.* She didn't want Ardelia seeing her man bare-assed.

"This house is *amazing*. When I was a kid, I'd play princess, but I never thought I'd be, like, in an actual castle."

"It's *not* a castle, and it's a devil to heat in the winters. But as the eldest, I'm the official steward, so it's up to me to keep it Bristol." She ran her hand along the door frame. "I come here between films to check on her. Daddy's in Monaco, and my brother's barely ever here. She's kind of my pet project." She smiled at Cherry. "Like you!"

"I think I just got compared to a house," said Cherry.

"Oh, you know what I mean. I like introducing people to culture, showing them new things. And *wait* until you see my art collection. And the *food*!" Ardelia placed her wrist to her forehead. Such an actress. "The staff will be here tomorrow morning, and we'll have a proper meal. Just tinned stuff at the moment."

Cherry stopped unpacking and turned. "The staff?"

"Just two of them. Oliver, he's the caretaker, and his granddaughter, Evelyn. She's just a kid and, between you and me, a sourpuss. But Oliver's a dear. He's like family. You'll love him."

Cherry didn't like the idea of being waited on. It was one thing at a restaurant, but in a *house*? Would Oliver come when Ardelia rang a bell? Would Evelyn say, *"Yes, mum,"* like the frog footmen in *Alice in Wonderland*? It was creepy and slavish. She decided she could be cooked for but not *served*.

"Don't make that face," Ardelia said. "It's not like I keep them in the dungeon with the stretching rack and the iron maiden. I need help keeping a big place like this. Speaking of"—she made devilish eyes—"how about a tour?"

"Sounds fun," said Cherry.

With these words, the bathroom door burst open and Lucas leaped out, completely naked. The steam didn't do much to hide his frame of mind.

"All right, baby, your man's spit shined and ready to—"

"Lucas!"

Too late he realized they weren't alone. Reeling backward, Lucas retreated into the bathroom. There came the squeal of bare feet on damp tile, a thump, and a curse. The door slammed shut again.

Ardelia had turned the color of cherry purée, eyes wide. Way wide. Wide in a way Cherry didn't like at all.

"Well." Ardelia cleared her throat. "Lucky you, I guess."

She turned slowly and stepped out into the hallway. The bathroom door creaked. Lucas had wrapped himself head to toe in towels and peered from behind the door.

"Is she gone?"

"You didn't hear us talking?"

"What?"

"We were talking in here. You didn't hear that I wasn't alone?"

"No!" He edged out into the room. "What's with you?"

"Just seems a little suspicious," Cherry said, looking away.

"Okay, *now* I'm getting the PMS vibe."

She whirled around to retort, but he'd already closed the door.

"The dining room," said Ardelia, flipping the switch with a flourish, illuminating a wall of windows and a long, elegant table. "Oliver is an amazing cook, and there's everything imaginable in the pantry."

Cherry doubted Liddell Manor stocked Yow-Gurts and cherry cola, but she didn't say anything.

"The causeway." Ardelia pointed left, then right, like a flight attendant. "The parlor. And the library."

"Wow." Cherry craned her neck until it hurt. Wooden shelves climbed to the second-story ceiling, each one crammed with thick spines, everything a faded brown. Some of the books were bigger than the dictionary at the Aubrey Public Library. Most of the shelves were behind glass, like museum cabinets.

"Why are the books behind glass?" Cherry asked.

"Antiques," said Ardelia, taking her by the arm. "Feel free to borrow any."

Cherry gawked at the towering, dusty spines. She imagined Ardelia up late with a fez and pipe, one of the foot-thick tomes on her lap. The biggest book Cherry had ever read was *Harry Potter and the Deathly Hallows.*

Ardelia led her through a connecting door under the spiral staircase.

"Through here is the music room. Do you play an instrument?"

"I took recorder in grade school."

Ardelia plunked a few notes on the chocolate grand. "That's the game room through there." She brightened. "Do you like chess? Spanner is positively brilliant. Beats me every time."

"Chutes and Ladders, mostly," Cherry joked. "And Candy Land. I'm a master strategist. Like, I *never* get stuck in the Chocolate Swamp."

Ardelia smiled with some effort. "Well, you'll have to teach *me,* then."

The tour continued, Ardelia going on about the tapestries; the doorknobs, which apparently once belonged to some king; the claw-foot bathtub that you couldn't actually use because it was older than certain U.S. states.

Cherry was nettled. Apparently you never knew a person until you went through their house, saw their DVD collection and the posters on their bedroom walls.

Ardelia wasn't just presenting her home; she was giving Cherry a glimpse into her subconscious, and it turned out there were vast places inside Ardelia that Cherry hadn't imagined. They were practically strangers.

From the drawing room, they reentered the marble foyer. "These stairs lead to the master bedroom, et cetera, and the second-story terrace. And that's everything! What do you think?"

Cherry groped for something nice to say. Ardelia was proud of her house. She'd spoken about the bathtub like some girls talked about T-shirts autographed by Beyoncé. "I'm surprised," she said.

"Oh?"

"All this old stuff . . . it doesn't seem like *you*. I mean, you own silver track shorts. You go to hotel parties."

"I see. You think I'm a vapid celebrity." She was joshing, but the accusation stung.

"No! Well, maybe when we first met. I guess it all makes sense. It's still a lot to take in, though."

Ardelia hugged herself. "The clothes and parties and things, they go away eventually. But *this*"—she gestured to the marble cherubs in the eaves—"this is *history*. This will *last*. And I want to share it with someone." She bit her lip, lost in her own thoughts. "I wanted to be a teacher before I became an actress."

"I thought you became an actress when you were eight."

"Well, it was an early aspiration." She nudged Cherry's elbow. "I'm glad you came. I like to show off the house."

"I don't think I'm the one to appreciate it," Cherry said.

"You will," said Ardelia.

They were quiet for a moment. The rain chattered against the high windows and in the distant, lonely corners of the mansion.

"Sorry about Lucas," Cherry said suddenly. The words clunked in the echoey room. "That was embarrassing."

Ardelia was already protesting, "Serves me right for hanging around your room like a school prefect."

"You wouldn't . . . I mean you're not like . . . You don't *like* him, right?"

Ardelia was genuinely confused. "What do you mean?"

"I mean, I would want to know if you thought he was cute. It's okay if you do. It's just, you're a celebrity and it's kind of hard for a girl to compete. . . ." Her face was hot. Embarrassment and anger tangoed in her chest, and it was so annoying how Ardelia was just standing there, looking stupid. Finally she seemed to get it. Her eyes turned to silver dollars.

"Darling, there is no way Lucas would ever go for a girl like me," she said. "He's yours, body and soul. That's obvious."

Cherry tried to laugh. "Right. Sorry. I'm being stupid."

"And besides," Ardelia added. "I would *never* get together with a friend's boyfriend. That's repugnant."

"Right. Repugnant," said Cherry, the word leaving her lips a bit reluctantly.

Ardelia smiled. "Come on. This week can't be all serious. Let's see if there's any good bubbly in the cellar. We can watch a movie on the big screen!"

She skipped toward the cellar door, a little girl in her childhood home again. Something caught Cherry's eye in the reflective brass vase by the staircase. She glanced up. Standing on the second-story foyer was Spanner, leaning over the banister, wrists crossed.

"Do you always eavesdrop on other people's conversations?"

"It's my home—I can do what I like," said Spanner.

"*Your* home?"

"I've lived here since I was nine years old." She smiled slyly. "Besides, I'd never eavesdrop. That would be *repugnant*."

Cherry tucked her hands under her arms. "Don't fall and break your neck or anything."

She followed Ardelia into the basement, happy the gloom hid her face.

Chapter Forty

Movie Stars and Swimming Pools

Cherry woke moaning and clutched at her temples. A Mack truck rumbled through her skull.

"I know that look," a voice said. "You'll want vitamin C and ginger ale."

She opened an eye. Sunlight was boring in through the bay window. It took her a moment to remember where she was. She looked left and saw the dent in Lucas's pillow. Sometime after the movie (something black-and-white, *Philadelphia Story*) they'd stumbled up to bed, wine-drunk and giggling. It was all they could do to pry off their shoes and drop onto the mattress before passing out.

She looked around the room for some sign of him. The person who'd spoken was bent over in the middle of the room, gathering Cherry's discarded clothing. The person stood. She looked about fourteen with nasty acne and an overbite. Cherry sat up. "Who?"—she winced and lay back down—"are you?"

"Eve," said the girl, stuffing the clothes into a wicker hamper she lugged with her across the carpet. "And I'm not the cook and I'm not your servant, so if you want something, ask Oliver. I just clean and do the washing."

It sounded like *dew ther warshing.* Her accent was different from Spanner's and Ardelia's. It was rounder and heavier, a bobbing pelican to their fluttery songbirds.

Cherry held a fist to her forehead. "I do my own laundry."

"They all say that the first day," said the girl, addressing an invisible listener in the corner. "Then it's, *Oh, Eve, I got a little stain. Oh, Eve, can you sew this tear?*" She scowled. "When you feel better, the others are by the pool. There's a swimsuit in the WC."

She left, slamming the door. Cherry's fillings rattled.

The shower was bliss. The taps conjured instant, lusciously hot water that stayed just the right temperature, and Cherry lingered, reveling in the endless supply. Lucas's toiletries were arranged on the vanity, clustered in a tight group as if afraid to take up too much of the spacious white marble. Cherry spread them out, along with her own things. They deserved to be there, after all. They were *guests.*

She considered her reflection in the full-length mirror. She'd put on weight since the fire. Mr. DuBois's Cajun cooking was delicious but rich, and her pointiest angles had softened. She was glad to see her chest was a little fuller, but that usually happened around her period. Would it all go to shit after the baby? In a way, Ardelia was lucky. She couldn't get pregnant, but then, she'd never have to put on baby weight or deal with breast milk or go through the Unthinkable Thing that happened when the baby came out—Cherry sure as shit didn't want to think about it. For now, she put on the navy boy shorts and bikini top slung over the towel rack, smacked her ass, and said to her reflection, "Damn if that ain't Cherry Kerrigan looking fine in her new swimsuit."

She made for the back stairs. As she passed the second floor, she nearly collided with a little old man coming around the corner with a breakfast tray. Tufts of gray fuzz clung to his scalp, and he wore spattered black overalls. A penguin in a paintball tournament. The breakfast plates rattled as he steadied himself.

"Oh, you scared the wits out of me." He spoke with the same bobbing syllables as Eve. "You don't want breakfast, do you? I'll have to put a new kettle on."

"I'm Cherry," she said, extending a hand to shake, then realizing he had no free hand to shake with. "Ardelia's friend."

"Oh! The American girl with the belly for rent!" He smiled, reminding Cherry of the sweet, sort of inappropriate old men who frequented Mel's for the early-bird special. "Look at you in your skimpies. This isn't a slumber party, dear."

Cherry laughed. "It's a *bathing* suit. Are you Oliver?"

"Unless my mother told me lies. I'll be preparing your meals, if that's fine with you."

"I used to work as a line cook, actually."

Oliver raised a furry eyebrow. "So did I! Aboard the HMS *Exeter*. Where were you stationed?"

"Burrito Barn," said Cherry. "Massachusetts."

"Never heard of the vessel." Oliver shook his head. "Well, it's a pleasure to meet you, Ms. Cherry, though you'll forgive me if I forget your name, what with the chorus o' young women running around this house."

"I'm the *nice* blonde," Cherry said, and Oliver's foggy squint vanished. He smirked.

"I'll have to keep an eye on you, I can see."

"Take it easy, Oliver," Cherry said, and headed down the stairs.

"At my age, I don't have much choice," he answered.

For two years, Vi had a pool, an aboveground that was terminally clogged with leaves and algae until the afternoon that Vi, Cherry, and two other girls performed an Omni-Cannonball and the sides split, flooding Mrs. Ravir's garden. Ardelia's pool was sunk into a raised patio on the side of the house, with a spectacular view of the grounds, the cherry orchard to the east, and a symmetrical and stuffy-looking garden, complete with a shady stone grotto, to the west.

The patio itself was white hot, the pool, blue crystal. A table and umbrella were set at one end, and Ardelia sunned herself in a skimpy green bikini (which made Cherry's good body feelings wither). Spanner, Cullen pale, sat in the shade with a magazine. As Cherry approached, Ardelia's phone hummed. Spanner picked it up and flipped a page.

"Hello, Chip. No, she's not available next weekend. Ardelia's recreational time is extremely limited, you know that. I *told* you not to call her this week. Well, you can try again, but you'll only get *me*. That's what I thought." She added a singsong "*Good*-bye."

"Morning!" Lucas waved to Cherry from the pool. He swam to the edge and sipped at a glass of orange juice waiting for him there. The drinking glass looked like it might be crystal.

"Is that my boyfriend, or did I just wander into a Kanye video?"

Cherry smiled at Lucas's bashful grin. He was enjoying himself.

"Morning, sleepyhead," said Ardelia. "Can you believe this weather? You must be a good-luck charm." She looked at Cherry over her shades. "How do you like the suit?"

"It's cool," said Cherry. "Kinda giving me a wedgie, though." She picked at the fabric around her butt. Spanner clucked.

"Good thing you didn't go with the thong," said a voice behind her.

Cherry spun so fast, she nearly lost her footing. Relaxing under his own umbrella, his stomach lily white and hairless, was Maxwell Silver.

"What the *fuck* are you doing here?" Cherry said.

"Cherry!" said Ardelia. "That's rude."

"You're supposed to be in the Netherlands."

"Nice to see you, too," said Maxwell. "How are you enjoying the *Lifestyles of the Rich and British*?"

"Shooting doesn't start for another three days," Ardelia explained. "Max's joining us for a few days." She hesitated. "I hope that's all right?"

"Oh, Cherry wishes she was the only one with a boy toy," Spanner said. She gave Cherry a smile dripping with honey. "Isn't that right?"

"Whose boy toy are you?" Cherry asked Maxwell, working to keep the grit from her voice.

Maxwell grinned around Cherry at Spanner and Ardelia. "I suppose I'm to be shared."

"No one wants to share you, Maxwell," Ardelia said, raising her paperback. "You're not a Toblerone."

Lucas laughed from the pool.

Cherry turned, feeling Maxwell's eyes on her back as she took the lawn chair beside Ardelia's. Ardelia said in almost a whisper. "Are you okay?"

"Yeah, why wouldn't I be?"

"I know he's a pig sometimes, but it's just an act. Ignore him. He's mostly harmless."

"You said he was the devil incarnate," Cherry whispered back. "And besides, I thought *you* were mad at him." She nodded toward Spanner. "Because of . . . you know."

Ardelia blinked slowly and hid behind her shades. "I'm not sure I follow you. But it doesn't matter, anyway," she added in a louder, more cheerful voice. "We're all friends here, aren't we?"

"Super-friends," said Maxwell. "Say, Lucas, you were going to show me how to do a jackknife."

"Can you believe this guy?" Lucas said to no one in particular. "What, they didn't teach you sweet dives at Oxford or wherever?"

Cherry expected this to go over like a lead balloon, but everyone laughed, even Spanner. Maxwell leaped up, tossed his shades onto the grass, and cannonballed Lucas. A plume splashed inches from the girls, who squealed and rained happy insults on the boys. Lucas had his arm around Maxwell's neck and was pretending to hold him under. Cherry's imagination roiled with alternate versions of this scene: Lucas, bat-shit crazy with jealousy, slowly suffocating Maxwell. Ardelia, furious at Cherry's betrayal, shouting herself hoarse.

The play battle raged toward the shallow end. Then Lucas lost his footing. He went down hard, clipping the cement edge before going under. Everyone froze. Cherry's mind went blank.

Lucas surfaced, waded slowly to the ladder, and sat on the grass.

"Oh!" Ardelia clapped her hand over her mouth. "Is he okay?"

Maxwell swam over, stuttering apologies. The paralysis broken, Cherry leaped to her feet and ran to his side.

"Are you hurt?" she asked.

He touched his ear, gingerly. "It's just a scrape."

"Baby, you're bleeding!" She turned his head. Blood trickled from his earlobe.

"Don't bleed in the pool," Spanner said. She rose slowly and came to Lucas's side. "Let me see." She tipped his chin, angling the ear toward the sunlight.

Maxwell held on to the pool's edge. "Well, don't I feel like an ass."

"You shouldn't have tripped him," Cherry snapped. Maxwell swallowed, looking like a scolded dog.

"It's okay," said Lucas.

Spanner rose. "Come with me. There's a first-aid kit in the pool house."

She cinched her robe and made for the tiny outbuilding at the edge of the patio. Lucas followed. Cherry was left crouching on the concrete, her heart thrumming in her throat.

"I really am sorry," Maxwell said, reaching for her shoulder.

"Why are you *really* here?" she hissed so Ardelia couldn't hear. "Are you fucking with me or something?"

Maxwell was wide-eyed and innocent. "I'm really not. I'm sorry, I didn't think it would make you uncomfortable."

She glanced in the direction Lucas had gone. "Well, it fucking does."

"Relax," Maxwell said, and she turned on him, ready to fend off his sleaze with her fists if necessary, but his look was serious, that of a longtime conspirator who knew how to hide things. "You need to *relax*."

Cherry swallowed, composing herself. "Excuse me."

She hurried to the pool house, a tiny cabana with wicker doors. In the shady interior, Spanner sat on an all-weather lounger. Lucas lay with his head in her lap, the damaged ear turned toward the ceiling. In one hand Spanner held a bit of bloody gauze, in the other a dropper of antiseptic. Something made Cherry stop near the door, just outside their line of sight. It was the way Spanner was leaning over Lucas, intimate but not sexual, her lips moving quickly, the words too faint for Cherry to pick up. Lucas looked straight ahead, his face expressionless.

Spanner dabbed his ear, and he winced, though not, Cherry thought, in physical pain.

Chapter Forty-one

"And Bless This Day in Our Hearts / As It Starts . . ."

After cucumber sandwiches (pale, flavorless wafers that piled in Cherry's stomach like rubber cement), Ardelia suggested a walk through the orchard. Soon Cherry's flip-flops were squishing through the wet grass. They went along, not talking, beneath the cherry blossoms hanging in damp clouds from their branches. Cherry couldn't enjoy the view. Her eyes stuck to the back of Lucas's neck, counting the hairs, studying the place where his hair stopped and smooth skin began. She wanted to reach out and touch it. He'd been quiet since the pool house. That was okay. Lucas could be quiet. He was a quiet guy.

This thought was the unsteady cap on her boiling panic. When she spoke up, her voice squeaked like a whistling teakettle.

"How's — ahem. How's your ear?"

"Still pretty tender."

She reached to touch it, and he flinched.

"Sorry." Unsure what to do with her hands, she hugged herself. The afternoon's humidity had started to break, and a cool breeze prickled the skin of her arms. Spanner, Ardelia, and Maxwell were a few rows ahead, talking loudly. Cherry cleared her throat. "What was Spanner saying back there?"

Lucas glanced sharply at her, then squinted at the sky. It had turned from blue to electric white. "That Maxwell was an asshole."

"Oh."

"And that I should watch out because he's a player and probably has a thing for you."

She laughed unsteadily, crazy with relief. "That's dumb. That's so stupid. Maxwell's slept with movie stars. Right? Why would he want me?"

"Does he?"

"Does he what?"

Lucas stopped and turned to her. "Does he want you?"

Something cold kissed the tip of her nose.

"He's not thinking about me," Cherry said, and nodded up the orchard path where Maxwell was trying to place his arm around Ardelia's bare shoulder. She dodged his touch, pointing out a bird on a high branch. Noticing Lucas and Cherry were missing, she turned and spotted them lagging behind. She waved cheerfully. "Hello! Have we lost you already?"

"Lovers' quarrel," Spanner mumbled, not too quietly. She peeled a flattened cherry blossom from the bottom of her shoe and flinched, glancing at the sky.

Maxwell winked at Ardelia. "Remember those?"

"We're fine," said Lucas, unsmiling. "It's fine."

The world flashed white.

"Oh, that looks like—" Ardelia started as thunder rumbled in the distance.

With a *crack* and a rush of breeze, it started to pour.

It was cool in the house, and the smell of fresh-brewed coffee drifted up from the kitchen. Lucas jogged ahead of Cherry on the stairs, not quite running away from her, but not waiting up, either. Ardelia called for Oliver to bring the coffee into the parlor. Cherry hesitated at the stairs, torn. Ardelia called for her to join them, and reluctantly she did.

Lucas probably wanted to be alone. It was probably a good idea not to go after him. Definitely probably.

"I'll be in my room," Spanner announced, and headed for the stairs.

A wild idea seized Cherry—to throw herself in front of Spanner's path and block the way. She couldn't bear another secret conference between her and Lucas, but

Spanner was heading for the other staircase, away from the room Cherry and Lucas shared.

She looked Cherry up and down.

"Someone's a little jumpy," she said. Then, glancing into the parlor where Maxwell and Ardelia had gone, she lowered her voice and murmured, "And you *should* be."

Cherry's hands balled into fists, her nails biting into the flesh of her palm. "Stay away from my fiancé."

Spanner smiled. She was getting to Cherry, and she knew it. With a flip of her ponytail, she turned and clipped up the stairs. Cherry had a decent throwing arm. She could probably take her out from here with that paperweight. . . .

"Cherry, come join us!" Ardelia called from the parlor.

She and Maxwell had arranged themselves on the high-backed couches, draped over the furniture like dirty laundry. It was a small, bright room with glass doors all around. Lightning flashed and turned the parlor into a film negative for an instant. Everything was rattling and popping with raindrops.

"We were talking in the orchard," Ardelia said. "And I was thinking, what about a little get-together tonight?"

"I thought you called it a glamorous garden party," said Maxwell.

Ardelia waved his comment away. "To-*may*-to,

to-*mah*-to. Just some family friends and a few local lord and lady mucks. I always throw house parties when I come home from a project."

"But not to fear." Maxwell leaned toward Cherry with a grin. "That's only part one of the evening. The mucks will be gone by midnight, and Ardelia's agreed to bring in some *fun* people from London."

"Yes, a two-part party," Ardelia said. "Sophistication and . . . the other thing. Sound good to you?"

"Um . . ."

Oliver toddled through the door with a tea tray of steaming mugs. He offered one to Cherry, and she took it, letting the heat work its way into her chilled fingers. She stared into the jet depths of the coffee and stalled. It was like a commercial: *Life getting way too complicated? Need a moment to think? Have a Folgers Moment!*

It didn't seem like a good time for a party. Two of the house's members had just stomped to their rooms in a huff. All was not well at Liddell Manor. But then, maybe a party would be a good distraction. And Spanner might be too distracted to spill any secrets to Lucas.

"What the hell?" said Cherry. "Sophistication and the other thing."

"Excellent!" said Ardelia. "Then it's done." She

snapped her fingers, and Cherry half expected the party to materialize around them, with the aid of movie-star magic.

Revitalized with caffeine, jogging up the stairs to their room, Cherry was beginning to feel better, more in control. This was good. A party would be good. She and Lucas would have fun together, and she'd show him how the only person she wanted to talk to, dance with, get silly with, was him. He'd realize it was ridiculous to suspect her of anything (even though it wasn't), and she wouldn't feel so guilty (even though she did). She checked her reflection in the hall mirror, assembling her smile. This was good. They were good at rebooting after a fight.

Except this wasn't a fight. This was something worse. This was a worry. This was a doubt.

Lucas was curled under the bay window with his sketch pad. He looked like a little kid. She wondered suddenly if their babies would be artistic. (Whoa, where had *that* thought come from?)

"You doing a new tag?" she said.

"Yeah. I guess. I don't know."

His hand made bold swoops across the page, followed by a series of angry squiggles. She wished she could see what he was drawing.

"They're going to throw a party tonight," she said.

"Some of Ardelia's neighbors and then some of her friends from London."

"Right."

"So."

"So."

He bit his pencil and considered his sketch pad, eyes narrowed. "Yeah," he said finally. "I'll probably not do the party, if it's okay with you."

"Sure, of course," she said quickly. "If you're not in the mood."

"I'll just chill up here."

"That's totally fine," she said. "I'm not really in the mood for a party, anyway."

"No," he said, meeting her eyes for the first time since she'd come up. "You should go. Ardelia's throwing it for you."

"You think?"

"Yeah, I'm sure," he said. "You should definitely go. And you'll have fun."

"I don't know about that."

"I do." He put the pencil back in his mouth and squinted at his drawing again.

"Okay," she said. "I'll go to the party."

"Okay," said Lucas.

Then, with a small nod, he tore out the page he'd been working on, wadded it into a ball, and tossed it in the trash.

Chapter Forty-two

Sophistication

The guests began to arrive at nine. Neighbors drove in from the nearest estates, men and women Cherry did not recognize as celebrities. Ardelia introduced them one by one, but Cherry instantly forgot their names. There was an older couple, Lord and Lady Cardigan, and their younger counterparts, Mr. Silk Shirt and his fiancée, Ski Tan. There was a young Sir Overbite and his friend Mr. Scarf. They all seemed stately, rickety. These weren't the Hollywood types of Maxwell's parties. These were a different species entirely.

"Inbreeding," whispered Maxwell. "Bones like vermicelli."

Everyone gathered in the vaulted living room. Oliver stoked a fire, and Eve, recast as a caterer in black skirt and white top, served drinks. The scene looked like a page from an L.L.Bean catalog or, thought Cherry, the cheesy

Murder Mystery Dinner Party Vi hosted on her twelfth birthday. Watching the guests, with their swirling snifters and stinky cheeses, Cherry felt as if she were looking into her future, or the next year of her life at least, as Ardelia's Stay-at-Home Baby Carrier.

She kept thinking of Lucas, brooding in their room. She wanted to go upstairs and make it all better, but she didn't know how. How do you apologize for something you haven't admitted to? How do you reassure someone about something they have every right to be pissed off about?

And as a constant reminder that things were teetering on the edge of complete disaster: Spanner. At least at the party, Cherry could keep an eye on her. The demon girl moved like a chess piece through the room, precise and rod straight, always a formal distance between guests. She smiled coolly, sipped her drink, laughed at Ardelia's jokes, and occasionally found Cherry's eyes and glared.

Maxwell, to Cherry's surprise, avoided the other guests and clung to the edges of the room, pretending to admire Ardelia's bookshelves. He circled around to Cherry and winked.

"I know what'll turn that frown upside down." He tried to refill her drink, but Cherry covered her glass.

"You in a bear trap?" she asked.

"Okay, I can tell you're not very happy with me." He refilled his own glass instead. Making sure the other guests couldn't hear, he leaned in and said in a nervous whisper, "Though honestly, I'm not sure why. You certainly seemed to know what you were doing. And for what it's worth, I rather thought you *liked* me. I was a little hurt when you told me to piss off."

Cherry rolled her eyes. *"You told Spanner."*

"She guessed, actually," said Maxwell. "You know how she is. She's like Sherlock in stilettos."

"Well, that's . . . good to know, I guess."

He cleared his throat. "Anyway, I didn't mean to . . . well."

She glanced at him. Maxwell wasn't in his element here. For some reason, Ardelia's fancy friends weren't *his* kind of fancy. Examining the little circle, she saw Spanner wasn't entirely comfortable, either. She wasn't really participating so much as standing sentry while Ardelia had fun and was charming. Cherry pictured herself round with Ardelia's baby, carted around to parties on a Hannibal Lecter handcart.

"Look how natural she is," Maxwell said, meaning Ardelia. "You see? Old money knows old money. These chumps won't talk to you unless you've got a title. Or your ancestors played squash with Oliver Cromwell."

"What do you mean?" said Cherry. "You're rich and famous."

He looked at her sideways. "There's rich and then there's *rich*. No one had heard of me before *Heavy Metal*

Pirates. I was doing dentifrice commercials in Cardiff. If this period Oscar bait doesn't win me an award . . ." He shrugged. "I don't know. Back to Cardiff, I guess. Good luck getting laid, then, Maxwell."

Ardelia looked up from her conversation and gestured for Cherry to join them.

"You'd better head over there," Maxwell said.

"I really don't want to."

"This party's all for you, you know. Ardelia's making sure you have their approval."

"Theirs?" said Cherry. "The James Bond villain society? Why?"

"These people's opinions matter a lot more to her than box-office receipts," said Maxwell. "These are the *family friends*"—he added a posh lilt to his already polished accent—"don't you know."

"Cherry, come join us," Ardelia called, gesturing with a little more force this time.

The window was open. She could always make a run for it. "Wish me luck," she said.

"God speed, pilgrim," said Maxwell.

She ventured into the circle of guests. The only free seat was next to Lord Cardigan's wife, Lady Frosted Hair, whose skirt suit seemed like an elaborate system of trusses and heavy buttons designed to keep her upright.

"Everyone, this is my new friend Cherry," said Ardelia. "She'll be staying at Liddell Manor next year."

"Possibly staying," said Spanner. Her normally plaster-pale cheeks had the slightest hint of pink. Cherry couldn't tell if she was drunk or . . . nervous? No, that was impossible.

Lady Frosted Hair's gaze lingered over Cherry's cowboy boots. "Do you ride? We'd love to have you down to see our Arabians."

An image: Lady Frosted Hair playing piggyback with a guy in a head scarf.

Horses, Ardelia mouthed.

"Oh!" said Cherry. "I don't know if I can ride a horse when I'm—"

"Cherry's not much of an equestrian," Ardelia put in quickly. "But I'm sure we'd love to come watch when you have your next showing."

"Uh, right," said Cherry. She raised her eyebrows at Ardelia, who cleared her throat.

"Who's having brandy?" Ardelia said. Spanner rose, but Ardelia stopped her. "Cherry and I will fetch it."

She went to the dry bar, and Cherry followed.

"They don't know why I'm here," said Cherry.

Ardelia shushed her and replied in a whisper, "They're very old school. They don't talk about unpleasant subjects." She began to decant brown stuff into glasses. "Frankly, the fact that I'm an actress is a big disappointment to them. The Deens are a bit of a local curiosity. The *entertainers,*" she added with mock condescension.

"But it's not your fault you can't have a baby."

"Just, *please,*" Ardelia said, her eyes full of worry, "try not to discuss anything . . . *controversial.* And don't curse! *Please* don't curse."

Ardelia returned to the booze-warmed circle, and Cherry followed. She saw how Ardelia transformed around these people. The lightness went out of her laughter; her tone was at once more clipped and more slippery. She was playing a part, Cherry realized. Auditioning for the role of Stuffy Person. The transformation was total—and unsettling.

Cherry settled onto the couch beside Ms. Ski Tan, who was finishing up a story about her latest trip to Tuscany.

"And it was fine, you know, but I'm so *done* with Tuscany. Isn't everyone just *done* with Tuscany?"

Her fiancé nodded. "Quite done."

"Now it's Croatia, you know," Ski Tan went on. "But soon everyone will be done with Croatia, too."

"I guess you'll have to go to the moon," Cherry said.

"I'm sorry?" Ski Tan tilted her head, earrings jingling.

"Eventually you'll be done with the whole planet," Cherry said. "And the only place to go will be the moon."

Lord Cardigan laughed. "Quite right! And then perhaps Mars!"

"Oh, Mars is lovely this time of year," Cherry said,

trying to match his inflection. "And the Martians? Lovely people."

They were laughing, all but Ski Tan, who still looked confused, and Ardelia, whose smile was sharp enough to cut glass.

"Have you met the Martians?" Cherry said to Lord Cardigan, eyeing Ardelia as she did. "Lovely little green persons. Though am I allowed to say that? Green persons? I suppose it's Persons of Greenness now."

"Oh, yes! Ha, precisely!"

She had them all laughing now, dry laughter in odd rhythms, as if none of them quite remembered how it was done. These were the sorts of people who farted once a year and had to leave the country to do it.

"Cherry is quite the comedienne," Ardelia said through her teeth. "We just love her sense of humor."

"Oh, you'll have to watch out for this one, Spanner," Mr. Silk Shirt said.

Spanner gestured for Eve to bring another drink. "And why is that?"

"Another sharp mind in the family?" Silk Shirt chuckled. He winked at their host. "You'd best hope Ardelia isn't secretly in the market for a new talent manager."

Spanner lowered her untouched drink and cleared her throat.

"Oh, you are too much," Ardelia said with a laugh, placing her hand on Silk Shirt's knee.

"Oh, Spanner's gone all red!" Ski Tan said.

"Ah, so we've found your Achilles' heel at last, Spanner," Silk Shirt added.

They laughed, and it wasn't quite cruel laughter, but then again, no one seemed to see how upset Spanner was, least of all Ardelia, who laughed along with them, *her* friends. "Oh, look," Ardelia said. "She *has* gone red!"

"Ardelia, hey—" Cherry started in a low voice.

"You'll have to excuse me," Spanner said, rising. "I'm not feeling well."

She left the room, leaving an uneven silence behind her. Cherry stared at Ardelia, dumbfounded. "What was that?"

"Hmm?" Ardelia said, appropriating Spanner's abandoned drink. "What was what?"

They'd just laughed a girl out of the room, and no one seemed to notice or care. And Ardelia should. That was *her girl*.

Something turned sour in Cherry's mouth. She met Ardelia's eyes. "You're a bitch."

There was a moment of stunned silence, and then the room erupted in laughter, the poshos turning red and wiping their eyes, in absolute hysterics. The only ones not laughing were Cherry and Ardelia. Ardelia was shocked, stung.

"Oh, you *must* keep this one, Ardy," Ski Tan said. "She's *precious.*"

"Excuse me," said Cherry, rising.

She needed a moment.

There was a half-bath off the main foyer. She checked the medicine cabinet for aspirin but found only skin cream and a box of tissues. The space under the sink was immaculate. No cleaning supplies, no wadded-up plastic bags. There was, however, a blue-and-yellow box, and Cherry wondered who in the house might need it. She recognized the label: 90 SECONDS OR LESS!

Chapter Forty-three

And the Other Thing

The first portion of the night's festivities was winding down. Lord Cardigan stretched and checked his watch. "Well, we should probably be shuffling off, then. It's after Luella's bedtime."

"Oh, don't go," Ardelia said without much enthusiasm. She seemed relieved. "We'll do brunch later this week."

Ardelia waved from the veranda as the last car disappeared down the orchard road. She let out a long, unsteady sigh. "Well, that was frightful."

"You were mean to Spanner," said Cherry. "I can't believe I'm actually defending her."

Ardelia scowled at her. "*You* were rude to my friends. Thank God they didn't realize you were making fun of them."

Cherry had to admit this was true. "Well, sorry about that."

Ardelia sighed and slipped her arm around Cherry's waist. "Apology accepted. No one's at their best with that crew." She kissed Cherry's cheek. Her breath smelled like wine. "And don't fret about Spanner. She's a big girl. She needs to loosen up, anyhow. Speaking of, where did she run off to? I need her for the second part of the evening."

Panic jumped into Cherry's throat. She might be with Lucas. She pictured her dripping poison in his ear.

"I've got to find Lucas," she said.

"In a moment," said Ardelia. "The other guests are arriving."

The wind had begun to kick up, and the evening's second contingent appeared over the tree line: a thundering, bright helicopter swooped low over the house and into the rear garden.

"And now the late-night crew," said Ardelia. She checked her reflection in the brass vase and arranged her hair. "Ready for round two?"

Cherry was ushered, dragged, toward the French doors. The garden was a maelstrom of light and noise, with the trees and trimmed bushes trembling and turning away from the helicopter descending onto the terrace landing pad. A mini-monsoon washed over the rim of the fountain, and twigs and leaves scattered into the shadows.

"They're making a mess already." Ardelia sighed.

The helicopter blades slowed as the cabin door slid open, and younger, flashier guests climbed down onto the terrace, some of them already holding drinks, the women's sheer dresses clinging in the stiff wind, the men's ties whipping over their shoulders. As a clique, they were loud and abrasive like the helicopter, a laughing, jangling hurricane of color and noise. Cherry wondered why Ardelia had invited them at all. She didn't seem happy to see them.

"You've got to please everyone all the time," Ardelia said, as if reading her thoughts. "Besides that one in the white suit is a record producer, and I'd like to do an album someday." She said this with a laugh, but it wasn't a joke, really.

"You've got to kiss a lot of asses when you're famous, don't you?" Cherry said.

Ardelia's smile faltered. She slipped an arm around Cherry's waist. "Yes. Which is why I need you to keep me sane."

A few of Ardelia's snooty neighbors lingered, even as the helicopter contingent blundered in through the French doors, the women carrying their high heels, the men carrying some of the women. The man in the white suit, the record producer, was pulling Maxwell into a bear hug.

"Welcome back, Maxwell. The empire's been lost without you."

Maxwell grinned. "Eddie, how's tricks?"

Eddie shrugged and removed his sunglasses. His eyes looked exhausted, even as the rest of him twitched with energy. "Shambolic, sweetie. Cynthia's up a tree with Charlie Chang and won't come down again until the album's finished."

"Poor dear," said Ardelia. The two exchanged air kisses. "Eddie, have you met Cherry?"

Eddie squinted, puffed out his cheeks like a massive albino frog. "Cherry? Charmed. Ed Oruther. I'm in music. What are you in?"

Cherry looked to Ardelia for help here. "Cowboy boots?"

Eddie computed, then burst into a wet guffaw. He leaned on Ardelia, slightly unsteady, though Cherry couldn't tell if this was due to drinks or the platform shoes he wore. "Absolutely brilliant. And where's Spanner? Did she finally have that massive aneurysm?"

"I thought she could only be killed by a stake to the heart," Cherry added. Again Eddie's face went limp, then contorted into a horrible mask of glee. *A dead albino frog,* Cherry thought, *that someone keeps electrocuting to life.*

"Well done," Maxwell said in her ear. "You're a natural."

Cherry excused herself and went to the bar. Eve was gathering glasses onto a tray.

"Have to hide the good snifters from the rabble." She gave Cherry the once-over. "You're looking like misery on a monument. What's with you?"

"Is this what it's always like here?"

"Like what?"

"Phony?"

Eve laughed, but Cherry could only sigh, watching Ardelia and Maxwell. They were dancing with the new guests now, Eddie twirling Ardelia under his arm awkwardly. Cherry placed her glass on Eve's tray. "Busing's the worst."

"Beats washing dishes."

"I hear that."

Cherry left the party. It was easy to get away from the noise in such a big house. While the living room and parlor were bright and clamorous with music, the foyer, the library, and everything beyond were dark and sleepy. An old house in an old country, just biding its time until quieter, more sensible tenants moved in.

She let herself wander toward the master bedrooms, all the way to the end of the hall, before she realized what she was doing—looking for Spanner. She found the other girl's room opposite Ardelia's. She hesitated at the cracked door, imagining a grand, spotless chamber of black curtains, candles, and stone floors.

"The lair of the beast," Cherry whispered to herself as she pushed in.

It was a plain, small room, very untidy. The desk was covered in paperwork, unopened mail, a humming laptop, its shelves and cubbyholes stuffed with folders, files—Ardelia's personal finances, maybe. The bedside supported a neat stack of scripts. One lay open on the comforter, red scribbles in the margins, and on the far side of the bed a heap of rejects piled nearly to the lip of the mattress. Everywhere was *work*. But this wasn't the buttoned-down, pencil-skirted Spanner she'd seen. It was as if all the girl's loose threads and frayed edges were stashed here, in this private space, where she kept her life's clutter.

There was a beautiful view of the rear garden, but what drew Cherry's attention was a frame on the wall, the only decoration in the dark paneled room, visible from both the bed and the desk, like a little altar. In the photograph, two girls, ten years old or so, sit in bright sunlight, the grinning brunette with her arms around a laughing blonde. The little blonde is laughing so hard, her eyes are shut, mouth open in spontaneous joy. They look like sisters.

Below the photograph, etched into the wall in wild, childish lettering, was *Ardy and Gracie. Best Friends 4 Always, 1999*

Spanner Grace. Gracie Spanner.

Suddenly she thought of Vi and that afternoon in 7-Eleven while Vi was taking the pregnancy test. She remembered her fantasy: she and Vi raising the baby together, the little life tying them together forever. Of course Spanner didn't want Cherry to have the baby. Who wanted to be replaced?

On her way back downstairs, she ran into Spanner coming up from the pantry. She carried a bottle of wine and a single glass. She really *was* red in the face, and her eyes were puffy. Spanner Grace was not having a great night.

"Drinking alone?" Cherry said.

"Where are you coming from?" She glanced over Cherry's shoulder toward the bedrooms. "You weren't in my room, were you?"

"Um, no," said Cherry.

Voices from the party below resounded nearby. Spanner nodded over her shoulder and led Cherry down the corridor, wobbling a little more than usual in her high heels. They came to a secluded alcove under the stairs.

"Tell Ardelia you're out," said Spanner. "*Now.* Or I tell Lucas everything."

"Everything what? I still don't think you—"

"I'll tell him you got high out of your mind and hooked up with Maxwell Silver in his hotel room."

"Oh." Cherry swallowed. "How did you know?"

"I quizzed the Kendras."

Smug, menacing Spanner was gone. This was drunk, desperate Spanner. This was a hurt little girl.

"Okay," said Cherry. "Just give me a second—"

"No. Find her and do it now. No excuses. Get it done."

She left, tripping a little as she made her way to her room and locked herself inside, a frayed edge.

On the ground floor, Oliver was opening all the French doors, and the party was spilling out into the rear garden. The guests had begun to disperse over the lawn. Eve was arranging drinks on a mobile bar and preparing to push it out onto the patio. Ardelia was overseeing this operation.

"The rain seems to have stopped, so let's make it a garden party, right?" Ardelia said when she saw Cherry. "I've got a hundred quid that Bethany Monk falls in the fountain."

"I need to talk to you," Cherry said. "Alone."

"Certainly. This way." She led Cherry through a connecting room into the foyer. Their heels clicked on the marbled floor. She smiled at Cherry. "What's up, buttercup?"

Cherry took a breath. Away from the party, in the vaulted, empty room, everything sounded so *loud*. "The answer is no."

Ardelia's face was impassive. "To what?"

"I'm not having the baby."

Ardelia lowered her glass, holding it in front of her hips like an offering. "What? Why?"

"Why?" She hadn't thought this far. "I just . . . I won't. I don't want to."

"But what about the money?" Ardelia said. She was a little drunk. "You'll have a place to stay and——"

"I mean, I *can't*," Cherry corrected her. She'd wanted to do this quickly. Execution style. This was torturous. "Something came up. I mean, something happened. And it's my fault, and I'm sorry. But I can't."

"What on earth are you talking about?" Ardelia set her glass on an end table. Some of its contents sloshed out, splashing on the floor. "I don't understand this."

Cherry shook her head. "Don't ask, okay?"

"I'm asking! I think I deserve to know!" Her eyes narrowed. "Is it Spanner? Has she done something?"

"I hooked up with Maxwell!"

Her words made the foyer sing. That or the sheer force of them had given Cherry tinnitus. She felt numb. It was like that chilled moment after being slapped, before the burning and the tears came.

Ardelia looked utterly perplexed. "That doesn't seem like you."

"I know." Her knees felt weak. She might collapse. "It——"

Something in Ardelia's eyes cut her short. The other

girl's gaze had drifted over Cherry's shoulder and up. She turned.

Lucas was on the stairs. His eyes met hers. He wobbled a bit, as if unsure whether to run back up. Instead, he brought his suspended foot down and without breaking stride, without looking at her, moved past them toward the front door.

"Wait—!" she started, but he was already gone. The door *thump-cracked* as it slammed behind him.

"Oh fuck, oh fuck, oh fuck."

She fought back the need to be sick. She felt dizzy. She rushed to the door. She could see him through the beveled glass windows. He walked with hands in pockets across the road and into the orchard. She opened the door to follow him.

A hand rested gently over hers.

"Don't chase him," Ardelia said. "Give him a bit."

"Fuck, fuck, fuck," Cherry cursed over and over again, her breath hot and wet in her throat, the world going wobbly like the treated windows. A surge welled up inside her, and she threw open the door and ran after him.

Chapter Forty-four

Snap

The rainstorm had left the ground soft. The mud pulled at her shoes as she ran through the orchard, ducking under the branches. She looked up one row, down another. It seemed impossible to lose someone in the wide avenues between the trees, but she couldn't see Lucas. She called his name, turned a corner, and there he was, leaning against a large cherry tree. When he saw her, he turned, but she called to him again, and he paused beneath the branches, his back to her.

"I know that saying *I'm sorry* doesn't mean anything—"

"Yes, it does."

"I'm *sorry*," she said, gasping it. It was airsickness all over again, the same upended feeling, that turning-inside-out feeling, of expunging something toxic from within. "I'm *so sorry*. We made out—it wasn't sex. It wasn't . . . anything! I wanted to tell you. But then, I swear to God, I thought all that would do was make you feel like shit and make me feel a little less guilty. So I thought, *Okay, I'll just deal with it on my own because Lucas doesn't deserve to feel bad.* But now I know that was totally stupid. And then there was the fire, and the offer from Ardelia, and I just don't know what in the clear-blue fuck is going on anymore."

He reached up to grab one of the lower branches. He pulled on it, testing its strength. The leaves shimmered and rained, and a few blossoms shook loose.

"I've been *so mad* at myself," he said at last. "For being jealous. I felt like such a jerk. Like a possessive, controlling jerk. I didn't like him, and I didn't want you talking to him." His shoulders pinched, like her gaze on his back was causing him physical pain. "When?"

"A few weeks ago," Cherry said. "The night of the fire."

"You said you were with Vi."

"I was," said Cherry.

"Oh, Jesus. Was it some kind of sick threesome?"

"No!" She wanted to strangle him. She wanted to hold him and press her face into his. "Don't be like that."

He turned to her, and his expression had softened. He wiped his hands together, brushing away the grit from the branch. "I don't know if I can let this go."

"I know," she said.

His eyes found hers. "I couldn't say this before, but I think I'm allowed to now."

She braced herself for the terrible force of his hurt, his anger, but Lucas didn't seem angry now. He seemed almost relieved.

"You've changed," he said. "At first I thought it was a good thing. Like you were letting loose a little bit. Staying out late, meeting new people. And then when Ardelia hired you, well, it looked like you felt good about yourself. Like you felt *smart*. And I've always known that you were smarter than you thought." His mouth soured; he shook his head. "But this isn't about *you*. It's just about your *body*. Is that all you're good for?"

"No. Ardelia respects me. She trusts me. *That's* why she asked me."

"She asked you because you're desperate." He held his hands palms up, weighing invisible values. "Money for your body. You know what that job description sounds like to me?"

She was inches from him before his mouth began forming the word, fist tight, arm pulled back for the same right hook that downed Olyvya Dunrey. But she stopped herself. This close, she could see the tears in his eyes, the tilt of his chin as he almost imperceptibly turned his cheek to meet the punch he knew was coming. He wanted her to hit him.

She put her palm to his cheek. "I'm sorry. You deserve better."

She turned and moved back toward the house. She could almost hear the snap of the rubber band that pulled him away, over the trees, across the sea, back to Aubrey.

Chapter Forty-five

The Garden of Earthly Delights

The party had moved into the back garden, and the house seemed empty, abandoned. Ardelia was waiting for Cherry by an end table crowded with half-empty champagne flutes. She wrung her hands, approaching the other girl carefully.

"Did you talk to him?"

Cherry nodded.

"Come with me."

She steered Cherry toward the stairs, her grip gentle but brooking no resistance. Eve emerged from the parlor with a tray of used glasses. Ardelia motioned for Cherry to go upstairs. Ardelia hung back and spoke to Eve in a hushed voice, barely loud enough for Cherry to hear.

"Eve, there's an upset gentleman in the orchard. Please retrieve him and take him to the kitchen. Have Oliver fix him something warm. Make him comfortable, but keep him out of sight."

"I've got to take the plates through!" the girl bleated.

"Just *do it*," Ardelia growled. Eve hurried toward the kitchen with her dishes, and Ardelia joined Cherry on the stairs. She smiled and ushered her through the house, down a long windowed hallway, to a pair of double doors.

The master bedroom was vaulted and opulent. Between two standing mirrors sprawled an immense canopied bed, its silky coverlet lounging over the edges and draping across the floor. In the far corner towered an enormous scalloped vanity. Everywhere Cherry looked, she saw herself in polished and reflective surfaces, everything silver and white—except for a small black panel tucked in a corner, the only blemish in the room's sterling complexion.

"Here, fresh air," Ardelia said, taking her through a triptych of French doors leading to the balcony.

There in the cool, still-damp night air, Cherry lost it. She began to sob and shake. Her heart was shattered, and the thousand still-beating pieces raced through her bloodstream, taking their separate pulses to her fingertips, her toes, her joints. She might shake apart.

Ardelia helped her to the deck lounger.

"Breathe, darling. Breathe."

"I . . . I can't . . ."

Ardelia disappeared and returned a moment later with a glass of water. She pressed something small and round into Cherry's palm.

"What's this?"

"Valium," said Ardelia.

Cherry pushed it away.

Ardelia offered her a glass. "At least have a drink."

"No." She shoved the glass. It tipped from Ardelia's hand and smashed on the balcony's tiled floor. Cherry felt cold water splash her toes.

"I'm sorry," she said.

"That's okay. That's all right." She felt Ardelia's palm on her forehead. "You're so hot, you poor thing. You're going to give yourself a stroke."

"Yes, please."

Ardelia laughed. "See? You've still got your sense of humor."

Cherry caught her breath, quieting her own sobs. She pulled her feet up onto the lounger, pressing her face to her knees. Ardelia sat beside her, wrapping an arm around her shoulder.

"I'm *horrible,*" Cherry said at last.

"You're not horrible."

"I'm the worst person." She looked up, seizing the idea. "I am. I'm Hitler. I'm Osama bin Laden."

"I think you're selling those two a bit short."

"He's never going to forgive me!"

"Oh, sweetheart." Ardelia held Cherry's face into her shoulder and rubbed her back. Up and down. Side to side. The gesture was familiar. Her mother used to do the same thing when Cherry was a girl.

"What do I *do*?"

Ardelia was quiet a moment. The sounds of the party below washed over them like rain.

"Well, I can have Oliver drive him to London. I'll pay for his flight home — don't you worry about that."

Cherry pulled away. "What? I mean, what do I do to make him forgive me?"

"Oh." Ardelia looked a little confused. "I don't know if there's anything you *can* do."

"So I just give up? Lose him?"

Ardelia licked her lips. "Darling, I'm not sure how to say this, but . . . these things happen. Hearts get broken. I know it may not make sense right now, but in time you'll move on. So will he."

"Jesus." Cherry edged away. "That's not what I thought you'd say."

"What did you think I'd say?"

"I don't know, that I shouldn't give up? That we'll get through this?" She added in a softer tone, "Don't you think we'll get through this?"

Ardelia bit her lip. "I think *you* will," she said.

Cherry stared at the patio tiles, the sparkles of broken glass. This was really happening. She wanted to run, but she wasn't sure in what direction. Down into the orchard, to find Lucas, or the other way. Into outer space.

"Come here," Ardelia said, helping her to her feet. They stood at the railing and looked down into the garden. The party was in full force. Couples and conversational circles cast weird shadows over the flower beds. A few of the guests had taken off their shoes and waded into the fountain, lounging against the weird blue orb in the center. A woman tripped and fell ass-first into the water. Everyone laughed. No one was worried. Everyone was all set forever.

"Look at where you are," Ardelia said. "Your life is changing. You're moving on. On to such incredible things." She squeezed Cherry's hand. "I know it hurts now, but think about all the people in the world hurting right now. How many of them get *this.*" She gestured to the party below, the laughter, the buckets of champagne, all the sparkling things. And the garden itself, the estate's rolling hills and beyond. "You know," Ardelia went on, smiling conspiratorially. "You and I could go to Rome. Stand in the Trevi Fountain. Eat the world's greatest food! There's too much to *experience* in life to be stuck with one man." She put her hands up. "I'm not saying you and Lucas are done for sure, right? I mean who knows what tomorrow will bring. I'm just saying that if things *don't* work out, there are *benefits.*" She seized Cherry's wrists, holding them together as if they were shackled. "You can do *anything* you want. You're *free* now."

And Cherry felt a chink in the long, solid wall of misery, the tiniest crack where fresh air was seeping through. For an instant, it was like she could squeeze out through that crack, let go of Lucas, let go of herself, and escape with Ardelia to anywhere she pleased. She'd never thought she could abandon herself so easily, but then here she was on a movie star's balcony in another country. Anything was possible.

It was terrifying, how easy escape seemed.

"I think—" Cherry started.

"Don't think," said Ardelia.

Someone knocked on the bedroom door. Eve's voice found them on the balcony. "Ms. Deen? They're asking for you."

"I'm going to head down," Ardelia said. "You stay here as long as you want. When you're ready, I'll see you out there."

And then she was gone, and Cherry was alone on the balcony, above the whole world.

Chapter Forty-six

The Secret Room

Her limbs felt heavy. The entire world was a loud party in another room. She felt a cramp and, wincing, holding her side, hobbled into the private bathroom.

Cherry closed the bedroom door behind her and locked herself in the spacious bathroom with its Jacuzzi tub and sleek modern sink like something off the Starship *Enterprise*. Feeling dazed, thinking and not thinking, she considered herself in the standing mirror, and thought about it, the physical reality of holding a baby in there, in her belly. Her tummy—tan, soft, and happy behind her hip bones—would expand and harden into a tight leather drum, pucker pink, navel like a divot on a huge golf ball. Her feet, hands, and breasts would swell to tender bags with blood, water, and milk—a noxious, hot soup ready to burst and trickle at the slightest prick. She'd crave dirt, cry, pull her hair in wild mood swings; a crazy, bloated hag, lolling in her own nasty on a velvet couch. It was a nightmare. She wasn't "carrying" anything. She was tossing her body into a turbine, grist for someone else's happiness. It was a sudden, hot, horrible thought.

She'd never felt so trapped. It was not just her body up for purchase, but her *life*. Ardelia wasn't renting her womb for a year—she was buying Cherry *whole*. From Aubrey. From Lucas. From her family. From herself. For $250,000.

She stepped out into the dark of the bedroom and felt a draft across her damp hands. It came from the panel by the bed, the cool whisper that ruffled the nightstand doilies.

The flat black panel slid aside. The small anteroom was cool, tiled like a bathroom, the far wall a bricked-off archway that must have once led to what Ardelia had called the *Galerie des Liaisons*. On the floor was a squat safety box with a keypad, its door hanging ajar like an invitation. But what drew her eye more was a cardboard crate, flaps bent back, packing kernels spilled around its base. The thing inside was pinkish, like a faded basketball, and as she lifted it from the box, it flopped awkwardly, making a rubbery *whoof* sound. She held it to the light. There were no fake nipples or distended navel, but she guessed what it was immediately. A fat suit. A fake pregnant belly and breasts.

The double doors squealed in the bedroom. Cherry

stepped out of the little anteroom, holding the suit in her arms like a wounded animal. Ardelia froze on the threshold.

"That room is private."

"What do you need this for?" She turned the suit and held it to her own body. The curves didn't quite line up. This was no one-size-fits-all fat suit. It was a custom job.

"I knew you wouldn't like it. That's why I kept it from you." Her voice cracked, pleading. "I was going to tell you."

"When? Second trimester?"

"Cherry—"

Laughter tumbled in from the hallway, followed by Maxwell, tie undone. He tripped over the carpet and put his arm around Ardelia to steady himself.

"Hello. What's going on here?" He squinted at Cherry. "What's that? Are we sumo wrestling?"

Someone followed him in. Spanner. "You can't be sneaking off like this," she was saying. "People will think you're—Oh." She took in the scene and tacitly closed the door, muffling the party outside. She crossed her arms. "So, this is happening, is it?"

"You're going to *fake* a pregnancy," Cherry said. It was out there. Saying the words seemed to shift the air pressure, change the spin of every electron. "You're going to keep me in a house getting fat and sick while you go on talk shows and the red carpet looking round and beautiful." A new wrinkle unwound itself in Cherry's brain. The blue-and-yellow boxes in the downstairs bathroom, the ones that said SURE! on the side. "You *can* get pregnant." She looked at Spanner. "She can, can't she?"

"It's complicated," Ardelia said.

Cherry looked to Spanner again. "Did you know about this?"

Spanner's eyes studied Cherry's. She looked tired. "Yes."

"Cherry, nothing's changed." Ardelia struggled to keep her tone even. "The pay's the same; the job's the same."

"It's *not* the same," Cherry snapped. "Before it was helping a person who wanted a baby but couldn't have one. But you *can*. You'd just prefer *not to.*"

"Oh, I could have told you that," Maxwell said. "We had a little scare a while back, didn't we?"

"Shut *up*, Maxwell!" the two girls shouted in unison. Maxwell's red cheeks reddened even more.

"You don't know what it's *like*," Ardelia said, pleading now. "You've got to be *perfect*. All the time. Everywhere. For everyone. You think *People* magazine cares if you've got swollen feet? Or if your tits are leaking on the *Today* show? They still expect you to be perfect, even while you've been *taken over* from within! And you certainly can't have someone *else* do it if *you can,* because that's *exploitative*. . . ." She couldn't go on, overcome by the unfairness of the world. Instead, she took a small step toward Cherry. "I really do want a baby, Cherry. This is the only way. Span, tell her."

Spanner was quiet, and Cherry braced herself for her icy bile. But instead the other girl shook her head.

"I'm sorry, honey."

"See?" Ardelia said, then snapped around. "Wait, what?"

"I told you not to do this," Spanner said, her tone quiet, even. "I told you this was bad for you. This was crossing a line."

Ardelia made an exasperated sound. "Oh, *not* this again."

"It's good she found out," Spanner said. "It can't go on like this."

"What is she talking about?" said Cherry. She felt dangerously close to losing her grip on the situation. She shook the wobbly belly at them. "Explain!"

Ardelia turned her back. Spanner looked as if she didn't know what to do with her hands. She had no cigarettes or cell phones or props to shield her. She folded them over her stomach.

"I told you I would do it," she said. "That if you wanted someone to carry it, I would, as your friend." Her hands dropped. "But no, you preferred me as an employee."

"I *need* you," Ardelia said to the wall. "You *know* that."

"And now, as your *oldest* friend," Spanner went on, "Ardelia, as your *only* friend, I'm telling you, do not become the sort of person who does . . . this." She waved to Cherry and the fat suit. "I know you want this baby, but you've got to take responsibility for it, Ardy. I can't let you make this mistake."

Cherry felt her fury drain away. She felt limp and lifeless as the fake belly in her arms. She let the suit drop to the floor. It bounced, lolled, and landed curves up. Trembling pink Jell-O.

"You should listen to your friend," she said.

Ardelia turned back and hugged herself, looking small and petulant. Something crumbled behind her eyes, and behind the crumbling wall, something black was waiting. "You sanctimonious bitch. High-and-mighty Cherry Kerrigan. So good and pure. She doesn't need fancy clothes and good food, just give her Pixy Stix and track shorts, thank you very much." Ardelia pointed a painted, sharpened nail at Cherry's chest. "Don't make like this is about *friendship*. You want the *money*. Just like everyone else. Ardelia Deen"—she bowed dramatically—"Ardelia Dollar Sign, more like. That's all anyone sees when they look at me."

Maxwell had backed himself into a corner and was searching furiously for a line of escape. He cleared his throat. "Do you really think that, Ardy?"

She ignored him.

"You," Cherry said, slowly and clearly so there was no mistaking her words. "Have. Ruined. My. Life."

She kicked the fat suit so it bounded across the carpet like a mutant tumbleweed. She pushed between them, jerked open the door, and ran out into the hall.

"Oh, shit, oh, Span, I've fucked everything up," she heard behind her.

"Come here, honey. It's going to be okay."

Chapter Forty-seven

Cherry

She went down the stairs, kicking off her heels halfway down to quicken her progress, and made straight for the front door. She'd walk to the coast, into the water, and dredge the sea until she reached Cape Cod, the Mass Pike, and the bridge to Sugar Village and the sweet-smelling dead pond. She was three rows into the dark, damp cherry orchard, the stars blinking through the petals so pale they were almost transparent. And then she stopped.

She didn't have anyplace to go.

She didn't have a trailer. She didn't have a home. She didn't have a Lucas. All she had was herself, a person she barely knew and didn't particularly like.

She trudged on until she came to a small brook. An ancient tree gripped the big boulder by the water, its exposed roots winding over the granite and into the soft earth. She felt the rough wood of the trunk and thought of their elm back home. This tree was probably so much older. Older than her neighborhood, older than her country maybe. She wondered if their elm would ever get that old, and if their names, carved in its side, would still be visible after hundreds of years.

She ran her hand along the bark, feeling its rough edges, and then she felt it. The smooth patch at shoulder level, the bark stripped away, the letters etched into ancient wood. A single word. Small and awake as a heartbeat: CHERRY.

"What are you doing out here?"

She jumped at his voice. He came strolling down the hillside, kicking loose the pebbles and dirt and letting them tumble into the brook. Even in the low light, she could see his eyes were red and raw.

"You did this?" she said, her hand on the sharp word in the wood.

He was quiet. She'd stumbled into his private gloom, tracked her own misery into his, here by the water.

"I'm sorry," she said, trying to find more words, a joke maybe. "I have nothing."

He looked confused. "What do you mean? I'm here."

"You don't want to be with me," she said. "I don't know if I'd let you take me back, even if you did."

He looked up into the branches, and losing his eyes

was like losing him in miniature, all over again; she didn't even have his full attention. But then, no. He was just trying to hide his tears. "No. That part's changed. It's changed. But we're still *something*." He looked at her. "We're still family."

She came to him carefully, worried he might vanish. But he was solid and stayed in her arms when she held him. He didn't move at first, but then, stiffly, his arms encircled her. He felt so sturdy, so permanent. And Cherry felt so shaky, like a leaf ready to drop off in autumn. Her legs felt weak, and she lost herself, falling against him. He caught her. He helped her up, put his arm around her shoulder.

"Are you okay?"

"I'm not feeling too good. I keep getting these cramps." She blinked. It was hard to concentrate. She felt drunk but hadn't been drinking. "I feel kinda woozy."

"Let's get back to the house."

He led her through the orchard, pointing out the smaller roots, helping her over the large ones. She tried to walk on her own, but her feet felt weightless, floating out from under her. Soon he was supporting her entirely, and Cherry felt the ground fall away. The stars were swimming through her vision now, and she realized Lucas was carrying her through the orchard as she drifted in and out of consciousness.

"I hate . . . damsels . . . in distress," she whispered to him.

They crossed the road, and she felt the even rhythm of the stairs, and then the light and echoey music of the front foyer undulating around her. She closed her eyes and squeezed her arms around his neck, and suddenly she was back in their elm in Aubrey, between their trailers, her arms around the trunk, her body hidden by the waxy summer leaves. She pressed her cheek against the smooth bark. It was smooth where Lucas had once carved their names, but the names were somehow still there, beneath the surface, burning with life.

"We're here," a voice said, and she opened her eyes, and they were in the downstairs bathroom. There were three mirrors, three panels here, Lucas with his arms around her, Red Guy and Green Guy, and all over again he was saving her life.

"In and up," she mumbled, and Lucas was there, helping her sit beside the toilet and holding back her hair. But she didn't feel queasy. The blood began to return to her head. She was on the bathroom floor with her fiancé, and Ardelia and some strangers were crowded around the door, looking worried.

"I didn't see how much she had to drink," said Ardelia. "Did anybody?"

"She's had nothing but seltzer," said Eve.

"I'll call an ambulance," said Spanner.

"Let's give her some space," said Lucas, standing and spreading his arms, barring the crowd. When he got them through the door, he closed it, and they were alone.

Cherry pulled herself onto the toilet seat. The light-headedness was replaced by pounding. Light spots danced in her vision. "That was scary. God, my head."

Lucas crouched in front of her. "Do you want aspirin? Not sure if that's okay if you're feeling faint. . . ."

She swallowed, still unsteady on her feet, and reached out for the counter. Lucas checked in the medicine cabinet. There were sanitary pads, some tile cleaner, and a blue-and-yellow box Cherry recognized, the Sure! test.

"Wait," said Cherry.

Oh.

"What is it?" Lucas asked.

After a while, Cherry opened the door. Ardelia was sitting on the bottom step of the master staircase. Spanner stood by the window, and Maxwell was slumped against the wall. Ardelia stood, hands folded, looking worried. They waited for her to speak.

"Well?" said Ardelia. "Is everything all right?"

"I'm not sure," said Cherry. "I think so."

"What was it?" said Spanner.

Cherry put her hand over her stomach and laughed. She grinned at them.

It *was* pretty funny.

"Well," she said, "I'm pregnant."

Epilogue

YOU ARE CORDIALLY INVITED
To a Post-Commencement Pig Roast

AT THE HOME OF
Lucas DuBois, Cherry Alice Kerrigan, and Baby Bump
128 Endicott Street, Worcester, MA

Thursday, June 27, 2013

Attire Is Casual (Gowns Acceptable)
BYOB RSVP TTYL

...

Cherry's hands ached from rolling burritos. She wiped
sweat from her forehead with the back of her hand, took a
long swig from her lemonade, and folded the last of thirty.
Vi was propped on the counter. The girls had changed
out of their commencement gowns—Vi into a tank and

shorts, Cherry into a breezy sundress. Despite the two mini–oscillating fans, both were slick with sweat.

"They look *fine,*" Vi said. "Don't . . . no! Don't reroll!"

"This is a matter of personal pride." Cherry redid the last burrito. "I can't let people think I've lost my touch."

"For burrito rolling?"

"It's my stance—that's the problem. I should be closer to the counter." She rubbed her tummy. At eight weeks, there was a just-visible bulge. "Sorry, Baby Bump, but it's true. You're ruining the burritos."

"Hey, don't blame Bump." Lucas came in through the side door with bags of ice in both arms. "You'll hurt his feelings."

"Or hers!" Vi corrected.

"Oh, those look *heavenly.*" Cherry hugged Lucas, pressing the bags of ice between them. "I love you, but you know this is just for the ice, right?"

He laughed. "I'll try not to take it personally."

"Cherry!" Pop bellowed from the yard. "Where are those damn burritos?"

It wasn't much of a yard, just a few square feet of scrub grass, a patio table, and a George Foreman Grill, all secreted away behind the tenant house on Vernon Hill. They'd been calling it "Shangri-La."

"Don't rush the pregnant woman!" she shouted through the window.

Lucas hefted the bags of ice into the freezer. The rest of the fridge was stuffed with barbecue supplies. So far the kitchen was the only room in the tiny bottom-floor rental that looked lived-in. Everything else (there wasn't much else, just a living room, bedroom, and bathroom) was piled high with half-unpacked cardboard boxes. The barbecue was doubling as a housewarming.

"What time are people getting here?" Vi asked.

Cherry hefted the burrito tray, balancing it on her tummy. "Any minute, so could you start setting out the chips? Oh, and call Stew. He was supposed to be here an hour ago with paper plates."

Vi saluted, hopped off the counter, and squeezed past Cherry into the next room.

"I wish you'd take a break," said Lucas.

"Just try to make me sit still. You think I'm bat-shit crazy *now*?"

She looked around at the chaotic kitchen, the spilled seasoning, the tortilla wrappers overflowing from the trash bin.

"Home, sweet home," she said.

He kissed her forehead. "Heaven."

"My feet are killing me."

"We have mildew."

She smiled. "Heaven."

"Cherry!" Pop bellowed from the lawn.

"I told you I'm coming!"

"No, not that! I think . . . you've got a visitor."

She hesitated, then handed Lucas the burrito tray and hurried down the stairs leading to the street, which in a few minutes would be lined with the cars of friends, extended family, even a few teachers Cherry'd invited, everyone from her old life she wanted to continue on into the new: the new home one town over; the new receptionist job at the fertility clinic up Vernon Hill; the new marriage after Labor Day; the new baby due in February.

Ardelia was paying the cabbie. She stepped out onto the sidewalk, and they hugged.

"I didn't know Worcester *had* cabs."

"I'm only in town for a day. Decided not to rent a car."

"Oh," said Cherry. She didn't know where to put her hands. It was so strange to see her. It was like someone doing an Ardelia Deen impersonation. "What brings you to the States?"

"I got an invite," she said, "to an important event." She removed a crumpled piece of paper from her purse. It was a printout from her e-mail account. In the body of the message was Cherry's BBQ invite. But Cherry hadn't sent it.

"Hello, Lucas," Ardelia said. Cherry turned. Lucas stood on the porch, leaning against one of the supports.

"Hi, Ardelia. Glad you could make it."

Cherry turned back. The starlet smiled weakly. "I hope . . . that's okay."

"Well . . ." said Cherry.

The mosquitoes hummed. She could feel her feet throbbing.

"Well," said Ardelia.

Cherry sighed. "You better go around back before someone spots you and calls the press."

It was eight thirty, and the sun-kissed, pork-saturated guests had all trailed away. The kitchen was a disaster area, the yard an atrocity. Pop, Stew, and Lucas were in the den watching television, and Cherry smiled to think of Lucas in the big easy chair, in *his* living room, the man of the house. A sunburned Vi was asleep on Cherry's bed. The sun was still setting.

Cherry and her guest lounged on the front porch overlooking the street. Both girls were damp with sweat, holding cold glasses of lemonade to their temples. The day's heat was just beginning to break, and there was electricity in the air. Late-night thunderstorms were expected.

"I can't believe Olyvya Dunrey cried," Cherry said, and they both laughed. Ardelia sighed.

"A lot of people claim to be my number-one fan, but I actually believed her."

Cherry took a sip, cleared her throat. "I'm, uh, sorry we didn't talk much."

"You were a busy hostess," Ardelia said.

"I mean, at all," said Cherry. "After everything."

"Oh, yes." Ardelia considered her ice cubes. "There's no reason for you to apologize for that." She glanced at Cherry. "You received my letter?"

"Yeah. It was very thoughtful."

"I meant it. All of it."

"It's okay," said Cherry. "It's . . . we're past it now."

Heat lightning turned the sky a living white. She'd have to run inside and close all the windows. Unless Lucas remembered to. Her brain felt foggy. She was so exhausted. The rain would feel so good.

"You're working?" Ardelia asked.

"And going back to school," Cherry said. Ardelia looked surprised. "I know, right? I'm training to be a counselor. They've got a service for young women up at the clinic. Sometimes they need someone to talk to." She smiled. "I like to talk to them."

"That sounds perfect."

"What about you?"

"A new project. Science fiction, actually. Robots. I'm the villain. I thought you'd like that."

Cherry chuckled. "And Spanner?"

Ardelia cleared her throat. "Spanner and I have parted ways. Temporarily."

"You fired her?"

"No! No, I didn't want her to go. But Spanner decided she needed some time on her own. Which I suppose is a good thing. She's gone home to see her parents." Ardelia did a little internal math. "This is the longest we've been apart in sixteen years."

Cherry refilled their lemonades from the big pitcher. She liked the rattle of the ice. It was a cooling sound. She sat back, glass balanced on her tummy.

"I saw your pictures in *People* magazine," she said. "We get it at the clinic. You know, for the waiting room."

"Oh, yes." Ardelia twirled her finger in her lemonade.

"So . . . you really went to a fertility clinic?"

"Yes, I really did."

"You should have called me. I could have hooked you up."

Ardelia laughed. "Yes, well."

"And?"

"And I'm going to wait until I'm eight weeks to announce it but . . . I am officially, well and truly pregnant." Ardelia raised her glass. "You think this would just be lemonade if I wasn't?"

"That's a change."

"Spanner convinced me," she said. "And you did."

They were quiet a moment. More lightning.

"I just kept thinking what my daughter might think

of me, if I did it the other way." Ardelia set her glass on the table. It made a soft *clink.* "I wouldn't want her thinking of me the way you do."

"Hey, I don't . . ." Cherry wasn't sure what she thought of Ardelia. But she didn't hate her. "It sounds like you've changed."

Ardelia thought about this. Her eyes searched Cherry's. "You haven't."

"Yes, I have."

Cherry leaned back in the lounger, putting her swollen feet up on the porch railing. Ardelia looked down at her own stomach, resting her hand there.

"So, when are you due?" Cherry asked.

"March 24."

Cherry thought. "That's the day we met. March 24."

"I hadn't thought of that." The two girls looked up at the sky. "We should have a joint shower."

Cherry looked over and smiled. "That sounds awesome."

The sky was deepening to pink and lavender, the houses and trees turning to dark silhouettes against the sky. She could smell barbeque and her own sweat, and feel the mist of her breath off the cold, cold lemonade. Sprinklers were sputtering, and there were kids, brand-new kids, screaming somewhere, laughing, playing late-evening tag the way she and Stew used to, until they were called in—*five more minutes* becoming *one more minute* and then *right now!* Someone was playing music, and Cherry thought she could hear a train whistle, long and low, taking someone away, taking someone home.

Any second, it would rain. She could feel it.

"Everything's going to be different now," said Ardelia.

"It always is," said Cherry.

ACKNOWLEDGMENTS

To paraphrase one of my favorite authors, Cherry had a most difficult birth. She owes her existence to many people. First, to my agent and mentor, Scott Treimel, who suggested I write a book "about pregnancy" and who guided me through many versions of this story. If Cherry has a godfather, he is it. Second, to my superlative editor, Deb Noyes-Wayshak, who had the vision, patience, and fortitude to help me shape and refashion Cherry's story until it was just right. She is undoubtedly Cherry's godmother. Third, to all the folks at Candlewick Press and Walker who contributed their suggestions and insight, in particular my U.K. editor, Lucy Earley, who, among other things, honed my Britishisms.

My deepest gratitude to my best friend, Evan Simko-Bednarski, who talked me out of many trees, and Helena Fitzgerald, who talked me off many ledges. Thanks to my close friend and colleague Vicki Lame, who read many versions of this book and was its champion from the get-go. Thank you to Antonio Elmaleh, Anne Williams, and Cathy Ann Horn for their warmth, wisdom, and hospitality. Thank you to my mother, Kate, who is so much a part of this story, it's embarrassing. Thank you to my father, John, who is forever my first and greatest role model. Finally, thank you to Sarah Elmaleh, my constant companion, my love, and my muse.